The Missing Diamond
A Crown Jewels Regency Mystery
Book 1

Lynn Morrison

Anne Radcliffe

Marketing Chair Press

Cover design by Melody Simmons

Published by

The Marketing Chair Press, Oxford, England

LynnMorrisonWriter.com

ISBN (paperback): 978-1-7392632-8-7

Contents

Dedication

To Harriett, who loved England so much there is a family story about her smuggling fine china back from it.

Prologue
1813

In life, Thaddius Percy, heir to the duke of Northumberland, had been somewhat of a drunk and a profligate, prone to excess of every kind. It was a curious twist of fate, then, that the herald of his death would be an unassuming man. The estate's stablemaster, no less.

In his sturdy, well-worn and much-mended brown waistcoat, the stablemaster cut a rather drab figure, especially when compared to the livery of the butler. The stablemaster pressed his lips tightly, trying to show little expression, but the set of his shoulders revealed a corded tension.

The duke had employed both men for years, and they knew that even when delivering dire news, their master expected certain protocols. Silence stretched between them as the stablemaster stopped to change out of his riding boots into soft-soled leather shoes. The better to protect the carpeting.

Together, they walked down the opulent main corridors instead of through the normal servant's pathways. The lovely teal of the walls, normally so restful, provided no succour as they headed to the study.

At the far end of the long hallway, the study's mahogany

door stood open. Their master stood at the window like a withering black shadow, scowling at the bright light of day. The Breaker of Northumberland was not quite as intimidating as he had been in decades past, but both knew that His Grace's tongue and wits were still plenty sharp enough to savage the unwary.

That tongue—that cruelty—had been what earned the duke his nickname.

They paused before crossing the threshold into the study, taking a moment to collect themselves. Truly, it seemed like hesitation, not contemplation of duty. With the inappropriately gay, bright sunshine flooding the room, it seemed almost as if the heavens themselves were celebrating the black news of a man's death.

Perhaps they were.

"Your Grace," the stablemaster said politely, imbuing his voice with a note of regret. He even made a proper half-bow to the lord's back, though the duke did not deign to turn to face them. "Your son, Earl Percy... I am sorry for your loss—"

Gideon Percy, Duke of Northumberland, lifted his hand swiftly in interruption, secretly pleased that it did not betray him with a palsy, as it so often did these days. Rather than press his luck, he quickly returned the hand to rest on top of the other on his cane. "I care little for platitudes. What I care about is knowing how it happened."

"An accident during the hunt, Your Grace. At a full gallop, Lord Percy miscalculated a jump he attempted. The ground was slick with mud and his steed faltered, throwing him when it failed to clear the deadfall. The Earl's neck was broken by the fall. He died quickly," explained the stablemaster.

It was only with great effort that Gideon resisted the urge to rage at his servants. Instead, he bowed his hoary head briefly, struggling to remain calm, lest his failing body betray him. "And the horse?"

"A badly broken leg." A pause. "We were forced to put him down."

"Which animal was the fool riding?"

The stablemaster darted a glance to the butler, who gave a half shrug and remained silent. "He was riding Sovereign, Your Grace."

At that, the duke spun around, losing his temper. It was only because he needed the support of both hands on the top of his desk to keep himself upright that he did not use his cane to sweep everything upon it to the floor. *"You let him take Sovereign!"* he said, his bass voice crackling with fury.

The stablemaster's face took on an ashen hue, but to his credit, he did not cower or snivel. "I could not sway him into taking a more seasoned mount, Your Grace. I did try, I swear."

Gideon did not doubt his stableman, but the truth did not cool his rage. The duke knew Thaddius had most likely been indulging in strong spirits before his ride, as well. A snarl tightened his jaw.

Of course, Thaddius would have died in the same way he had lived: in the most inconvenient and disappointing manner he could muster. That he had done it atop the back of the jewel of Northumberland's breeding program—a rather unseasoned young stallion who hadn't seen nearly enough time as a stud to recoup his investment—was just more salt in the wound.

"Get out," the duke said curtly, and gestured to the butler to shut the study door, turning away again.

Behind him, the butler and the stablemaster exchanged another look. Then the stablemaster left with the air of a man granted a reprieve from the gallows. Several minutes later, once he could see the stablemaster crossing the lawn outside, the duke finally turned back to his butler. "I trust you to see to most of the arrangements."

These men had spent more than half their lives together as master and servant, yet the duke had ensured that the gulf in station never once diminished. If they had not breached this divide during the death of the duke's favoured elder son some thirty years past, the butler knew full well they would most certainly not do so now. There would be little grieving over Thaddius.

"Of course, Your Grace," the man nodded.

He required no further instruction. After all these years, he knew his master as well as he knew himself. The butler had often taken decisions on his own, finding it easier to handle matters than require the volatile Breaker of Northumberland to face the facts that he was growing ever more infirm. Now, it appeared the butler would have to resume the old ways a while longer since the other son, heir apparent, had got himself killed. "Would you like me to send word to the front, to the young Lord Roland?"

Gideon surreptitiously tested the steadiness of his right hand, curling it into a fist. "You may write the message to secure his release. The missive to the son... I shall do that task myself," he replied, turning to seat himself at the grand desk. The butler bowed and left his master to the task.

Thinking for a moment, the duke dipped his quill and wrote tersely to Thaddius' son. His grandson. The young man who now stood next in line to inherit Northumberland.

Roland,

I must inform you that your father has passed. The event is as regrettable as it was foreseeable. For want of better character and judgement in the man, we have been left in the position you are required to assume a mantle of responsibility rather sooner than you expected.

Accompanying this letter is a communication intended for your commanding officer. It is imperative that you be released from service forthwith to attend familial obligations, and that you return to Northumberland with all due haste so that you may prepare adequately to return to society.

I trust the crux of the problem is understood.

Gideon Percy

Duke of Northumberland

1

The sun was setting in Mayfair, and the lamplighters were already abroad, working to combat the growing shadows on Grosvenor Street. The two men riding on horseback drew some curious looks as they passed. Some might attribute it to their military dress. More likely, it was rather because the two men of such clearly unequal stations were committing the faux pas of riding side by side.

"You do not have to come with me," Roland Percy said irritably to Thorne. He held himself with the stiffness of someone who was too drunk to be astride without the risk of falling off. Fortunately, Arion was a warhorse and steady as a rock, despite his master's condition. "You are a valet, not my nursemaid."

"With you as you are?" Thorne replied evenly. "I would be a dunce if I did not. You do not have to go out tonight. You are in your cups already, and you set such a pace to London that we arrived days before our own luggage will. I expect the dandies of the ton can wait until tomorrow."

Indeed, Roland Percy, now Earl Percy, had only arrived in

London this very afternoon. By evening, he already found the walls of the townhouse too stifling to bear. After a decade of service, commissioned officer though he had been, the townhouse felt more like a shrine to vanity and debauchery than a home.

It had been his father's townhouse. Rather, it had been the entailed property Thaddius had maintained as his principal residence in London. The duke had allowed Roland to occupy the property now in his late father's stead—and use or dispose of his father's belongings there however he saw fit, by the by.

The drapes were bold, the furniture and ornamentation chaotic. It had given Roland an instant headache, and he wanted to do away with the lot. Come daybreak, he would get Thorne to get rid of all he could and hide whatever he could not.

All the house had to commend it was a very well-stocked wine cellar. Roland had promptly—and perhaps unwisely— used it to fortify his wits following the trip. After most of a bottle of Port, it somehow seemed the more intelligent choice to head to White's rather than go straight to bed. Then, upon considering the fact that he would reintroduce himself to the ton, he decided that he couldn't bear to undertake the journey as sober as he was. He had finished the bottle and part of another.

"Come. We can ride and take the air, then head back to the house," Thorne coaxed when Roland did not immediately reply. Roland's drunken state was as uncharacteristic as the length of this latest black mood. Clearly, his employer was more troubled than he had ever been.

The letter from the duke had found them at their winter camp near Ciudad Rodrigo. Their location was the result of months of frustrating withdrawals to a defensible location following the misbegotten siege of Burgos. Roland had seemed disgruntled at being torn between two duties. Abandoning the line at such a crucial moment had likely felt nearly a dereliction, but of course, the family had to take precedence.

If he had seemed sombre from Portugal all the way to Northumberland, the next trip south to London was worse. Thorne knew only that Roland had been ordered to join the season and that he should endeavour to be married before the end of it. Thorne did not know, not exactly, what else The Breaker had said to Roland. Roland would not speak of it, but it weighed heavily upon him.

"This—all this," Roland waved his hand vaguely toward Grosvenor Square and the surrounding houses, "it is nothing but another mission. We must review the enemy's posture and put our backs to forming a strategy. The season begins this week, and there is no time to be wasted."

"The *enemy*?" Thorne repeated, brushing his forelock back from his face so that he could give his master a long, sideways look with his faded blue eyes. "What a curious way for the duke's new heir to describe his fellow nobles."

"More curious than the fact that my valet is escorting me to my club? More than the fact that I allow you, lowly individual that you are, to speak to me in such an inappropriate fashion?" was Roland's droll reply, meeting the blue eyes with his own dark brown ones.

Thorne grinned, knowing it for a fair strike and that there was no insult in it. There was too much history between them. Roland had applied to his grandfather over a decade ago, at age seventeen, to buy a commission and the ability to leave his family estate. Thorne had gone with him, enrolling in service and serving as his batman and personal protection on the battlefront. Upon Roland's recall to England by his grandfather, Thorne also accompanied him, ready to fulfil any role needed by his employer.

They were of the same age, and both had dark hair of similar shades, though Roland's parted left instead of Thorne's middle part. Amusingly, they had been often mistaken for one another from a distance, especially when in uniform. Simply put, Roland had grown to respect and trust Thorne more than any other man in his life. There were debts of honour between them, and Thorne had earned the privilege of speaking to Roland plainly a hundred times over.

"If we are off to meet the enemy in battle, then at least you have dressed for the occasion," Thorne said, nodding at Roland's service uniform—the only fit clothes he had. Thorne himself was wearing one of his two sets of civilian clothes, but Roland had been dismayed to note how worn his man's clothes were growing.

He should have noticed sooner, if for no other reason than because Thorne would never complain of such things. The state of both of their wardrobes was another urgent matter and part of his haste to get to London. Another thing to attend. Tomorrow. He exhaled.

Thorne understood where Roland's thoughts were immediately. "Yes, there is much to do, but again, none of it is so pressing that it cannot wait until after a trip to St. James'."

"I cannot stand to sit on my hands," Roland muttered. "It is too late today to attend to the hundred other things that urgently require my attention, but at least I can take action in this. Besides, my grandfather seemed rather adamant that I had been gone from society too long. So, what better place to dip my feet into the waters to check for sharks before fishing for a bride?"

"Fishing for sharks with your feet is one thing, my lord, but there are better places to learn what bait might catch a woman."

Nettled, Roland's head whipped in Thorne's direction. "Bait? I am now heir to the duke of Northumberland. What more do you believe I need to dangle to woo a woman? I will have ambitious mamas and simpering debutantes clinging to my breeches like nettles, as it is."

Thorne wisely said no more, since Roland was not in the state of mind to hear it. Also, they were now within earshot of the club's footmen, and if he tried to argue with his employer, there would be whispers and looks. Nodding his head to Roland, Thorne continued on his way back to the house.

⁓

Forget the sharks, Roland thought. The scene at White's was more akin to a cockfight. Though bloodless, it had just as much chest-puffing and strutting as one, at any rate. The fighting was subtle, prone to sharp words instead of claws, but still vicious.

Roland had sobered up—somewhat—on the ride to the club, but the gentlemen he became acquainted with soon rectified that issue. The flow of brandy quickly drowned and silenced whatever small part of him knew it was unwise to keep drinking.

It began innocently enough, with toasts. Drinking to his return to London, to his health, to future victories on the battlefront against the scourge Napoleon, to his late father, and to the future in store. He had begun by sipping politely at every toast, but his snifter kept being topped.

"Our dear Percy is nigh half-seas over," an old acquaintance, Lord Barbour, claimed in amusement.

Roland straightened his slumping posture. "I am *not*," he spoke firmly, if rather slowly. "And if I were, it would be your fault."

The men laughed in agreement, amused by his lack of control. Some laughs were more polite than others. There would be whispers. Aspersions cast. Roland could not bring himself to care; this pageant of noble behaviour was a farce. There was nothing gentle about the gentlemen of high society.

"So, you are off to the market this season," grumbled a young gentleman by the name of Lord Henry. "Lord Percy shall leave crumbs for the rest of us, eh?"

Lord Barbour, who had long been firmly espoused, took pleasure in teasing the young popinjay. "There shall be plenty of lesser women to choose from, Lord Henry. Remember, Percy here can only wed one! Perhaps he has a specific quality in mind, like blonde hair or a lovely singing voice. All you must do then is choose from the types he does not prefer."

Singing or hair colour? *Zounds.*

"That character I seek would be the manners and breeding suitable to one day be duchess," Roland replied shortly. "I imagine that Lord Henry should have many unsuitable women to choose from."

There was a round of laughs at Henry's expense. Another wit toward the back shouted, "Then her looks are of no consequence?"

Roland scarcely cared. Not about looks, hobbies, or his future wife's character. Marriage was naught but a transaction to secure mutual benefits for both parties. His mother and father had mostly lived rather separate lives. By every indication, they both had preferred it that way. Rumour had it that Thaddius Percy had never returned to his mother's bed to even attempt to secure the 'spare' to his heir.

Once he had done his duty and secured an heir of his own, he rather expected his life to be the same. But he answered, "Of course, a pleasant visage would be a boon, but little in that regard cannot be fixed by simply turning down the lamp." That caused another great boom of laughter, and even a bit of knee slapping.

"It would seem, then, that a stout pair of child-birthing hips should be the primary requirement for your wife," muttered Lord Henry.

One man sat in the back, although his bright blond hair prevented him from ever going wholly unnoticed in any company. Alone among all the younger gentlemen, Lord Peregrine Fitzroy was the rare familiar face to Roland. They had both attended Eton, and observers might have characterised their relationship more as adversaries than friends.

Doubtless, this was why Fitzroy had been watching Roland's evolving drunkenness with a smug twist to his lips. Aiding it, even. Roland had seen how the man's tongue was still quick to denigrate. Fitzroy was quicker still to play the part of a mischief maker when the opportunity arose, as it did now.

"Roland, a gentleman of the ton is not supposed to pick his wife the way he would pick a horse," he remarked. "I think instead you will find it rather more like an arduous campaign. Their mamas are formidable strategists, after all! You have been fighting the French for so long, I wonder if you know a lady's mind well enough to be up to her challenge—much less her mother's."

Twirling his goblet, Roland was careful to look unconcerned. "If you want to compare the marriage market to a war, Peregrine, then it takes little to imagine their objective. My grandfather wishes to secure the future of the title. Certainly, there will be no shortage of willing candidates who would want to be a duchess someday. Then all that I must do is choose the most advantageous match the season has to offer."

Barbour grinned. "No need, then, to set out with a map and a shovel to find such a treasure, Percy. Her Majesty the queen will do half the work for you. Just wait for one of the young ladies to win the queen's approval at her presentation, and you can try to snatch this season's diamond of the first waters from the grasp of the other men of the ton."

"Her what—?" the words escaped Roland's lips before the recollection struck. Queen Charlotte was presented with the new debutantes during the season proper, and the queen's approval of their beauty and grace of manners was a highly sought-after prize.

Fitzroy smirked. "See? *Lord Percy* has all but forgotten civilisation." The way Fitzroy's gaze lingered on his uniform as he said it was nearly a slight.

Disgruntled, Roland cast a look about the club and the well-tailored men within it. Crisp tailcoats, expertly tied cravats, and polished Hessian boots completed their ensembles, making each gentleman a paragon of elegance in the dimly lit, wood-panelled room. Internally, he sneered, unable to envision these men ever dirtying their hands in service. Most especially, he could not see Peregrine Fitzroy do so. He likely fussed with his appearance more than a woman did her own.

"I find greater purpose on the field than in parading like a fop, *Pip*," he replied, using the childhood nickname that Peregrine had hated. But even as he said it, his thoughts snagged upon Barbour's idea. Why *shouldn't* he start his search with what the ton thought was the top of the list? It was as good a starting point as any other. Perhaps better—even if it required him to dress for a ball.

"Truly, spoken like someone more at ease with soldiers than with gentle ladies. Men, let us not concern ourselves with Lord Percy; he clearly shall prove to be no competition for the diamond's hand," Fitzroy assured them, deliberately filling Roland's glass once more to the top. "Should you want for ungentle company, Roland, I hear that Lord Lancaster's daughter will make her debut."

"The Lancaster girl?" Lord Henry shuddered. "Her visage commands such attention one cannot look away, no matter how much one might wish to."

"No. Lord Barbour provided a most excellent suggestion. I

shall propose to the diamond of the season," Roland said, thoroughly tired of the conversation.

"You could propose, but anyone may," Fitzroy pointed out. "It is the result that matters. What if the young lady diamond decides she could do better than you, Lord Percy?"

"She could not!" Lord Henry tried to defend Roland. "Percy is likely to be the most eligible bachelor of the season. What woman would not be amenable to courting him?"

"One who believes her gentle husband should prefer a ball to a battlefield, mayhap. What say you, Percy? Would you care to wager?" Fitzroy asked, now in his element. "The end of the season is a popular time for declarations of love. Think you can win the diamond's heart by then?"

Under the pressure of Fitzroy's mocking grin and his deprecations, Roland's anger at everything that had come to pass crystallised abruptly. Betting for romance was a foolish notion, particularly amongst the members of the ton. "Winning her heart is of no consequence. Her hand is the only prize I seek, and I will obtain it.

"Wonderful. Then there is only the amount of the wager to be decided. How much of your newly inherited wealth are you willing to hand over when you fail?"

"Is my reputation not wager enough?"

Fitzroy waved the suggestion aside. "Where is the fun in that? I can hardly dine out on your dented honour."

Roland thought for a moment, and then dipped his hand into his coat pocket, pulling out a handful of coins. "Just a meal then? The contents of my pocket should suffice. I've got twelve shillings, two pounds sterling, and a single milréis. What do you say, Fitzroy?"

Fitzroy surveyed the room, judging whether the other men deemed the offer acceptable. Thoroughly entertained by Roland's barbarity in making a bet upon the hand of his future bride, the gentlemen seemed to agree. "By the end of the season?"

"I have no need for your generosity," Roland said, slapping his purse on the table. "All of you may stand witness. This pile of coins says the diamond of the season will accept my engagement by the end of May."

2

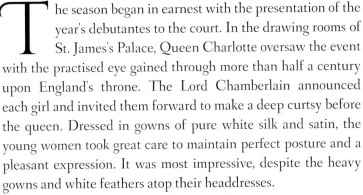

The season began in earnest with the presentation of the year's debutantes to the court. In the drawing rooms of St. James's Palace, Queen Charlotte oversaw the event with the practised eye gained through more than half a century upon England's throne. The Lord Chamberlain announced each girl and invited them forward to make a deep curtsy before the queen. Dressed in gowns of pure white silk and satin, the young women took great care to maintain perfect posture and a pleasant expression. It was most impressive, despite the heavy gowns and white feathers atop their headdresses.

Queen Charlotte inspected every debutante with great care. Although the ton's gossips would have the final say on which woman outshone her peers, seldom did Queen Charlotte's bestowed favour not predict the recipient of the title. She searched their countenances for any hint of wilfulness, insipidity, and any other aspect which might mar their standing. Every young woman hoped to win the title of the queen's diamond of the first water.

Every young woman, except one.

That young woman was Lady Grace Tilbury, the third child

of Earl Tilbury. Born and raised on the family estate in the rolling hills of the Cotswolds, Lady Grace received the education appropriate for a girl of her standing, including embroidery, singing, and playing the pianoforte. Her mother had given strict instructions not to mention the additional things she had learned by listening in on her brother Felix's lessons. Beyond this direction, her parents had turned a blind eye to her precociousness, happy for the reprieve it offered from Lady Grace's more extravagant efforts to capture their attention.

Lord and Lady Tilbury could not have foreseen the ramifications of that decision. Unlike most girls of her age and station, Lady Grace had discovered that a wide world existed beyond the confines of her family estate. Thus, she feigned interest in trying her hand at the marriage market—mostly because it would allow her to travel to London. In London, she was confident she would find a lifestyle that would capture her interest. Sheltered as she was, she knew only that she did not desire to follow in her mother's footsteps, as her older sister Mercy had done. She could think of little worse than ending up married and heavily pregnant within two years of leaving home.

And so it was that when Queen Charlotte took one look at Lady Grace's unremarkable chestnut waves, freckled nose, and twinkling eyes of an ordinary shade of hazel, she summarily dismissed the young woman without a single question. Far too impertinent, the queen decided before waving her away.

For her part, Lady Grace took no offence, happy enough to have simply survived the occasion without tripping over the long train of her elaborate white court dress.

Two weeks into the peak of the season, with a half-dozen balls and many afternoons of paying calls behind her, Lady Grace sat at the dressing table in her Mayfair bedroom and watched her reflection in the mirror as her maid, Elsie, finished twisting her thick tresses into a simple braid. Elsie wound a piece of ribbon around the bottom of the braid, knotting it twice. Both women knew it was a vain hope that the braid would survive the night. Lady Grace's hair had a mind of its own, much like its owner.

"Will you need anything else, my lady?"

"No. It is late; you should turn in."

The maid finished tidying the room and banked the fire before she left. Grace waited until she could no longer hear the woman's footsteps in the hallway before rising from her seat. She hurried across the room and opened the door, checking to ensure the hallway was empty. Dressed as she was in her night rail and wrapper, she tiptoed along the hallway, her slippered feet making no sound, until she reached the door to the next room. She twisted the knob and opened it wide enough to slip inside without knocking.

There was no need to announce her arrival or request permission to enter. Lady Charity Cresswell, her best friend and current host, sat propped up on her bed with her back leaning upon a veritable mountain of feather pillows. Grace scurried across the room to the other side of the bed, removed her slippers, and slid under the covers.

The more poetic members of the ton likened Lady Charity's appearance to that of an angel. For certain, her golden locks and the thickly fringed blue eyes captivated the hearts and minds of every man she passed.

Innocent though she was, like her dear friend Grace, Charity had approached the marriage mart with single-minded determination. She would settle for no less than the most highly sought-after bachelor. Tonight, after dancing until the wee hours in the ballroom of Almack's, Charity had pulled out her inkwell and paper to make a note of those she had met.

While Charity listed the sets she'd danced and the names of

the men who had accompanied her during, Grace picked up the well-thumbed copy of Debrett's Peerage that lay between them.

"Drat, I cannot remember whether I danced the first quadrille or second with Lord Henry."

"It was the first," Grace replied without looking up. "You danced the second with Lord Dunstan, although why you allow that dullard to escort you around the floor is beyond me. *Lord Dunce-tan.* Yes, it has a ring to it."

Charity's hand flew to her mouth to stifle laughter before she reached over and swatted her friend on the arm. "You are terrible, Grace. You must stop referring to him that way. If you do not, eventually you will end up uttering those words in company."

"And so what if I do? I am sure I am hardly the first to find the man to be a pompous fool." Grace pictured the man in question. The ridiculous man in his breeches, coat, and waterfall silk neckerchief reminded her of a peacock spreading his feathers. "Please tell me you are not seriously contemplating wedding him."

Charity cast Grace a mulish glare, but could not hold the serious expression for overlong without a giggle erupting. "He is ridiculous, is he not? I have no need to lower my standards when there are plenty of other available men for my consideration."

Grace reached over and plucked the paper from Charity's lap. She skimmed the names, reading them aloud. "Lord Henry, Lord Dunstan, Mr Simpson, Sir Elliot, Lord Percy... What of Lord Fitzroy? He is not completely odious."

"Lord Fitzroy is only here because of familial obligations, as well you would know if you paid more attention to our fellow debutantes rather than the matrons. His sister, Lady Lark, was presented at court along with us. He puts in an appearance at his mother's command and escapes to the card room at the first opportunity."

"He is young enough and handsome enough, even so. He will have to take a wife at some point. Who is to say you cannot bring him around?"

Charity gave Grace's suggestion due consideration and then shook her head. "No, he will not make his choice this year. I am sure of it. If the title had not passed to him so soon, if his sister had not been making her debut, he would likely still be abroad pursuing his own interests. I do not intend to wait for any man. Everyone knows that the best and the brightest are engaged by the end of the season. It is my duty to follow suit. Looking at my options, Lord Percy rises to the top. He has also already inherited his father's title and is next in line to be the duke of Northumberland. I will be hard-pressed to do better than that."

Grace handed the paper back and wagged her finger at her friend. "You are the queen's favourite and have your pick of the litter. No one would dare tarnish your name. I say, what is the rush? One must not make the most important decisions in life under duress.

Charity sighed heavily. She set her pen and paper aside to give Grace her full attention. "You are far too interested in my prospects. What of your decisions? I find your approach to be most perplexing. You never gave the impression of being set against marriage before we came to London."

"I am not dead set against it," Grace hurried to correct her friend. "I think it would be nice to marry... someday. Or if the right man comes along and offers the right thing, I would not refuse out of hand. But Charity—! There is so much to see and do. The men explore the world and do not settle down for years and years! Do you not want to have even a taste of that same adventure?"

She waved her hand. "We do not get years and years. If we do not land a beau soon, they question what is wrong with us. But nevermind that. How will you know which man is right for *you?*" Charity countered. "It is hard to find a husband when you spend most of your time on the edge of the dance floor."

"That is so I do not embarrass myself by stepping on their feet, revealing how poor my mother's choice of given name was."

"And," Charity teased her, "what are the criteria by which you consider a man to be the right one?"

"Well... I will let cold logic, not fleeting emotions, guide me —although a touch of romance would be nice. I think I should like a man who wishes to travel to other countries. Perhaps he would like to take me with him, and that would be wonderful. Those names on your list would be aghast at me wanting to travel. So, I will take my time, and if I do not find a man who shares my desires, I will wed someone with one foot in the grave and wait until I am a widow."

Charity buried her face in her hands and her shoulder shook. It took Grace a moment to realise her friend was laughing.

"Oh Grace, you are a jewel in your own right. One day, someone else will come to this recognition and sweep you off your feet. When they do, I will remind you of your intention to wed a near-corpse."

Grace rolled her eyes dramatically. "Be my guest. But enough of me. My mama will arrive next week and I will move into our London house. Our opportunities to speak openly about such matters will become scarce. Let us review your list and discuss. Shall we begin with Lord Percy, as he is top of your mind?"

"He is most eligible," Charity reminded Grace. "His lineage is without flaw, and I can aspire no higher than a dukedom should I desire to remain in England. What do you think of him?"

Grace had no trouble bringing his visage to mind. Often

enough, she had seen him paying attention to Charity, offering to refill her glass or escorting her onto the ballroom floor. Beyond that, she had precious little to add. "All I know of him is that the man seems to only have eyes for you, Charity. I cannot recall him dancing with a single other woman. I am certain he will soon ask your father's permission to court you."

Charity relaxed against her pillows, her eyes getting that faraway look that they did whenever her daydreams came to the forefront. "He already did."

Grace gaped in surprise. "He did? And?"

Charity shrugged. "My father has granted that the final say is mine. It would be nice to be a duchess, I think, though Lord Percy is... well, quite rough around the edges. There is no romance in his soul."

Grace bit her knuckle to keep from laughing. "As if that matters to our mamas."

"Truly," Charity said with a half smile. "Still! It is nice to be fawned over a bit. Receive flowers and words of poetry. So no, I have not accepted—not yet. If we cannot have any assurance in enjoying a marriage, we can at least enjoy the game. Besides, if I take away their hopes of landing Lord Percy too soon, all the other ladies will despise me."

Grace cleared her throat, causing Charity to turn her way. "Those ladies already despise you now for the terrible crime of being both beautiful and kind."

"Yet, you do not. For that, I am truly grateful. But Grace, you must not hold back from me, out of fear of upsetting our friendship. Are you certain you do not care for any of the men? You are not in the least captivated by Lord Percy's darkly handsome good looks, despite his manners?"

Grace needed no time to consider. "I value our friendship over any man, Lord Percy included. Should you marry Lord Dunce, however..."

"Grace! You are dreadful!" Her laughter filled the air. She threw her arms around Grace and hugged her. "You are like a sister to me, one by choice rather than by blood. I could never marry someone who might drive a wedge between us."

"I cannot foresee that happening. We do not want the same thing. From what little I have seen and learned, this world is big enough for us to both be happy without hurting the other."

3

Despite the damage he wrought to his reputation that first night at White's, you could be sure that Roland Percy received an invitation to every private event following that benighted wager. This was particularly true if Lady Charity Cresswell was expected to attend it.

His behaviour had been scandalous, and the ripples had spread through the days since. There were whispers and disapproving looks from a few. Some, aware of his previous detachment from society, were more sympathetic to his indiscretion. Yet many, many more of the members of the ton seemed entertained by him—much in the manner one might be entertained by a dancing dog act.

The story of his bet spread among the gentlemen, and others had begun to lay their own wagers on the outcome. No one wished to miss a moment of Lord Roland Percy's attempts to court the lady. For his part, he used the opportunity to mend fences.

This was how he found himself invited to the Fitzroy's ball, even though there was still no love lost between the two of them.

Truly, London was but another battlefield, albeit a more subtle one than he had yet experienced. Or perhaps one might better equate it to chess, given its rules about how the pieces could move. With this realisation in place, he had begun to bend his mind in earnest towards learning the strategies that governed the game.

Roland had not softened greatly in his stance regarding the members of the ton, but he did have to admit that the Fitzroy ballroom was quite lovely. The room smelled of flowers and beeswax. The candles alight in sparkling gold candelabras were suspended by nearly invisible strings, bringing a warm glow to every corner of the room.

That was only a fraction of the delights to be found inside. The grounds around the estate were similarly adorned, for the dowager Lady Fitzroy's extensive gardens had to be shown to the best effect. They were considered among the finest in London—second only to the queen's, naturally. Rumour had even had it that she had grown the exotic orchids in the arrangements herself.

Lanterns adorned the pathways, reflecting a lovely light off the glass cloches still protecting some of the more delicate outdoor plants from the chill of spring evenings. And a single harpist had been employed to play within Lady Fitzroy's glasshouse simply for the delight of guests visiting it.

The guest list numbered well above two hundred, many of whom already filled the floor. And despite the lavish setting and extravagant gowns, the men and women in the ballroom weren't there simply for the entertainment. They were at the peak of the season, and courting was in full earnest.

Standing on the sidelines, Roland watched as the string quartet played a jaunty quadrille, the couples forming two lines on the dance floor.

"Percy," came Lord Fitzroy's amused voice behind him. "I

did not expect to find you holding up our walls. You need not fear for our safety. I assure you, my house is quite sturdy."

Roland spun to meet Lord Fitzroy's gaze. "I appreciate the reassurance. I shall find other points of weakness in the household which need to be attended to," he replied dryly.

Fitzroy gave him a sidelong glance, uncertain whether these words were meant entirely in jest. In fact, they weren't. As he had prowled the estate this evening, Roland had not spotted a single discreet guard on the grounds for the event.

The lapse in vigilance Roland personally felt was unforgivable, even as he reminded himself that Fitzroy was also rather young to be the earl. Roland knew Peregrine Fitzroy was slightly younger than he, roughly five and twenty. Robin Fitzroy, his father, had been much older than his wife and had died of an apoplexy some years back. Patently, Peregrine had never been taught to know any better in the matters of defence.

Brushing off his words, Fitzroy continued. "I would have thought you would find no lack of willing dance partners tonight. To look at you, I understand why Cupid hung up his bow for the evening. Surely, he deemed firing an arrow at you an exercise in futility."

"The ladies are willing." Roland cleared his throat nervously, darting his eyes away from meeting those of yet another debutante who decided to strategically plant herself in his line of sight. "I am the one who is uninterested. I only wait for my turn to dance with the diamond." He nodded in the direction of Lady Charity.

Attempting to get to the courting phase with Lady Charity had been an exercise in frustration. If he had called upon her regularly, so also did half of the men participating in the season. While the ton gossips proclaimed Roland in the lead for the lady's hand, Lady Charity appeared to be enjoying the attention lavished upon her by other suitors. Calling upon a woman with a gaggle of gentlemen, at best he exchanged a word, perhaps two, before she turned her eyes to the next. It was maddening.

Of the woman herself, likewise, he had learned little. Lady Charity was attractive, he conceded, if one liked golden hair, fair skin, and rosy lips. He'd confirmed she had impeccable manners, a respectable family, and the same sorts of dull interests that all the women were into—embroidery, arranging flowers, playing some instrument, and raising children.

Roland took a moment to thank God he had not been born a woman.

"The Cresswell girl is leading you on a merry dance, thus far," Fitzroy commented. "As our good Queen's favourite, she has her pick of suitors, and she is taking her time choosing. Should you wish to gain her favour sooner, you will need to do more than simply escort her around the dance floor for a set. I would suggest a more romantic gesture, but mayhap you would be better served by expanding your horizons and dancing with other young women."

A knot formed in the pit of his stomach at the idea of flirting with so many women. "You may be correct, *Pip*, but I am disinclined to seek varied companionship for the moment."

"Come, Percy, we are no longer children, and you know better than to malign your host. Still, it is good to see you're still taking your wager seriously," Fitzroy said, hiding a grin behind his glass of champagne.

"How could I not, with half of the gentlemen of London reminding me of it at every chance?" Roland snarled back.

Fitzroy took a long look down his nose at Roland, as if divining the true cause for his bad mood. "I see. Well, perhaps you will allow me to do you a nicety," Fitzroy volunteered unexpectedly.

"If you mean to release me from my wager, again, I do not require your handouts."

"And miss a win at your expense? Not a chance, my thorny... friend," Fitzroy clapped him on the arm. "Have you made the acquaintance yet of Lord and Lady Tilbury's youngest daughter?"

Roland cast about in his mind for an image of the lady. "Not that I recall, and I fail to see how that is relevant if I am not planning to court her."

"Indeed. You have been most singularly focused. You must admit, however, that there is no good hunt to be found in a lame animal—that lame animal being you, Percy, and not the lady. So, I do but seek to make it a bit more sporting and entertaining. I should remind you the diamond does not stand in isolation. A word in the ear of her best friend might bring you an advantage. Come along," he said, heading off without waiting for Roland's refusal—

—which Roland would have uttered, had he not been left talking to the air.

Reluctantly, he followed in Lord Fitzroy's wake to another wall, where a young woman was standing quite alone—no smothering mother standing guard. She was vaguely familiar in the way all the debutantes of the season were by now, but he could not recall where he had seen her.

Fitzroy gave a short bow toward the young woman. "Lady Grace, has your family abandoned you here?"

Grace gave a somewhat wry smile to the charming Fitzroy. One corner of her mouth lifted, which caught Roland's attention immediately by the very fact that it seemed genuine and not the fawning, much-practised smile of every other debutante. "My brother is taking his turn on the floor with Miss Simpson. My mother invited me to join her while she went off to exchange some lively gossip near the drinks table. As generous an offer as that was, I much prefer to make my own

Lynn Morrison & Anne Radcliffe

opinions of people. I am sure my family assumed me perfectly safe for the moment."

"Of course you are," Fitzroy agreed smoothly. "My lady, allow me to introduce you to the infamous Lord Roland Percy, heir to Northumberland."

Obediently, her eyes turned Roland's way. He waited a heartbeat, but she did not offer her hand. So he accorded her a small bow and sized up Lady Grace. Despite the upswept coif, her hair was an ordinary chestnut. Brows of a slightly darker shade curved over hazel eyes, and she had inherited the faintest touch of a cleft to her chin. Other blushing, fluttering debutantes would lock eyes with him, clearly hoping to compel him to find them appealing. With Lady Grace, he sensed only cool appraisal.

Fitzroy interrupted his musings. "Our mutual acquaintance here, Lord Percy, would love to bend your ear about how to win the heart and hand of your dear friend, perhaps during the next set?"

Her eyebrows arched in disbelief at the bluntness of Fitzroy's request, but before she could frame a reply, he added, "Please, do not claim to have already promised the set to someone else. I have noted both you and Lord Percy have a propensity to remain on the side when the music plays! Come join myself and Lady Charity on the ballroom floor." And from there, he sauntered off to find his partner, leaving the two alone.

An extended silence fell between them as Grace blanked her face. He assumed she did not wish to show embarrassment at the slight—that Roland would seek her out only as a means to reach Lady Charity, and not for her own company at all. It was very much like Fitzroy to salt a gift.

Grace held her head high as though waiting for the inevitable—that Roland would turn heel, or worse yet, make it clear he was there for one reason only. How many other men

30

had made a similar attempt? As the dearest friend of the cream of the season, Lady Grace must spend much of her time standing in Lady Charity's shadow. Yet, she did nothing to step free of it. Roland found himself wanting to know why.

Before the moment of silence stretched overlong, Roland made an effort to smooth things over. "My lady," he said, clearing his throat. "Despite the way he acquainted us, it is still lovely to meet you. I would very much be honoured if you would allow me to escort you."

4

Grace wanted to refuse, but not for the reason Lord Percy likely expected. She had a certain amount of curiosity about this man whom Charity rated so highly. Had Lord Fitzroy left them with an introduction and the start of a conversation, she would have exploited the opportunity to peer inside Lord Percy's mind. Did the man truly care for Charity, or was he only interested in her beauty and dowry?

But now, the man stood across from her, waiting for a reply. Grace could scarcely tell him there was a reason she had spent the entire season avoiding the dance floor as much as possible. While her mother had bestowed her with a name she hoped her daughter would embody, nature had its jest in the end. It was only with great concentration that Grace was capable of keeping her left foot straight from her right, and her poise always chose to disappear at the most inopportune moments.

Dancing with Lord Percy meant half the ton watching her every move. It was sure to be a disaster. There was nothing for it, however, but to muddle her way through as best she could.

She sent a silent prayer to the heavens, requesting divine

intervention—or at least enough ability to avoid making a fool of herself. With a tight smile designed to hide her gritted teeth, she nodded her agreement and allowed Lord Percy to guide her onto the dance floor.

He led her confidently across the crowded space, through people standing in their way, as though certain everyone would clear from his path. They did. Worse yet, many turned to stare, desperate to know which woman had managed to lure the elusive lord onto the floor. As they took their place in line beside Fitzroy and Charity, Grace heard the other couples whispering her name.

She hated that it took this for people to take an interest in her. Most of these people had exchanged only the barest word with her. They asked her thoughts on inane topics like the weather, if they spoke to her at all. For certain, none had bothered to learn which topics truly interested her. Yet, she had no other choice. Grace imagined her spine as made of steel and turned her gaze to the only person she trusted in this room.

Charity's mouth dropped open when their gazes clashed, shocked to find her friend on the dance floor, and with Lord Percy, no less. For a moment Grace feared Charity would misinterpret the scene, but then Charity gave her a genuine smile brimming with encouragement.

"Oh, how lovely to have you join us, Lady Grace and Lord Percy. With all of us here, I'm sure this will end up being my favourite set of the evening," Charity said lightly.

Fitzroy laid a hand over his breast. "When accompanied by me, how could it be anything less?"

Grace barely managed to keep her eyes from rolling.

The reel began, and the couples executed the required footwork, crossing back and forth across the central line. Grace hardly dared to blink, she was so focused on getting the steps right.

Faint voices drifted past as the couples around them chatted while stepping in place. Grace knew she was expected to say something, anything to provide an opening for a conversation. Why else make the dances last so long, with so much time spent waiting one's turn to prance down the centre aisle? Yet, she dared not turn her attention from the dance.

While she counted the beats until the next turn, he finally decided to speak first. "Are you and Lady Charity enjoying your first season?" he asked her.

She was, but not in the way he imagined. That didn't matter. Lord Percy expected her to wax pleasant and respond with something vapid, so that he could then ask her opinion on housekeeping or raising children.

Then again, she realised, what would he care about those opinions either? He was not interested in her thoughts on children. He was not interested in her. So, she decided to respond instead with the truth. "I will own that it is much grander than our country fairs back home," she said, lifting her gaze long enough to glimpse his face. She shifted closer to him and added in a low voice, "I like those better, because *we* are not the animals being put upon display."

Her remark caused the man to miss a step in surprise. For a single heartbeat she celebrated the barb striking home, but with Percy's balance off, she realised she had to twist sideways or risk having her feet trampled.

Perhaps another woman would have executed the move with no trouble. Grace instead lurched sideways and bumped into Charity, who lost her balance as well. It was nearly a calamity, but the gentlemen managed to save them from certain embarrassment. Lord Percy, feeling her stumble, pulled Grace back enough so she would not crash into Charity with full force. Lord Fitzroy was able to deftly catch hold of Charity's waist to steady her.

Embarrassing, but not as disastrous as falling to the floor would have been. A hot flush scalded Grace's cheeks, but Charity rushed to apologise to Grace and Lord Percy as though the mistake had been hers.

How very odd, Grace thought, struck by the thought Charity was not merely covering for Grace's clumsiness. If ungainliness could be contagious, Grace had surely passed the disease to her dearest friend. Twice more, Grace noticed from the corner of her eye Charity getting her step wrong and ending up out of position. Perhaps her conversation with Lord Fitzroy was more interesting than the dance.

Once again steady on her feet, Grace was emboldened to needle Lord Percy again. "Shall we skip the pleasantries and move on to whatever you want to ask me about Lady Charity? We both know that is the only reason you have dared to dance with—"

Her sentence went unfinished because Lord Percy then met her gaze squarely, and the command of his presence nearly made her lose her step again. Rather than be offended by her inattention, he appeared both rueful and amused. "Someone other than her? For whatever poor defence it offers, bending your ear about Lady Charity was actually Lord Fitzroy's idea and not my own. I was not nearly clever enough to devise this scheme myself."

Rough edges, indeed. That promptly deflated Grace's sense of indignation somewhat. "Nevertheless, you still asked me to dance."

"Yes, well... While I may be a bit slow in the art of social dealings, I am not lacking in sense enough to make the gross error of being rude deliberately. Learning how to win Lady Charity's approval is much on my mind, but that does not preclude learning more about you."

Grace blinked at him in consternation.

Lord Percy cleared his throat. "You are fast proving to be a curiously direct creature. I must admit, it is a rather refreshing change of pace from simpering."

Grace's spine stiffened again. "You are being rather direct yourself, Lord Percy."

"That is how I prefer it. Thank you for this... *honest* dance, Lady Grace," Lord Percy told her, the faint amusement in his eyes fading as he looked away. "I would be grateful if you would commend me to the diamond. I cannot imagine she will accept someone who does not pass your judgement," he finished.

Grace was not so sure, but she would not reveal her friend's methodical approach to rating her suitors to the man atop Charity's list. Instead, she tilted her head to the side and gave him an appraising look, one which promised nothing. "I will take your request into consideration."

When the final strains of the violins hung in the air, Lord Percy gave her a deep bow of thanks and then turned heel after escorting her to the edge of the floor. Charity latched onto Grace's arm and practically dragged her off.

They did not get far. Grace's mother stood waiting on the side, her face alight with surprised pleasure at seeing her wayward child in the arms of such a man as Lord Percy. She wiggled her eyebrows at her daughter, reminding her to keep a smile upon her face. "Lord Percy asked you to dance? I wasn't aware you'd been introduced, not that I'm complaining. And you, Lady Charity, were stunning as always. You must take care with men like Lord Fitzroy. He is our host, but his reputation is not without blemish."

"One might say the same about most of the men here, perhaps even Lord Percy," Grace mumbled. Her mother rapped her on the arm with her fan.

"*Dear girl*, look at your hemline. Did you catch it on something?" Grace's mother said while looking at the bottom of

Grace's dress in dismay. "Never fear. Elsie can whip the hem up in no time. Lady Charity, would you like to accompany us? Your cheeks are quite pink. Best you catch your breath before rumours hint at a fever."

Charity patted her cheeks. "Thank you, no. I was upstairs earlier and found it to be stifling. I'll step into the garden for a moment. The cool evening air should do the trick."

If Grace's hem wasn't dragging, Grace's mother would never have let Charity go on her own, but needs must. "Do not wander out of sight, and for goodness' sake, don't stand in close quarters with any man!"

Charity pledged to remain within sight of the doorway and hurried off before Grace's mother had second thoughts. Grace's mother hustled her daughter out of the ballroom and through the corridor to the main staircase. She led the way to the room set aside for the use of the lady guests.

At her mother's side, Grace entered a lovely parlour, decorated in shades of pale rose. Along the far wall stood maids from the various houses. Elsie was waiting patiently with the others, ready to attend to any grooming needs or wardrobe emergencies such as this. Deposited there like a sack of barley, her mother left with instructions to return downstairs as soon as she was put to rights.

Although Grace was happy for the chance to sit, she felt somewhat guilty that the maids could not do the same. How tedious it must be for them to stand like statues for hours on end, while their mistresses twirled and drank below. Grace encouraged her maid Elsie to avail herself of a low stool while seeing to the tear in her gown.

Elsie was a mouse of a girl, but a veritable genius with a needle and thread. Despite the difference in their station, Grace had grown to consider her a kind of friend this season. In a trice, Elsie set temporary stitches to hold Grace's hemline for the rest of the evening, chattering away at her mistress in an attempt to soothe Grace's ruffled nerves.

"Did you tear your hem dancing? Was it with someone handsome?" Elsie asked slyly. Grace had been reading her stories; Elsie was a hopeless romantic.

"*Handsome*, yes," Grace admitted, albeit begrudgingly. Lord Percy did amply meet the definition of the word. "But not the man for me. I will tell you the rest later."

Grace stood to check the fall of her dress, and someone bumped into her from behind. She whipped around to apologise, but stopped short. The plain dress identified the woman as a housemaid. The poor thing was already stumbling away, muttering under her breath, earning dire looks from all she passed.

Elsie's eyes widened, and she covered her mouth with her hand. "Good grief! One of the Fitzroy servants appears to have made a little merry with the punch herself! The poor thing clearly has no head for it. I hope someone sends her to bed before she is caught."

Grace's gaze followed the drunken maid until she exited the room. She glanced around, checking whether someone would go after the girl. When no one moved, Grace suggested, "See if you can find someone before she embarrasses herself."

Elsie bobbed her head and stood from where she'd been kneeling. Before she could depart to undertake her mistress's instruction, there came a crash from the corridor.

Grace and Elsie exchanged worried glances. Without a word, they rushed over to the doorway. A cold marble bust had rolled to a stop not far from their feet. The cause of its demise was still there — the merry maid was no longer quite so gay. Her wild gaze swept over her surroundings, as though seeing them for the first time. She lurched forward, caught her foot on the carpet runner, and went falling-face forward, toward the wooden banister.

The banister gave with a great crack, sending the girl over the edge, tumbling down to the unforgiving marble floor.

For as long as she lived, Grace would never forget the horrible sound nor the echoing scream. Yet, something compelled her to check whether the girl had survived. Without a care for her own safety, she rushed to the now bare edge of the balcony and glanced down. The slim form, swathed in black, lay sprawled atop the broken wood, her unseeing gaze forever fixed upon the sky. Beside her knelt none other than Lord Percy.

Their eyes met. A woman's scream rent the air.

Elsie grabbed Grace's arm and pulled her away from the edge.

Grace's heartbeat echoed in her ears, pounding so loudly she could neither hear nor think. She had to get away. "The servant's staircase! Where is it?" Elsie shook her head, still in shock from what they'd seen. Grace lowered her pitch, adopting the strident tone of the Tilbury butler. "Show me, *right now!*"

Elsie rocked sideways, but finally moved. She guided Grace to a hidden door in the panelled wall. It swung open to reveal a narrow staircase made of plain wooden boards.

Grace scooped up the bottom of her gown and clutched it tight, giving little regard for the unseemly amount of ankle on display. She hurried down as fast as she dared, trusting Elsie to follow. Luck was on their side. They passed no servants coming the opposite direction. In fact, they made it all the way to the ballroom without encountering anyone.

Inside the ballroom, chaos reigned supreme. Husbands searched for wives, mothers for daughters. Grace searched the room until she spotted the tall white feather that adorned her mother's head. Once again, she brushed aside all rules, clutching onto Elsie's arm as she barrelled her way across the busy room.

"Mother!" Grace cried.

Her mother spun around; her face drained of all colour. She swayed at the sight of her daughter, alive and well. "Thank goodness!" she exclaimed. "I heard a woman fell from the upper floor and I feared the worst."

"It was a maid," Grace murmured, keeping her voice low.

"You saw?" her mother screeched, drawing the attention of everyone around them. She drew herself up and issued directives, like a general charging into battle. "Elsie, run ahead and call for the carriage. Grace, we're leaving. I'll hear no arguments."

Grace had no intention to disagree. Her mind played an endless loop, starting from the rolling marble head and ending with the broken banister. Her body wracked with chills as the reality of what she'd witnessed set in.

A woman had died before her very eyes. The only other person to witness her death was Lord Percy.

5

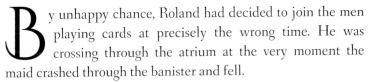

B y unhappy chance, Roland had decided to join the men playing cards at precisely the wrong time. He was crossing through the atrium at the very moment the maid crashed through the banister and fell.

Roland's shock lasted only a second before his reflexes jumped into action, and he sprung to where the wretched girl landed. Even as he moved, however, he suspected his haste was wasted, because the girl had made no effort to right herself or cushion the landing. The fall was not far, but she struck the floor with her head and neck.

He knelt by the maid's side as her last breath left her lips. She did not take another.

Stunned, he glanced upwards. As he did so, he spotted the most unexpected white face peering down at him from the upper level. "Lady Grace?" Roland asked the air. A horrified shriek behind him pulled his attention, and the lady disappeared from view.

He could find no more time to spare a thought for what he had seen above, for the crash had been heard, and shortly there would be others there. He removed his coat, covering the dead maid's features.

"Oh!" The dismayed woman moaning behind him spun him around. "Oh, my!"

"Lady Fitzroy," Roland said, expecting that said lady would be useless in dealing with this unexpected crisis. Already, it appeared that she might faint, and he made ready to catch her. "Discreetly, if possible, please find your son."

She appeared stunned into immobility, and at any rate, discretion had been a hope too far. Curious faces had already begun to peer into the atrium. "Would it be possible for someone to send for Lord Fitzroy?" Roland said, projecting his voice slightly, as he tried to conceal the body from their view with his own.

Two grim-faced servants arrived, Lord Fitzroy himself on their heels. But Fitzroy had never seen death, at least not such as this, and he seemed at a loss of what to do. Fitzroy's mother, the dowager countess, predictably swooned and had to be escorted by another gentleman to a chair.

Seeing no other choice, Roland began issuing terse, quiet orders. "It seems the evening has come to an unfortunate and early end. We must remove the body to somewhere more private so that the guests may leave," he instructed the servants. "We need the guests to be moved back into the ballroom and attended while her body is moved and the floor is cleaned. Where is Lady Fitzroy's maid with the smelling salts?"

Fitzroy, grey-faced but still moving, nodded to the servants and came back to life. Together, the two moved towards the major doorways, encouraging the guests to leave the atrium and return to the rooms in which they had been enjoying themselves for the moment, though Roland could hear the buzz of whisper and speculation already running rampant.

In the end, Fitzroy escorted most of the gentlemen back into the card room, and Roland found himself once more in the opulent ballroom. Like a horde of hornets, the Fitzroy servants swarmed, following the orders of the butler, Fitzroy, and ironically, still Roland himself. Roland did what he could to ease the growing discontent between split up families who were expressing fears.

Once the body was removed from the atrium and the blood cleaned up by a sobbing maid, the dowager Lady Fitzroy recovered herself enough to order the footmen to retrieve conveyances, and took it upon herself with Lord Fitzroy to personally escort each guest out with the most profuse apologies for a ruined evening. Roland allowed split parties to cross through the atrium as they sought their husbands and daughters, and the crush of guests lessened.

Roland took a breath of relief that this ordeal was in hand—until he heard Lord Cresswell's rising voice the next room over.

"Where is she?" the man demanded of Lord Fitzroy. "My daughter. I cannot find her anywhere!"

"Lord Cresswell," Lord Fitzroy said. He was attempting to sound soothing, but it was an arduous task when Fitzroy himself appeared as disconcerted as Charity's father. "I have not seen Lady Charity since we had our dance. But we will locate her forthwith, I promise. Perhaps she is out in the garden... one of the upper rooms..."

Roland's brows drew down, and a tightening grew in his gut. Lady Charity could not be found? The queen's Diamond herself was *missing*? A flash in Roland's mind recalled Lady Grace's moon-pale face staring down at him, horrified, from the banister.

His feet took him to where Lords Cresswell and Fitzroy argued quietly, and both men stared at Roland with a mixture of hope and worry. "I could not help but overhear," Roland said. "You say Lady Charity cannot be found? Where are the

Tilburys? Perhaps they may have seen her. Grace Tilbury and your daughter are quite close, are they not?"

Fitzroy barked a call for the butler. The man appeared in the doorway, from where he had been overseeing the carriages, helping keep the exodus rather orderly. The butler shook his head. He had not seen Lord and Lady Tilbury depart. It seemed that they had already left well before the other guests.

Roland's brows grew lower. Surely Lady Grace's family would not take Lady Charity with them without informing someone. He hoped he was wrong, even though the results of that would be... well, rather sinister.

"Percy," Fitzroy said to him once Lord Cresswell stalked away. It was unnerving, Roland owned, to see Fitzroy completely disarmed of his suave assuredness. "If we cannot locate her—if the diamond is not here?"

"It will be quite the scandal," Roland finished for him. "We must send for the Runners. And if you have a stableboy to spare, I would like them to retrieve my own man, Thorne. He may be of use in helping conduct a search. I trust him, implicitly, in all regards." Fitzroy nodded and saw it done.

The butler finished sending off all the families—save the Cresswells—before Thorne and the Runners arrived. That was about the only small favour they received out of this wretched evening.

Roland explained to Thorne all that had transpired—well, save the spotting of Lady Grace at the site of the maids' death—and Thorne's normal calm demeanour drew into a frown. "Do you believe the lady eloped?" he asked.

Roland gave Thorne a matching, considering frown as he thought over the details once more. Lady Charity's many callers. Her refusal to formally name suitors. A mysterious, untimely death. Lady Grace. "It may be possible," he replied slowly. "Certainly, that will be the conclusion the others will draw, eventually."

Thorne shifted uneasily. "What do you want me to do?"

"I want you to go with the butler," Roland said finally. "Check every servant's corridor, stairwell, and room hidden in the maze of the house. I cannot help but think Fitzroy and Cresswell may overlook these as they scour the house."

Nodding, Thorne departed.

Once unencumbered by guests, the search began in earnest. The Fitzroy mansion was to be scoured from top to bottom at Lord Cresswell's insistence, every public nook and cranny. Roland joined the men, somewhat predictably, on the fourth floor as they threw open some of the guest bedrooms in search. Aware that there were servant's quarters above, in the attic, Roland hoped Thorne would check these in addition to the hidden passages, so he did not fuss about the aristocratic oversight.

As the guest list of the ball largely had their own residences in London, none of the many guest bedrooms and associated sitting rooms were in use. There was no privacy being impinged upon by the rough search. The muslin cloth covering the desks and tables were tossed, and every stick of furniture peered beneath. Lady Lark's bedroom and sitting room, also on this floor, received decidedly more care, he noted.

On the third floor, as he searched Fitzroy's study with the escort of a footman, he could overhear the butler as he denied Lord Cresswell free entry to Lord and Lady Fitzroy's bedrooms, saying it would be highly irregular, singularly inappropriate for anyone to enter besides himself and the lady's maid! Lord Cresswell grumbled about it, but even as upset as he was, he recognised the truth of the butler's words, and he moved on to the reception rooms of the next floor down.

Zounds, Roland thought to himself. Lord Cresswell must truly be upset if he was trying to cross such boundary lines.

Libraries, studies, reception rooms, and morning rooms proved similarly vacant. All twenty or so of the public rooms and guest rooms of the house were empty of any young debutantes besides Lady Lark herself, snivelling on a fainting couch next to her mama with one of their lady's maids in the main sitting room.

Before the search moved on to the outside, they regrouped with the searching footmen and servants. Glancing at Thorne, Roland only received a headshake in reply; nothing of note had been seen.

So onward they went, splitting up as they exited through different doors to check every portico, front and back. They looked along the walls, inspected every lawn pathway and well-groomed garden spot that a young lady might shelter peacefully from the party, including Lady Fitzroy's glass-roofed conservatory. They even explored the more practical walled gardens that grew the herbs and vegetables for the household's medicinal and culinary needs. And from there, the search extended outward to the rest of the grounds. Every tree and bush was examined.

It was a fruitless effort. All they found was Lady Charity's ivory fan, its white feathers dusted with dirt, abandoned beside a stone garden bench. For as Thorne, Roland, the Runners and the men within the Fitzroy household determined after a long search that lasted the rest of the hours of the night, Lady Charity was nowhere to be found.

6

Grace shifted beneath her warm bed covers, finding her muscles stiff from hours of disuse. She must have been exhausted the night before, as she had no recollection of having gone to bed. She opened one eye into a narrow squint to judge the hour.

A wan face swam into view. "My lady? Lady Grace?"

Grace slammed her eyes shut again. Lying abed late into the morning was a welcome concession following a night of dancing. Whatever Elsie wanted could wait until Grace was ready to rise.

Elsie patently disagreed. She poked a finger into Grace's shoulder and called her name again. "Are you awake, my lady? You *must* wake up!"

The worry in Elsie's tone pierced through the veil of sleepiness. She blinked to clear the gumminess in her eyelids. Her mind was equally sluggish, and her mouth as dry as a desert. She commanded her mouth to ask what Elsie wanted, but what came out was barely intelligible. "Wha-err-nt?"

Instead of answering, Elsie leapt to her feet. "Her ladyship needs to speak with you. I'll fetch her."

Grace blinked again and more of the cobwebs fell from her mind. She forced herself into a sitting position and reached for the glass of water that always sat on her bedside table. Despite being room temperature, it rated among the most refreshing drinks of her life. Now thinking clearly, she glanced around, searching for clues as to why her mother was so desperate to speak with her.

Her gaze swept her bedroom. The fire roared, chasing the damp from the room. Atop her white lacquered dressing table, the bottles of scent and boxes of powder formed a neat line. She shifted to get a better view of the far corner. Her gaze landed upon the skirt of her ball gown draped over the tall, wooden screen. The memory of staring down at it while counting the steps to the quadrille rose to her mind. She'd danced with Lord Percy. Had she embarrassed herself in front of the ton?

The answer eluded her. She took another sip and furrowed her brow, telling herself to concentrate. How long had she slept to recall so little?

Memories swam through her mind. First came Lord Percy's face when she made her remark about women being on display. He had stood, mouth agape, but he had not frowned at her bold remark. Another picture rose to mind. Charity, spinning off-kilter, and her rosy cheeks at the set end. Grace recalled her mother sending her upstairs to Elsie to repair the hem of her gown. Upstairs, where she witnessed something else...

Grace's stomach lurched. The maid. The crimson stain spreading beneath her head. Grace shivered as she recalled Lord Percy's dark eyes staring up at her in shock.

Why had he been there? Had he recognised her, or had he been reacting to the tragedy unfolding at his feet? Elsie had grabbed her arm and pulled her away so quickly. It was possible he had not caught a clear view of her face.

From there, her recollection turned into a whirl of

memories. Her mother had bundled her into the carriage. Once home, Elsie had pressed a hot drink into her hands and instructed her to drink it all. The honeyed liquid had slid down her throat with ease, the sugary sweet taste disguising the dose of laudanum that left her, even now, thick-headed.

Grace thought once of chastising her mother for drugging her, but just as quickly discarded the notion. That cup of tea was the only reason she'd had a good night of sleep. For once, she was willing to admit, perhaps her mother knew best.

Any goodwill she had evaporated when the self-same mother burst into her bedroom, slamming the door against the wall in the process.

"Where is she? Did you know? Of course you did!" her mother exclaimed, looking furious.

Grace sloshed the water in her glass as she jumped at her mother's harsh tone. "Where? *Who*?"

"Don't play smart with me, young lady. I've been too lenient with you, but you never seemed to mind. And this? This is how you repay me? We'll be ruined!"

Grace set the glass aside and opened her mouth to accuse her mother of being melodramatic. Yes, she'd seen the maid fall to her death, but it had been a terrible accident. Surely others had witnessed her strange behaviour in the moments before her death. Witnessing a tragedy was hardly cause for ruin.

But then Elsie slipped into the room, standing out of sight of Lady Tilbury's venom. The girl was petrified. Dark shadows marred her face, and her eyes were red. Had Elsie spent the night crying over the accidental death of a stranger? Grace knew her too well to believe that was the case.

As the berating continued, her mother's tone ranged higher, her words as sharp as glass. For much of her life, Grace had wished her mother would pay her more attention. Yet, this was certainly not what she had in mind. There was nothing for it but to endure. Grace waited for a break in the harangue to ask for some clue what she was about. Anything. Finally, Lilian Tilbury stalked over to the bed and loomed over her daughter. "I shall only ask you this once. Where is Charity?"

"At home?" Grace ventured tentatively. The question made no sense. Her mother knew Charity had gone outside while Grace went upstairs to fix her hem. Grace had come straight back down and rushed into her mother's arms. When would she have encountered Charity?

Her mother rocked backwards. She took a deep breath and launched into Grace again. "She is most certainly *not* at home! No one has seen a sign of her since she walked into the Fitzroy gardens, and believe me, they have looked, young lady!"

"I do not understand," Grace gasped. She struggled to grasp the meaning of her mother's rant, her mind recoiling away from the horrid possibilities.

Lady Tilbury paid her child no mind, so caught up was she in her rant. "High and low, behind every shrub and statue. Lords Percy and Fitzroy made certain to check every possibility, even going so far as to send someone to question your father at dawn. As if we would have brought her home without telling her parents! The girl walked out, and I want to know where she has gone. You are going to tell me."

Grace's mouth gaped, her jaw having dropped at some point during her mother's rant. She had no answers, but plenty of questions. "Charity is gone?"

"Are you daft?" her mother gasped. "Have you heard a word I have said? She has run off with some man. By now, she is likely halfway to Gretna Green. She has ruined herself. If you knew about it... if you are covering for her, your reputation will be black with tarnish."

"Charity would *never* elope!" Grace sniped back. How dare her mother suggest such a thing. "She had nearly a dozen suitors, Mother! An unblemished reputation. She had not even given a man permission to court her. Why would she throw that away? And on whom?"

Her mother's face dropped, and she moaned. "She *must* have eloped. It is the only answer I can stomach. Tell me she chose to leave, Grace."

Tears sprang to Grace's eyes. Her mother's voice had lost the harsh edge and now carried a depth of pain she had never seen. Fear stole up her spine, its icy fingers sinking into her mind.

If Charity was gone, it was not by choice, especially if Lord Percy remained in London.

Grace reached out a hand, desperate for reassurance from her mother. It hung in the air, unmet.

Lady Tilbury had no time to coddle her daughter. There were far more important matters demanding her time. She drew herself up, calling upon the poise gained through years in high society. "Get dressed. We must be seen paying calls if we are to separate your name from hers."

"*Separate us*? You cannot be serious, Mother! We must search for Lady Charity. Lady Cresswell will have need of us— of you, Mother. You are her dear friend."

Lady Tilbury's stance softened. She stretched her hand toward Grace, but pulled it back. She balled her hand into a fist and clutched it against her mouth.

Grace's spirit rose from the dark depths of despair. Her mother would unbend. Grace would apply everything she knew about Charity, leaving no stone unturned until her friend was safe and whole at her side.

Her mother shook her head. "I am sorry. You have a kind heart, my dearest girl. But London is no place for such sentiment. If you are to come through this crisis without blemish, you must do exactly as I say. Charity was an

51

acquaintance, no matter how it looked to anyone else. You are horrified by her actions, and had no more warning than anyone else of her plans. Do you hear me?"

Grace sat frozen, her mother's glare burning into her forehead. She would find no quarter. Her head tilted forward, the barest minimum, but enough to satisfy her mother that she would play along.

And she would... for a short while. Just as she'd always done. Her mother's attention would soon shift to something else. When it did, Grace would slip into the shadows and stop at nothing to find out the truth.

7

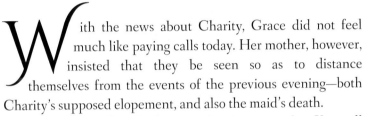

With the news about Charity, Grace did not feel much like paying calls today. Her mother, however, insisted that they be seen so as to distance themselves from the events of the previous evening—both Charity's supposed elopement, and also the maid's death.

"Come, we will walk, for it is a lovely, sunny day. You will feel more yourself," Lilian Tilbury said to her daughter.

So, Grace allowed herself to be dressed and coiffed, like a doll, for the walk to Lady Ashton's. Or perhaps it was the Ashbrook's. Grace's mind was a thousand leagues away, and she had not paid any attention to her mother's prattling.

As they descended the front stairs, however, a very unexpected gentleman was dismounting his horse and handing his reins to the footman at their front walk.

"Lord Percy," Grace's mother gasped.

Grace's eyes had been pointed downward, studying the walk, but she lifted them at her mother's exclamation. Immediately, they squarely met the piercing, dark brown gaze of the lord, and a chill settled in her bones despite the warm sun on her shoulders.

He was clearly trying to maintain a pleasant expression, but he looked somewhat tired and drawn. "A fine day for a walk, Lady Tilbury," he greeted Grace's mother. "I had hoped to pay Lady Grace a call, but perhaps today is not convenient?"

"We are expected elsewhere this afternoon," Lady Tilbury admitted, both practically beside herself with excitement that Lord Percy was here and torn with indecision. "Oh! But we had decided to walk on our way to pay a call to another house. If you do not mind that we are heading in the direction of Lord Ashbrook's, you are most welcome to accompany us. It is no inconvenience for us to enjoy the fine weather with you in our company!"

"I should be delighted to take a walk with Lady Grace and yourself," he mentioned briefly with a small bow.

Lady Tilbury fluttered excitedly, shooting glances at Grace. Her expression clearly spoke volumes about her hopes for Grace and some gentle courting of Lord Percy, but Grace knew his intentions had nothing to do with courtship. When she met Lord Percy's eyes, she recalled the shocked clash of eyes that had happened as he stood below the balcony, looking up at her from beside the body of the dead maid.

"Lord Percy," she greeted him neutrally.

He offered Grace his arm, nodding politely at her mother. Lady Tilbury cooed excitedly and stood back to give the couple some privacy. Seeing no choice for it, Grace took his arm, feeling an unpleasant flutter of nerves in her belly.

Her touch upon his arm was so light, he could barely feel it there. He could not feel any warmth from her hand through her kid leather gloves. He glanced over, searching for some hint of how she felt. Grace kept her eyes downcast, revealing none of her thoughts.

Roland walked a few steps, tugging Grace along. It looked like demure hesitance on her part, but Roland knew it was anything but.

"Your mama is clearly excited about your prospects, but I am sure you know what my intentions truly are," Roland said to her as they walked, bringing his arm closer to his body, nearly pinning her fingers. This tugged Grace ever so slightly closer to him so he could keep his voice low.

Grace slanted a look up at him from beneath her eyelashes. "I shall try to hide my disappointment that you find me unsuitable to call upon otherwise, Lord Percy."

Roland closed his eyes in a brief regret at his unintended slight, even as his lip curled in amusement at her outspoken annoyance. At least Lady Grace did not seem to care that he wasn't sizing up her marital worth. "My apologies. If it may appease you at all, I do appreciate that in a conversation, you tend to get straight to the point, even if you have a knack for sharpening the edges of it. I take it you have been informed of the news?"

She took a long breath and ignored his barb. "Yes. I heard this morning. And I heard we were questioned whether she had come home with us."

"Fitzroy and I explored every possibility, yes," Roland agreed. "But no one has questioned you."

"Why ever would someone question *me!*" she exclaimed quietly. "And why should it be *you*, of all people?"

"I was with the search party," he answered vaguely. "As you are her close friend, I feel I must ask, because indeed, who else would think to do so? Did she have plans to elope after all? Is that why she had yet to show any overt favouritism? She already had her eye set upon some less suitable match?"

It was the most logical conclusion—and one that most of the ton had already made, as predicted. He had already heard the whispers about how Charity had found an opportunity during the fuss of the maid's death to make her escape and had taken full advantage.

The girl beside him shook her head and pitched her voice so low he could barely hear it. "I cannot imagine Charity ever doing such a thing. From what I knew, she had every plan to marry as well as she could this season."

Plans to marry highly and well, as most ladies desired. Without conceit, Roland admitted to himself that it seemed unlikely Charity could find a better suitor than himself this season if her goal was to marry well. Yet, she had not fawned over him as the other debutantes did. He had assumed she was waiting for him to make a romantic gesture, but what if it were something more?

"You seem so certain," he finally replied. "And yet, I keep thinking of last night. You ask why I would be the one to question you, as if you pretend I did not see your face over the broken banister. I was the only one who saw you there. Imagine my surprise, then, when we tried to locate you to ask whether Charity was in your company and discovered that your family departed so precipitously. Who else might pose questions to you about it without creating a scandal?"

Grace's pale face grew a shade whiter. "Then I suppose we have you to thank for keeping our name from this afternoon's gossip columns, Lord Percy."

Roland did not relish it, but a part of him found satisfaction in rendering the sharp-tongued Lady Grace somewhat at a loss. "I suppose you do, and you may show your gratitude by satisfying my curiosity. For I cannot help but wonder what you might have had to do with that poor girl's death."

Grace nearly tripped over her own feet, and Roland

steadied her. "I can scarcely credit you as a scheming murderer, and yet, she fell in a most peculiar way. And there you were, right behind her," he continued, his voice growing hard. "Oh, perhaps such a foul deed was not the intention at all. Perhaps you were only aiming to create a distraction for Charity to slip out, and it went awry."

"*No*. A terrible coincidence," Lady Grace finally choked out. "I had been upstairs to fix my hem after our dance. The Fitzroy maid—I did not touch her. But... I did follow her."

Roland's eyebrows drew down again. "Why?"

"She—the maid—she was behaving a little strangely. My maid and I thought she must have been in her cups."

Roland's face tipped down towards hers, studying her wide-eyed expression as he considered this. If the maid had indeed been drunk, she could have fallen. It could be a coincidence, as Lady Grace said. And she did seem to be earnest regarding both Charity and the maid.

Then Lady Grace turned her face away, returning to studying the cobblestones.

Roland was not entirely certain she was telling the truth. Even if she were, there was still the possibility that Lady Charity had secrets she had kept from her own fastest friend. She may have still eloped, leaving Lady Grace none the wiser in order to protect her reputation.

Perhaps the maid had been simply a terrible accident.

Something about this story, however, did not entirely sit well with Roland, and he could not quite put a finger on what it was. The two of them concluded their walk towards the Ashbrook estate in a thoughtful silence.

8

Following that unsettling *tête-à-tête*, Grace wanted nothing more than to return to the safety of her bedroom, where she'd be free to vent her frustrations upon her pillow. Her mother, however, would hear nothing of the sort. She all but dragged Grace along on her afternoon of paying calls.

Of course, Charity's disappearance was the only thing anyone wanted to discuss.

Lady Tilbury was quick to put an end to that line of conversation. She rebuffed any attempts to suggest Charity and Grace were more than acquaintances, despite the numerous times they'd been seen together. Her innocent daughter Grace would never even think of disappearing from a ball, and certainly had no idea of anyone else's plans on that front. She'd then casually drop mention of Lord Percy's visit, turning the conversation away from the matter of the missing Diamond and onto the suggestion that her daughter might be a suitable replacement.

Through it all, Grace kept a smile pasted on her face. She nodded at what she hoped were the appropriate times. Now and again, she'd murmur a quiet phrase of agreement with whatever was being discussed. For once, she was grateful that calls rarely stretched beyond a quarter of an hour. By the time they said their hellos, drank tea, and prattled on about the weather, there was precious little left for other discussions.

It was near four when her mother proclaimed their visits done and agreed to return home. After handing her pelisse and hat to the footman, Grace rushed up the stairs. Her bedroom door beckoned, and she answered the call. She ignored her mother's admonitions against running in the house, her slippered feet padding across the wooden boards until she found the solace she so craved.

But even there, in her bedroom, she was not to be alone. Elsie was inside, needle in hand as she whipped a proper stitch into the hem of Grace's gown. Seeing her there reminded Grace of something she had heard the night before, and had paid no attention to. Hadn't Charity mentioned going upstairs at one point? Perhaps Elsie had insights to offer.

Elsie felt her mistress's gaze upon her shoulders and gathered her things, offering to leave, but Grace commanded her to stay. The young maid watched with trepidation as Grace perched upon the nearby chair and fixed her in her gaze.

"How did Lady Charity seem to you last night?"

"Beautiful, as always, my lady. She had on a fine gown, almost as nice as yours."

"She came upstairs before I did. Had something gone wrong with her dress or her hair?"

"Not that I'm aware of. She came in, sweat dotting her brow, and proclaimed her desire to put her feet up for a brief rest. A footman moved a chair and footrest for her, while her maid helped her sit without crumpling her gown. She didn't stay long, though. As soon as she'd caught her breath, she set her glass of punch aside and asked her maid to tidy her hair. With every man there wanting to dance with her, it's a wonder she got away at all."

Grace was well aware of how popular Charity was with the eligible suitors. She had watched from the side as Charity spun round and round the floor, always in a different man's arms. It came as little surprise that Charity had used an excuse to sneak upstairs for a rest. But then, why had she looked so peaked after she'd come down? This was hardly the first ball of the season. By now, both girls were well aware of the demands of such an event, and spent the day resting in preparation. It was still early in the night, not yet even midnight.

"Did Charity speak to anyone upstairs?"

"No, my lady. It was early, and there was little for us to do. We maids were indulging in a cheeky natter while we waited. As you know, it's rare we get time to chat with servants from the other houses. I hope you don't mind," Elsie added in a quiet voice.

"Of course, I do not mind! I feel bad enough that we keep you up until all hours, waiting in the room in case we have need of you. If you have found a way to pass the time, all the better." Grace's mind wandered off, wondering what the lady's maids discussed when their mistresses weren't around. If she asked, Elsie would answer. But Grace didn't want to pry. It was none of her business, and besides, she trusted Elsie to speak up if they'd talked about anything relevant to Grace or her family.

There was, however, one person Grace could ask about. The Fitzroy maid. Grace had told Lord Percy that the accident was a terrible coincidence. But was it truly? She wanted nothing more than to banish that memory from her mind, but she'd force herself to relive those moments if it helped her find Charity.

Grace took herself back to her final moments with Charity. They'd swirled on the dance floor, where Charity had mistimed her steps. When the set ended, Charity's cheeks shone pink.

She had seemed otherwise fine, but only to the casual observer. Grace felt certain that something had been wrong. In all the balls they had been to so far, she had never seen Charity lose her footing. She never turned the wrong way. Even when they had danced in the privacy of Charity's bedroom in the weeks leading up to their debut, Charity's performances had always been perfect.

The night before, Elsie had suggested the Fitzroy maid had overindulged. Could such a thing have happened to Charity? Charity had always been so careful to avoid drinking to excess—but she never abstained. What if perhaps she had accidentally consumed a stronger beverage than she had expected and felt the effects?

Replaying Elsie's words in her mind, Grace thought quickly. Elsie had said Charity had a glass of punch. Grace had as well, however, and it had not left her reeling.

Grace reached over and took the dress from Elsie's hands. She set it aside and then clasped Elsie's hands in her own. "We have not spoken about what we saw last night. It was a terrible, *horrible* accident."

Elsie bit her lip and looked at the floor. Her breath shuddered out. "I'm all right, miss. There's no need to discuss it."

"But there is, Elsie. Something was wrong with Charity during that last set. She was off balance. Not nearly as badly as the maid we saw, but enough to make me wonder if there is a connection. You said you thought the maid had nipped a drink. Did you see her do that?"

Elsie shook her head. "No, but I wasn't keeping an eye on her. To be honest, I didn't even know her name. She passed through the room from time to time, seeing if we needed anything. It was far too busy below stairs for us lady's maids to add to the crush."

"Then why did you think she was drunk?"

Elsie flushed. "I shouldn't tell you this, but sometimes the servants — not all of them, or even most of them, mind you — finish the half-empty glasses. They say there's no point letting a perfectly good drink go to waste. I assumed that was what she'd done."

But whose glass would the maid have finished? Elsie had already said it had been quiet. Grace knew little about the ways of the servants. Would the maid have ventured into other rooms? If she had not...

The drink could have been Charity's glass of punch, and the maid had finished it after she left. But no... Grace knew that the punch hadn't been unusually strong. Certainly, a single glass, even had Charity left it mostly full, would not have put the maid so deep within her cups.

Unless... Grace's stomach turned as she suddenly considered a more terrifying prospect. What if the maid hadn't been drunk at all?

For the first time, Grace wished she could believe the rumours about her best friend. It was easier to imagine Charity safe and sound, riding off with a secret love, than to face this possibility. But face it, she must, for no one else was interested in discovering the truth.

9

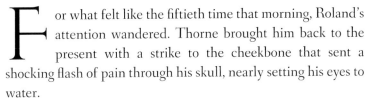

For what felt like the fiftieth time that morning, Roland's attention wandered. Thorne brought him back to the present with a strike to the cheekbone that sent a shocking flash of pain through his skull, nearly setting his eyes to water.

The dark-haired servant dropped his fists. Mindful that there were some gentlemen milling around the outskirts of the ring, watching, Thorne said in a low voice, "I did not realise your plans this morning included a wish for me to beat you soundly."

Furious with himself for the lapse, Roland grunted and launched a series of strikes with his knuckles that had Thorne backing up towards the ropes. Thorne, canny man that he was, kept his cool and went on the defence, blocking patiently while Roland tired himself out. And then he let loose with a stunning left jab that hit Roland in the gut, knocking the wind out of him.

"This is pointless," Thorne said, brushing his forelock out of his eyes and dropping his hands again. "Your mind is clearly elsewhere. The question is, where is it?"

Roland could not answer, even if he wanted to. Which he didn't.

"Ah," Thorne grunted in understanding. "You have that sour-lemon face you always get when you think of family. Which I take to mean you are preoccupied with your failures thus far in securing a lady to bear the next heir of Northumberland."

"Clearly, you have too much time to think about what my face suggests," Roland muttered. "Perhaps I should give you more work."

The man grinned at Roland. "Mayhap it is love? Does the diamond's eloping truly sit so poorly? Were you enamoured after all?"

Thorne was right in one respect, at least. With the Fitzroy ball two days past, and no word one way or another about the diamond, Roland had thought to find an outlet for his black mood in pugilism this morning, but if he could not keep his mind to task, this trip to the training rooms was a futile outing. To his everlasting dissatisfaction, the nightly balls had rendered them quiet. Many of the men there preferred to watch and gamble rather than take their turn in a bout and risk blackening an eye.

He wanted, almost, to beat something bloody. Naturally, the amiable and ever-reliable Thorne was willing to oblige him in a match. However, even in the worst temper Roland could imagine, he would never let his feelings overwhelm his sensibilities, especially if it might result in harm. He could never, never imagine abusing someone in his employ.

"It is not love, and *of course* I was not enamoured. It sits poorly that I have spent so much time attempting to court her and I have nothing to show for it." Roland replied testily once he regained his breath. "Otherwise, I do not care that the diamond perhaps found a different husband."

Then he straightened and turned his back on his sparring partner, heading for the ropes.

"Perhaps Lord Percy cares about the loss of his wager," Lord Henry said, for he was standing near enough to the ring to overhear this last. "I certainly know that *I* am, for I had bet ten shillings on his success with the Lady Charity, and as a result, I am ten shillings poorer this morning."

Roland was annoyed yet again at the reminder he made that disreputable bet, and while drunk besides. But he kept his feelings from his face. Mostly. Despite Roland's efforts to be the perfect gentleman in every regard, Roland's jaw would grow tight when something frustrated or angered him, and he knew Thorne would see it. "I am sorry to have disappointed you, Lord Henry. I hope you could afford the loss."

Now Lord Henry's face pinched in anger. "We are all, of course, subject to our occasional lapses in judgement over assessing the character of a person, are we not? I thank you for your concern, nonetheless."

Thorne looked from Roland to Lord Henry, clearly understanding Henry's subtext. Henry was taking umbrage and was suggesting that perhaps it was Roland's character he had misjudged—not the Lady Diamond's. He put his hand on Roland's shoulder to forestall his reply, steering him out of the ring.

"I say, Lord Percy," Henry called out, his voice taking on a falsely jovial tone behind them. "Since I am reminded of my debt, I wonder. Have you yet repaid yours to Lord Fitzroy? If you must wait for funds to clear, I would be happy to provide you a small loan."

Roland managed to keep his temper. "Thank you, Lord Henry. I shall remember your offer, should I ever have need of it."

Thorne pointed with his chin, indicating a quiet bench

away from Lord Henry where they might pretend to watch the next participants who had taken the ring without being overheard. Once they were seated, Thorne gathered his words. "It has been most clear that you have been rather... troubled since Northumberland. You have not spoken of it, but I know the manner of your grandfather well enough to imagine His Grace was somehow responsible. What did he threaten?"

The flash of fury, commingled with the barest tinge of fear in Roland's dark eyes, confirmed to Thorne that his speculations were deadly accurate, and had struck a blow to a most sensitive spot indeed.

"Ah," Thorne said simply.

"While waiting for my return from the front, the duke had much time to think upon the generosity of my allowance. If I have not secured an engagement before the end of the season, I shall find it reduced," Roland said, gritting his teeth.

As he was no half-wit, Thorne knew that this would very likely mean Roland would be unable to afford to keep a household staff—even if he were the only one. "I should hope you aren't overly concerned for my prospects," he said with a grin, attempting to ease the mood.

The muscles in Roland's jaw and shoulders relaxed, but only a tad. "Never."

Roland did not speak about the other conditions that The Breaker had had plenty of time to think about writing into his will. If Thorne suspected there had been additional codicils that played a part of the duke's threat—a deduction which Roland knew Thorne was eminently capable of making—neither man decided to speak of it.

As was proper.

"So, what shall you do now?" Thorne asked him, ever to the point.

"I... must begin again, sifting through the balls to find

another woman suitable to court, I suppose. Worse, for I may have to call on several at once now. Also, I must endure the Lord Fitzroy's smirk about it for the remainder of the season, with my money sitting in his purse."

"You have no one else to blame for pinning your hopes on one lady alone. The only other lady you've spoken to this entire season you practically branded a murderess to her face. If speed is of the essence, she may not consider your attempt to call fondly."

"Lady Grace?" Roland nearly exclaimed with a laugh. "She..." He spread his hands, trying to frame his reply as he thought about the chestnut-haired waif of a woman. Unbidden, the image of her face came to mind as she goaded him by comparing the women of the ton to animals at a country fair. She had had one slender eyebrow raised at him in challenge, as if defying him to argue against it.

For a moment, he pondered the possibility of courting Grace, given that he hadn't done so until now. She came from a noble line—albeit barely. Pretty enough in a more provincial sense, he supposed, but with none of the striking beauty of her friend. Nor any actual grace at all. No. "I can only imagine what Grandfather would think of that choice. She is all... left feet and claws."

Thorne snorted. "If that is the mark of one's worth, I must warn you I have heard from the other servants of your dancing."

"Nevertheless," Roland said, finally regaining his aplomb, "even without the murder accusation, I believe she may despise me already. So, it matters naught, and my search goes on."

Thorne's blue eyes roved this informal boxing club while they talked, noting that a few more gentlemen had entered. But they, too, seem disinclined to hop into the ring. At first, Thorne did not pay them much heed, but their curious behaviour finally commanded his attention. And once it had Thorne's attention, Roland's eyes soon followed.

What had caught Thorne's notice was that the knot of men talking did not face the ring at all, as they would have if they were spectators. They clustered tightly, Lord Henry among them, as though their voices were being kept low, and it was difficult to hear over the noise of the match.

Roland also marked this odd, secretive behaviour and decided it was time to stretch his legs. "Is there another wager afoot, Lord Henry?" he asked casually, leaving Thorne sitting on the bench as he approached the gathered men. "I may be interested if the odds are good, what with the debt to be paid to Lord Fitzroy."

The knot of gentlemen broke up, some looking guilty. But Lord Henry's face—it was difficult to decipher.

"There's a rumour out of the Cresswell household, though it is hard to credit," one of the newly arrived men admitted. "One of my footmen has a cousin working at the Cresswell house. Through him, I heard that a note of ransom arrived early this morning. What makes it so strange is that it was for some odd amount. Some two pounds, eleven or twelve shillings, and..." his voice trailed off as he tried to recall.

"Twelve shillings, two pounds sterling, and a milréis?" Lord Henry asked, his inquiry soft.

"Yes!" agreed the man. "The milréis. That was what made it so odd."

"*Quite.* That is quite odd indeed," Lord Henry agreed, locking eyes with Roland.

10

At the rattle of the doorknob, Grace stuffed the broadsheets she was reading behind her back. She glanced over to see Elsie slip inside, taking care to close the door softly. The maid had departed shortly after breakfast to visit the Cresswell household, ostensibly with the assignment to retrieve a pair of gloves Grace had forgotten during her last visit. In truth, she was under orders to find out what the Cresswell servants thought about Charity's disappearance.

Grace expected her to be gone for a while, and had snuck downstairs to retrieve the prior day's paper. Her mother only permitted Grace to read the fashionable world section, with its coverage of social gatherings and the latest ball gowns. If she wanted to know the outcome of Parliamentary debates or reports of lurid crimes, she had to pilfer the day-old newspaper from her father's study. Preferably when the room was empty.

Back upstairs, she had settled in a chair by the window in her bedroom to study the news for any clues. Thus far, she had discovered precious little. With Elsie's early return, it appeared all her sleuthing attempts were for naught.

"Back so soon?" Grace asked, leaning forward to get the paper back out. "Did they refuse you entry?"

"No, miss!" Elsie's voice trembled with emotion. "They hardly noticed when I walked into the kitchen. The house was in such a fuss."

Grace's heart hurt thinking about Charity's family. If only her mother would unbend enough to allow Grace to visit them. They must be devastated—the entire household. Grace could only imagine how it must have been. "I am sorry I sent you over there. It must have been a difficult situation."

Elsie hurried across the room and perched on the edge of the chair across from Grace. "You have no idea, my lady! They're saying Lady Charity has been kidnapped!"

Though Grace had already suspected something nefarious had happened, to hear her suspicions confirmed was still a blow. "Oh, Charity!" Grace exclaimed. "Two days wasted instead of searching simply because they believed she had eloped of her own free will. Whatever finally changed their minds?"

"Lord Cresswell received a note in the morning post with a demand for a ransom payment!"

Grace gasped and fell back against her chair, creasing the papers still tucked away. "A ransom! How much is it? Will they pay? What am I even asking? Surely they must pay!"

Elsie waited until Grace finished arguing with herself. "That's the thing. The amount of the ransom is so minimal and strange. Lord and Lady Cresswell don't know what to make of it. Is it some intended slight?"

Before Grace could ask anything else, the doorknob once again rattled. Elsie leapt to her feet and scooted away from the chair, hiding the evidence of her untoward, informal friendship with her mistress.

Lady Tilbury threw open the door and marched into the room. "Elsie, collect Grace's wrap and hat. We are going out."

70

Grace groaned aloud, too annoyed by her mother's untimely arrival to remember to bite it back. "*Must we*, Mama? It is not even visiting hours yet."

"I should think you would be pleased. After all, you spent much of yesterday desperate to visit the girl's family."

Grace scowled at her mother. The only family she'd asked to visit was the Cresswell's, and there was little chance she'd changed her position on the matter after a night of sleep. Yet, she drew a blank on whom else her mother might mean.

Lady Tilbury was still talking. "Lady Cresswell has need of us, my dear. Especially now that we know Lady Charity didn't leave on her own. We must show the family solidarity." Lady Tilbury waved her hands, hastening Grace on. "That dress is highly unsuitable for the occasion. And is that a newspaper tucked behind you? You will have newsprint all down the back of your gown."

Grace kept her mouth shut on the hypocrisy of the situation as her mother bustled around her room, issuing orders like a commander on the eve of battle. She was getting what she wanted, and if playing the role of dutiful daughter got her there faster, so much the better.

While Grace washed her hands and splashed water on her face, Lady Tilbury opened her wardrobe. After careful consideration, her ladyship chose a grey silk gown cut in the empire style, with slashed sleeves and darts along the front. "This is sombre enough without straying into mourning wear. Elsie, help Grace into this."

Grace despised the dress for the very reason her mother had chosen it. To make matters worse, the grey leeched all colour from her face. The Cresswell home was bound to be popular, as yesterday's social pariah became today's sob story. Still, no one was coming to see Grace. Even though Charity would not be there, she would still be the centre of attention.

During the coach ride, Lady Tilbury instructed Grace on the proper facial expressions for the current circumstances. "Demonstrate your best concerned smile."

Grace adopted what she thought was a suitable shape by pressing her lips together.

"Far too disapproving. Can you turn the corners up a bit? No, that is too much! Like this," Lady Tilbury demonstrated.

After several failed attempts, Grace lost her patience. "Mama, I am genuinely distraught over Charity's absence, as well you know. Do you not trust my anguish to come through in an appropriate manner?"

Lady Tilbury sniffed. "Very well, but no tears. Your face becomes blotchy, and your neck turns red. You should ask Mercy to show you how to cry prettily the next time you see her."

Grace did not bother to point out that her sister Mercy had far more important matters on her mind, namely the recent birth of her first child. "I promise to remain ever stoic, while nonetheless expressing the perfect balance of sadness and hope. Is that satisfactory?"

Lady Tilbury rapped Grace with her fan for her impudence.

The coach came to a stop in front of the Cresswell home. Nestled discreetly just a stone's throw from the Grosvenor Square, their Georgian manor stood as a testament to the wealth and refined taste of its noble occupant, the well-to-do Earl Cresswell.

Ornate, classical columns flanked the grand entrance, evoking a sense of grandeur and stability. The brickwork was of the finest quality, a rich red that contrasted beautifully with the meticulously kept white stone detailing around the windows and doors.

The driver helped Grace down first. While she waited for her mother to descend, Grace paid little attention to the opulent entrance. Her gaze rose to the left front window on the third floor. Prior to their debut, on many an afternoon, she and Charity had peered through its curtains, watching the upper class parade around the square on their way to pay calls.

Those days were over now, and not simply because they had joined society. Grace held tight to the belief that Charity would return safe and sound. But would society accept their Diamond back into their midst? To that question, Grace had no answer.

A footman answered the door and Lady Tilbury handed over her card. He returned a moment later. "Lady Cresswell will see you."

Charity's mother rose when they came into the drawing room. Her brittle smile threatened to shatter into a million pieces, and her wan complexion left her as pale as her ivory satin gown. "Lilian, it is so good of you to come." If she, too, recognised how fickle was the support of Lady Tilbury and the other visiting ladies depending on whether their honour might be at stake, she did not say so.

Lady Tilbury took her friend's hands and squeezed them tight, smiling while lying through her teeth. "I wanted to come straight away, but Byron forbade me. You know how men are. They don't understand how tightly the bonds of sisterhood connect us women."

"You are here now, and that is all that matters. Oh Grace, you must be so upset as well. Someone has taken our darling Charity!"

Lady Cresswell invited the Tilburys to sit and sent the footman for a fresh pot of tea. "I do not understand any of this. How could someone kidnap my Charity? *Why?*" She carefully did not mention the obvious reason, that someone could have designs on Charity's virtue, perhaps to force a marriage where one had been refused.

"I heard you received a demand. For one as valuable as a diamond, they must have asked for a king's ransom," Lady Tilbury said.

"That is the strangest part; they did not. They asked for a very peculiar amount that sounded more like the contents of someone's purse than the value of a debutante, and set a delivery date that is a week away. As soon as William read the note, he rushed off to the palace."

"The palace?" Lady Tilbury and Grace gasped in unison.

Lady Cresswell nodded. "He was in too much of a rush to answer my questions. Said he would not stand for it, and the queen herself would surely intervene."

Lady Tilbury laid her hand across her chest. "My word! Let us pray he is correct. Our queen is strong and fearless. I would not want to be on her bad side."

A loud knock echoed in the front hall, catching the women's attention. Another one of society's matriarchs, no doubt, had come to feast at the high table of gossip. But when the footman appeared in the drawing-room doorway, he had no card upon his silver tray.

"Her Majesty requests the immediate presence of one of your guests, my lady. She has sent a carriage." He shifted his gaze until it fell upon Grace. "Lady Grace, Lady Tilbury, if you will follow me. I have your jackets and hats waiting at the door."

Lady Tilbury turned upon her youngest child and in a harsh whisper hissed, *"What did you do!"*

Grace hadn't a clue. Until this moment, she would have sworn the queen didn't even know her name. At best, she'd refer to her as the girl standing next to my diamond.

The footman coughed politely into his gloved hand, reminding them all of the need for haste.

"Go, Grace," Lady Cresswell encouraged. "Perhaps she has had word of Charity, and wants you to go along to collect her."

Grace's hopes soared, but as she slipped on her jacket, she dragged them back to the ground. She'd read enough newspaper articles to know such horrid tales rarely had a happy ending.

11

Thorne could read the postures of the men as they welcomed Roland into their cluster. There was trouble afoot, and it was of the sort that was of an immediate, dangerous variety to his employer. As quickly as he could without alarming anyone, he made his way closer, just in time to hear Roland respond.

"What, exactly, are you implying I have done, Lord Henry?" Roland kept his timbre light, almost casual.

Thorne knew better than to trust that tone of voice, and hoped Lord Henry was wise enough to cease in allowing his tongue to flap about.

"Would you feign ignorance even now?" the lord exclaimed, his face growing red. "A ransom comes for Lady Charity in the exact amount of your wager, and you are surprised that suspicion falls directly on your head for it?"

Roland planted his hands on his hips. "My Lord Henry, I hope I have misunderstood your words, for it feels like you nearly accused me of kidnapping the Lady Charity in front of these gentlemen. *Surely*, I must have been mistaken in my hearing, because you have no more proof than a ransom note for a figure that all the gentlemen of White's knew."

He paused briefly, giving Lord Henry a chance to open his mouth and recant. Lord Henry, however, was too angry to immediately backtrack. Roland nodded.

"Speak plainly, then, to correct me if I have it wrong, for I am sure it is understood that I would have to respond to such a serious, baseless accusation with a request to defend my honour. Oh, and Lord Henry," Roland said, dropping his voice to something very low, "I should warn you—I do not believe that any matter of honour truly serious enough to warrant a duel should be settled by firing impotently into the air."

Lord Henry's face changed colour again—this time from red to white, and the rest of the men there glanced around uncertainly. "You... I did not mean to imply your guilt, Lord Percy. Guilt is a matter for the magistrate to determine," he replied in a stilted fashion. "I only meant that it seems suspicious indeed."

Roland nodded. "That is fair, Lord Henry. But you must also agree it seems improbable, yes? For if I was a man of such low character, to win the bet, all I would have to be willing to do is sully the Lady Charity's virtue."

The men saw an out and agreed loudly, relaxing as the immediate danger passed. Thorne took this moment to step in.

"My Lord," he said in the carefully formal, ingratiating tone he scrupulously adopted when surrounded by other nobles. He knew Roland detested when he spoke to him this way, but Thorne had always worried about inadvertently causing damage to Roland's reputation. Certainly, Thorne cared more to adhere to the boundaries of propriety than Roland ever did. "The hour grows late; we must depart so you will not be late when you pay your calls."

"My apologies. Gentlemen," Roland murmured, nodding his head and taking his leave.

Outside of the training rooms, they hurried to mount and headed for Roland's city dwelling at a slightly risky canter. "What calls?" Roland finally asked his man once they slowed to a trot. They were approaching the districts where the wealthier lived and walked frequently, so too much haste would be both indecorous and suspicious.

Thorne's blue eyes met Roland's. "An excuse. But in retrospect, I believe a visit to the queen would not go amiss," he said.

"I would sooner stick my hand into a beehive," Roland answered mulishly.

Thorne turned to one side to hide his grin at Roland's petulance—a display Roland would allow no one else to see. "Truly, your steadfast composure despite the adversity of your noble birth moves me, Sir Barbarian. Every day I am reminded how profoundly grateful I am to have been born an untitled nobody."

Roland shot him an ominous look that spoke of long suffering, and Thorne laughed, before he continued. "It is a silly suspicion, as you say. Nonetheless," his man replied, continuing to sound inappropriately jovial about the whole thing, "if Lord Henry thought of it, despite his wit being as sharp as a wheel of cheese, you can be sure that others will as well. You should head off the rumour as best you can."

"I know," Roland sighed. "Let us hope I can do so before my grandfather catches wind of it."

At the house, Roland stripped to his breeches quickly and made use of the washbasin and cloth. He wished he could take a full bath, but alas, there would be no time. At least the soap, scented with citrusy-smelling bergamot, was refreshing. As he began towelling off in preparation to dress, however, he could hear a banging at the front door.

Thorne appeared in his room shortly after. "Two guards from the Palace," he said shortly. "They are here to escort you to a private audience with the queen."

"It would seem, then, that the queen is more inclined to head off *me*," Roland murmured in reply, pulling fresh clothes in haste.

"Aye." Thorne stepped in to help him with his collar and sleeves, straightening his shirt to sit properly as Roland did up the front. "Let us hope it is to head you off instead of offing your head."

"Sometimes you are an utter trial," Roland complained. But he set a hand on Thorne's shoulder, trying to convey all the words his lips could not, and Thorne gripped his shoulder in return.

In this cutthroat world of the ton, full of politicking, power games, and ostentatious displays of wealth, Queen Charlotte was wholly in her element. For the first thing that happened was Roland was quickly escorted to the large and richly-adorned council chamber.

The arrangement of the furniture indicated quite clearly that he was not welcome to sit. And if he entertained any further questions about the queen's mood when she made her summons, he was made to wait.

So, Roland stood, waiting patiently and wordlessly despite his inner seething, for about a quarter of an hour until Queen Charlotte finally swept into the room. As was appropriate, he bowed, lowered his eyes, and waited for her to speak to him first.

"Lord Percy," Queen Charlotte said coolly. "It was good of you to respond so promptly."

Roland raised his eyes, unsurprised to see Lord Cresswell had entered the room with her. "Of course, Your Majesty," he replied.

"I have been given to understand that you made an... interesting wager concerning your bid for the hand of my diamond of this season—the same young lady who seems to have gone missing at Lord Fitzroy's estate." Queen Charlotte made a slight gesture towards Lord Cresswell. "Lord Cresswell has brought it to my attention that he received a ransom note this very morning for the same peculiar amount you decided to wager."

Perhaps unwisely, Roland let his equally cool gaze meet the infuriated one of Lord Cresswell. "I have heard this myself, ma'am."

"And what do you have to say about this?"

"Your Majesty, Lady Charity's disappearance is shocking and weighs most heavily in all our hearts. The ransom note, however, was not mine. Lord Cresswell was not present when I laid my wager. If he found out about it, then I suspect half the ton's tongues have been wagging. If so, it is possible the note may have been sent by anyone," Roland said smoothly, ignoring the daggers of Lord Cresswell's eyes.

"Or mayhap the gossip is just convenient enough to shroud the truth in doubt!" he boomed.

"I presume you have some proof to back your claim, Lord Percy?" the queen said, lifting a finger to silence the irate Lord Cresswell.

"Yes, ma'am," he dipped his chin. "At the presumed time of Lady Charity's disappearance, I was assisting Lord Fitzroy with the death of one of his maids. My time was wholly consumed by this tragedy—quite publicly so. Then, once the guests had mostly dispersed, and we were made aware of Lady Charity's disappearance, I was part of the search. I would have had no time to either conceal the lady or abscond with her."

"Unless you had an accomplice," interjected Lord Cresswell.

"Who would that be, Lord Cresswell?" Roland asked the man. "My staff consists of a single valet, and I left him at my house that evening. Before this, I have been serving in His Majesty's army for the last ten years. What close friends at Lord Fitzroy's ball would you imagine I could trust to be an accomplice in such a heinous act?"

To that, Lord Cresswell had no answer. Roland let his dark eyes meet the queen's so that she could see he was in earnest.

Queen Charlotte resettled herself on her chair. "I heard of that unfortunate incident with the maid. Well, Lord Percy, if you speak truly, then it certainly appears someone is taking advantage of your wager to the fullest—either to aid in concealing their crime, or to misdirect searchers who might thwart an eloping. If half the ton knew of this wager, mayhap the young lady did as well, and sought to take matters into her own hands."

Lord Cresswell, who had been deflating somewhat, found a new reason to be apoplectic. "She would *never*—!"

"Lady Grace thought not—" Roland said at the same time. And he paused as abruptly as Lord Cresswell did at the realisation he had uttered the comment out loud. Both the queen and Lord Cresswell stared at him as if he had grown two heads.

"Do continue," the queen said, her eyes drilling into Roland's, "about how Lady Grace is involved."

Inwardly, Roland cursed himself for his thoughtlessness. As briefly as he could do respectfully, he explained Grace's relationship with Charity, Fitzroy's introduction of her to

Roland, and the dance they shared. "In fact, I was supposed to dance with your daughter immediately after the turn with Lady Grace," he added, turning to her father, "but she appeared to have left the ballroom."

Lord Cresswell nodded stiffly. The queen's own face was impassive, showing nothing at all.

"When I could not find her, I decided to retire to the card room, and as I was heading through the atrium, that is when..." Roland trailed off, gesturing expressively. "The next day, I paid a call to Lady Grace, to inquire about whether Lady Charity had plans to elope and whether she had used the disturbance to leave. Lady Grace said Lady Charity had no plans of the sort; the diamond's ambition was to marry well."

Drumming her fingers on the arm of the chair, the queen paused in thought. "I have the sense you did not believe Lady Grace. Not entirely, Lord Percy."

Roland straightened slightly, the only sign he allowed of his surprise that the queen had also sensed his misgiving. "That is correct, Your Majesty."

"Perhaps you would share with me the reasons why? Beyond, of course, the fact that one would assume Lady Charity should have been happy to accept you as a suitor, given her ambition to marry highly. I rather wonder at the reasons why she did not."

His jaw tightened as the queen deliberately poked the bruise to his ego with an arched eyebrow, but he took a breath and answered steadily. "I have little but conjecture, ma'am," he admitted. "The Tilbury family departed the party shortly after the maid's death. She was reluctant to talk about Lady Charity, to even look at me, when I called upon her." *I also saw her face in the very spot the maid fell*, he thought to himself, seeing her pale, horrified face looking down at him in his memory. But he was loath to bring her name up in direct connection to the maid's death. Reputations could be ruined by less, he reasoned to himself.

Before he could be asked more, an obsequious footman entered the council chamber, pulling the queen's disapproving stare away from him. The footman bowed deeply, then approached the queen to murmur somewhat to her directly.

"Perhaps," the queen said to no one in particular, straightening in her chair, "we shall ask Lady Grace about her involvement herself. Fortunately, I sent for her as soon as Lord Cresswell offered her name as Lady Charity's dearest friend. Do show her in."

12

For all the rush to cross town, Grace and her mother spent a full half hour cooling their heels in the palace corridor. A uniformed footman stood near the door, staring straight ahead, as though they were not there. It was true that a good servant was neither seen nor heard unless called, but Grace would have welcomed any hint about why she was there.

Yet, when the door opened, Grace regretted her fervent wishes to go inside. She stood from the bench upon which she'd sat and smoothed the skirt of her gown. Her palms left damp circles on the silk, the sight of which grounded her into the present.

"*Stop that.* You'll crease the fabric," her mother whispered. Lady Tilbury gathered herself and marched for the open door.

A polite cough stopped her before she got far. "My lady, you will need to wait here. Her Majesty has asked only for Lady Grace."

Lady Tilbury's eyes grew round in surprise. "As her mother, it would be appropriate for me to accompany—"

"Do you question the queen?" the footman asked, daring to arch an eyebrow.

Lady Tilbury baulked at his words. No one questioned the queen. She reached over and grabbed her daughter's wrist. In a harsh whisper, she imparted final instructions. "Curtsy, do not speak until she does, and never turn your back on her."

Grace knew all the rules for being in the presence of the monarch. They'd been drilled into her in preparation for her court presentation. Despite her penchant for high spirits, even she recognised there were limits.

She squared her shoulders, lifted her head high, and forced her legs to carry her through the open door, with no idea what she would find inside.

Her gaze naturally went first to the queen, seated at the end of the council chamber. Charlotte sat upon a heavy chair covered in red velvet, looking to all the world like a monarch upon the throne. Her perfect posture owed as much to the corset cinching her waist as to her training. Jewels glittered on her ears, slender throat, and wrists, and her powdered wig was an elaborate affair that stood high upon her head. Her dark eyes flashed, beckoning Grace to approach, but with care.

Grace lowered her gaze and dropped into a deep curtsy.

The queen's voice echoed in the room. "Rise, Lady Grace. We have questions which only you can answer."

Grace straightened up and risked a glance around the room. She'd assumed the queen meant the royal we, but she found they were not alone. Lord Cresswell stood near the queen's chair, his face flushed with some high emotion. And on the other side of the room, Lord Percy stared back at her, his impassive face and dark brown eyes wholly unreadable.

The last vestiges of hope in Grace's breast for good news about Charity flickered and died. She forced a placid smile upon her face. "I am at your service, Your Majesty."

"Tell us about the night of the Fitzroy Ball."

Grace wished she could wring her hands, uncertain how to

answer. "I attended along with my family. It was a pleasant evening, and everyone seemed to be in good spirits."

"Do you think I care about that? Skip to what happened after you danced with Lord Percy."

Grace gulped. How much had Percy said? She had no choice but to assume the worst. The queen had eyes everywhere, and likely knew all.

"After our dance, I noticed I had ripped the hem of my gown. My mother sent me to my maid upstairs, to have it repaired. While there, one of the Fitzroy servants was out of sorts. She stumbled awkwardly, eventually leaving the room. I heard a great crash in the corridor and rushed to check on her. She had knocked a marble bust from its pedestal. Before I could call for help, she fell against the balcony railing and went tumbling over the side."

"You witnessed this accident?" the queen asked, her voice growing arch as she turned her eyes towards Lord Percy. "How odd that Lord Percy failed to mention that you were present there."

Grace felt her cheeks grow cold. Lord Percy had not hinted at her involvement. She had said too much, but there was no going back now. "I was upstairs. He might not have seen me."

"Forgive me, Your Majesty. I was more concerned about Lord Fitzroy's guests on the ground floor," Lord Percy added.

Grace's mouth fell open. Lord Percy had nearly uttered a lie to the queen. To protect her? Quickly, she closed it again, but fortunately, no one noticed her surprise.

Queen Charlotte glared at Percy for speaking out of turn. She hushed him and set her sights once again on Grace. "And after this accident? How did you get downstairs to leave, and why? For Lord Percy noted that your family had left with haste."

"My maid took me to the servant's staircase, and we hurried

to the ballroom. My mother was there, searching for me. As soon as I told her what I'd seen, she demanded we leave at once. It was a terrible shock, ma'am."

"Hmm." Queen Charlotte pursed her lips as she weighed Grace's words. "You said your maid was upstairs. Did she see this servant woman imbibe?"

"I asked my maid this very question. The Fitzroy servant had been with the other maids for most of the evening. It is unlikely she had access to sufficient quantities of drink. Although I'm no expert, I found her behaviour to be very strange. She was unbalanced, as if intoxicated, but when she spoke, her words were not slurred. And then, there was Lady Charity's behaviour during the prior set."

"What has Charity got to do with a sotted maid?" Lord Cresswell asked, looking confused.

Queen Charlotte silenced him with a blistering glare. "Please continue, Lady Grace."

"Lady Charity made mistakes during the dance, as if she too was unbalanced. Yet she was always very careful not to drink to excess, and indeed I did not see her consume more than two glasses of punch in the whole evening. While no one is perfect, I have never known her to miss a step. After the set finished, Charity's face was flushed, and she complained of it being too warm. My mother suggested she accompany me upstairs, but she said she had been there earlier. She told us she preferred to step outside and let the night air clear her head."

"And that was the last anyone saw of my diamond," the queen concluded.

"I thought..." Grace hesitated. Her mother would tell her to hold her tongue, but her desire to find Charity compelled her to finish her statement. "I had a thought that the events might be connected, Your Majesty. If someone put something in Charity's drink while she was upstairs, and mayhap the servant finished it? It is a tenuous link, but I cannot abandon my suspicions. Especially now that Lord Cresswell received the ransom note."

Queen Charlotte's brows drew down. "That is a very serious suspicion to entertain, for you would imply then that there was a plot calculated to deliberately cause harm to Lady Charity and no other. If it is true, that means the ransom note could very well be in earnest."

Lord Cresswell barked a laugh. "For all we know, the ransom note is a sick joke, especially since the amount matches Lord Percy's ridiculous wager that he would marry my daughter this season."

A *wager?* On his possession of Charity, as if he was making a bet on a horse at the race? Grace's gaze flipped to her right, where it crashed headlong into Lord Percy's dark brown eyes. He lowered his head, silently admitting that Lord Cresswell spoke truly. Her hands fisted at her sides.

The queen's attention was on the opposite side of the room. With this last outburst, she had arrived at the limits of her patience with Lord Cresswell. Missing daughter or not, one did not speak out of turn more than once.

She glanced at the guard in the back of the room. "Please see Lord Cresswell out."

"Out?" Cresswell paled. "But we have no answers. What am I to do?"

"Go home and comfort your wife. When I have made a decision regarding payment of the ransom demand, I will send word. Until then, you are to do nothing. Do not think of crossing me in this matter."

Cresswell had the good sense to bow before taking his leave, but the tick in his jaw revealed his genuine sentiments. The queen watched him go.

While she was distracted, Grace turned again to Lord

Percy. He had lifted his head, but his gaze was fixed forward, toward the queen. He would not meet her eyes, and he did not look sorry in the least. If he thought that avoiding eye contact would allow him to escape her anger, he was sadly mistaken.

"You *wagered* on my dearest friend?" she hissed. "You are meant to be a gentleman. Have you so little honour?"

He flicked his gaze back to her, but his expression warned her to keep her head.

"While I agree the choice of his wager borders on being boorish, choose your words carefully, Lady Grace," the queen cautioned. Seeing Grace's upset, she tossed her head back and laughed at Grace's naivety. "Come, child. The season would be dreadfully boring without something to keep us entertained. Wagers are made all the time, in situations serious and otherwise. The royal purse has been known to partake in many of them. Have you still something to say?"

Grace flattened her lips together, pulling them so tight they turned white. She dared a single shake of her head.

"Let us return to the matter at hand. There has been no sign of Lady Charity since she ventured into the Fitzroy gardens two nights past. Her absence may or may not be connected to the servant's death. And now we have a ransom note." Queen Charlotte tapped her fingers on the arm of her chair. "There are messages implicit in the theft of my diamond and the significance of the ransom amount. I have a sense that someone is playing a most dangerous game, and it may be against me in part. It must end, and Lord Percy will see it done."

"What?" Grace blurted.

The queen ignored her outburst. "Lord Percy, I wish you to locate her before this... person's game is played out in its entirety. Consider this your penance for your lack of manners."

Lord Percy looked grim but put as good a face on it as he could. "Your Majesty, I am happy to assist in any way I can."

Grace choked at his sheer cheek. "How do you expect to find her? You are new to London, you know Lady Charity not at all, and furthermore, only cared about her because of the wager. I should be the one to lead the search."

For a moment, he could only stare at her, stunned. "*You?* But you are a *woman!*"

Queen Charlotte bristled at his response. "You say that as though it were a limitation, Lord Percy. Are you suggesting *I* am also incapable?"

"I, err—no, of course not, Your Majesty."

The queen was not impressed. "You have a reputation for having a head for strategy. If you wish to sway me, offer some counter arguments. Pray tell, without Lady Grace's aid, how would you mean to find a girl you barely know, in a town you have been absent from for years? She has the social connections and has already proven her powers of observation. I think perhaps she is correct; she is your best source of assistance for solving the riddle of our missing lady this season." Queen Charlotte shifted her head to look at Grace. "Is that right?"

"Yes, Your Majesty. I beg of you, please allow me to aid Lord Percy's search. I am willing to do whatever it takes to see Lady Charity's safe return."

Lord Percy was not willing to back down. "It is true that I have been away from society for a while and some aspersions cast upon my manners, but even I know there is the matter of Lady Grace's reputation. She can hardly travel with me unescorted."

The queen waved off his concern. "She has a lady's maid, as we have heard. I trust you will find a way to work together without blemishing either of your reputations."

Grace sensed she was on the verge of an unexpected victory. Even her mother and father would be unable to stop her from searching for Charity.

Lord Percy screwed up his face, his displeasure in diametric opposition to her satisfaction.

Queen Charlotte silenced him with her final statement. "I, too, wagered you would win the hand of the diamond. Perhaps you are unaware—I do not like to lose my bets. Find Lady Charity or I will declare a replacement. One way or the other, you will stand at the altar with a diamond, Lord Percy."

13

Roland's face felt numb as he listened to the queen's words. That Queen Charlotte never cared to be wrong in the eyes of the ton was bad enough, but with the queen laying a wager aligning with his own? Before, it did not much matter to him if he lost his own wager in the end. Now, he felt trapped by it.

He did not dare look in Lady Grace's direction, certain that she would be smug about his being hoisted with his own petard.

Until that moment, he'd considered the name and face of his bride as almost irrelevant. Indeed, at the time of his wager, he had been certain that whomever the queen had chosen as the diamond would meet his minimum criteria in beauty, breeding and manners. Lady Charity had, and he had been content in his pursuit.

With the possibility that the queen might thrust any random lady she deemed appropriate into the role of his bride? Roland already was having trouble getting to know Lady Charity, and he decided he did not actually like that idea of being rushed to the altar with a perfect stranger whatsoever.

It was a situation uncomfortably familiar to Roland, for he

knew somewhat of how forced marriages could be. Love was not important. But whatever else he had wanted of his bride, he had always imagined that both would go into the agreement willingly. A partnership.

Such foolish thoughts were unproductive, he chastised himself, gritting his teeth. Mayhap the idea he had of choosing had always been an illusion, a mirage. Did it matter whether it was his grandfather pulling his strings, or the queen? The result was the same.

He must turn now to what he could control.

"How would you like us to proceed, Your Majesty?" he asked.

The corner of Queen Charlotte's mouth drew up slightly as she contemplated the two of them standing before her. "Carefully, of course. No one must know what you are about. You must also manufacture a reason for being in one another's company, naturally. Perhaps you might let it be known, Lord Percy, that you are courting Lady Grace. Oh yes, I quite like that idea. It will give you a chance to hone your courtship skills with a woman... in the event you fail."

The queen's voice hardened on those last words, making it a veiled threat. No one would be happy if he failed. "Lord Percy, I recall your original wager was that you would be engaged before June, was it not?" she asked sweetly. "We shall try to keep you to this date."

"And of the lady herself?" Roland asked, desperately holding onto the fraying edges of his temper. "She has been missing for two days. There are already rumours she is likely ruined, and my reputation could go with hers."

He could feel Grace's calculating eyes upon him then. The queen looked unconcerned. "If she is truly ruined, then I will find someone else. Please do keep us apprised of any progress." With that, she called for a footman and whispered instructions his way before dismissing Roland and Grace from her sight.

~

As soon as Grace and Roland exited the council chamber, Lady Tilbury latched onto her daughter's arm and hissed, "What is going on? Why did the queen send for you?"

Grace did not bother to lower her voice. "Queen Charlotte is concerned about her diamond. She sought my opinion on the matter because I am closely acquainted with Charity. Given Lord Percy's involvement with the initial search, she called for him as well."

Lady Tilbury wanted to ask more, but Grace gave her no time. She pulled free and strode ahead. Outside the palace, Queen Charlotte had left a carriage at their disposal, with Roland's horse already tied to the back. The intent was clear: they were to leave together.

Lady Tilbury took the sight in stride. "My lord, I see you are already dressed for dinner. Would you like to accompany us home? I am certain Grace is keen to know you better, as are my husband and son."

Once again, Roland could not refuse. "It would be my pleasure, Lady Tilbury."

The carriage ride was one of the most horrible experiences Roland had suffered yet this season. Lady Grace's mother was in a tizzy about their esteemed guest. Grace, for her own part, was silent, staring out the carriage window as they returned to her home.

This left Roland to answer Lady Tilbury's thousand and one questions about his career with the army, the front, his family, and Northumberland. Of the latter two, he said as little as he could.

When they arrived at the Tilbury mansion, the ladies excused themselves to change for dinner. Lady Tilbury invited Roland to make himself at home in the drawing room and left their butler to see to his needs.

Roland settled in for a wait. There was a large portrait hanging over the fireplace—a family portrait, he assumed—with Lord and Lady Tilbury, an older daughter, a strapping young man, and Lady Grace.

Finally, bored, he inquired of the footman waiting in the hallway whether other members of the family were nearby, but it seemed that Lord Tilbury and his son, Felix, were out and not yet arrived home. So he looked around the drawing room some more, and then he thought carefully about what on Earth he was going to do now.

But before he could think much on the matter, Grace herself appeared in the drawing-room doorway. She took care to leave the door open as she entered the room.

"My lady," Roland greeted her neutrally, studying her face for a hint of her feelings. Her expression was strange. She seemed both angry and... determined? "I did not expect your arrival so soon."

Grace cast a furtive glance over her shoulder. She chose the chair opposite his and motioned for him to sit. "Listen carefully, as we won't have long before someone comes in. You *must* take this matter with the utmost seriousness. If you do not, Charity's life will be ruined!" she hissed.

"I beg your pardon!" Roland said. Though it was difficult to muster a sound of offence without raising his voice enough to capture the attention of the servants in the hall.

"It would not be fair! She has done nothing to deserve this, although I am certain you and the other suitors will cast her aside now that her virtue is in question. If we are to find her, you cannot treat this with casual insouciance."

Irritated, Roland put a hand to his chest mockingly. "You wound me with such a low opinion of my character."

Grace harrumphed. "A wound is certainly what you deserve. If I were a man, I'd call you out for that *ridiculous* wager of yours."

"My lady forgets that half the men of the ton were aware of this wager. Not only did they have nothing to say against it, many bet their own funds upon it. As did the queen," he said tightly. "No slight was intended to Lady Charity in the matter at all. You should compose yourself."

Grace gasped, her nostrils flaring as she spluttered. "Regardless of your so-called intentions, sir, a maid is dead and my best friend is missing. Your snow-white reputation is stained with blood. The only thing that remains to be seen is what you will do about it. Will you play out the hand the queen has dealt and help me find Charity?"

"*My* reputation, Lady Grace?" Roland said stiffly, tightening his grip on the arms of the chair. "You insist on painting me as a blackguard, though you need my cooperation in protecting the reputation of your friend. Quite bold of you, especially considering you were behind the maid before she fell, and only my silence prevents suspicion from falling on your own head. It might surprise you to know that I do not care overmuch for the queen's counterplan. We must either call a truce to put our energies on solving the matter, or else we can spend all night quibbling in circles again and again, and this ruse shall never pass."

Grace sniffed, but she did not argue. "Very well. Where do we start?"

Roland pinned her with a vexed glance and spread his hands, thinking. "If I were a runner, I suppose the first step I would do would be to attempt to follow Lady Charity's footsteps. We know where she was, approximately. We know where she intended to go. Or at least, where she said she would. I would guess I must figure out whether she made it to the gardens, and who might have seen her pass that way."

"The servants," Grace breathed. "Were the servants questioned?"

Pursing his lips in thought, Roland rubbed his jaw. "We asked only if they had seen Lady Charity," he admitted. "We did not ask who else might be about."

"I could call upon Lady Lark Fitzroy on the morrow," Grace said slowly, thinking. "That might give me a chance to speak with her and her housemaids discreetly."

Roland doubted Grace would make any headway, but he kept that to himself. If nothing else, it would keep her out of his way. "I will speak with Lord Fitzroy. He and I went to school together, and you have just reminded me I owe him some money."

Before they could make further plans, there was the sound of the great front door opening and shutting, followed by men's voices echoing in the hall. Roland got up from his chair, crossing over to the fireplace to put distance between them as Lord Tilbury and his son, Felix, arrived home.

"Lord Percy," Lord Tilbury said in surprise, entering to find them there. "I am surprised to see you. Did you have urgent questions for us regarding Lady Charity? I know Grace has been worried sick about the young lady."

"There has been no news on that front, I am afraid," Roland said, sidestepping the question carefully. He moved his gaze between Lord Tilbury and Grace's brother, whom he had not yet met formally. The young man looked nineteen, perhaps twenty, and his eyes sparkled with youth and mischievousness, though he put on a solemn face for the subject.

Nodding at Felix in greeting, Roland continued in the expectant silence, "I was actually invited here to dine with the family this evening, that I might... get to know Lady Grace better."

Lord Tilbury and Felix's eyebrows both climbed their foreheads. It was amusing, but Roland felt a twinge of sympathy —albeit tiny, to be sure—for Grace, that the two men of her family appeared so surprised at the possibility of her being called upon by him. Did they think she was unlikely to be able to make a high-ranking match? Daring a glance her way, he saw her staring at her lap, hands fisted on her dress. Almost as quickly as he noticed, however, she lifted her chin and smoothed her hands.

"Queen Charlotte called us both to the palace to discuss Charity's absence. Since it was so close to the dinner hour, Mama invited him to join us. If you two intend to dine as well, you had best change into suitable attire."

The dinner began awkwardly, but Felix and Lord Tilbury steered the conversation quickly into more comfortable channels. Lord Percy found he rather liked the young Tilbury heir, as he was witty and showed a great deal of kindness to his mother and sister. Grace had spent the first part of the meal quietly, and Felix had sought to tease her out in conversation. As she warmed up to the subjects, it did not surprise him in the least to discover that she was able to keep up with her brother even in more masculine pursuits of trade, the war with France, and politics. She patently ignored her mother's attempts to shush her.

Despite the beginning, the evening ended up being... surprisingly enjoyable. He had originally been sceptical about the value of her joining him in the hunt for Lady Charity—after all, what could a woman possibly contribute to this matter? By the end, however, he thought that perhaps there was a chance the queen had not been completely remiss in her decision after all.

14

Grace waved for the footman to take away her half-eaten plate of eggs and toast. Her appetite had been low ever since she'd learned of Charity's disappearance, but this morning, that wasn't the only cause.

She'd caught herself thinking of Lord Percy as she'd dressed that morning. Had her thoughts been filled with rancour, she would not have worried so much. Instead, when Elsie had nudged her from her stupor while twisting her hair into a tidy braid, Grace was horrified to realise she was smiling at a memory from dinner the night before.

Percy had proven to be an amiable dinner guest, offering an opinion on all topics raised. For someone as highborn and educated as he was, that came as little surprise. What had left a mark was the way he'd spoken of his time on the front lines. Grace had heard her brother wax poetic about battles and bravery. Percy did a little of that, as was expected, but he'd also mentioned the plight of the common soldiers. His face had glowed with pride when he recounted tales of the unit he commanded, not because he was their leader, but because of what they'd accomplished by standing together.

Perhaps that was why Grace had dared to venture into a conversation that was decidedly meant for the men. Her mother had cast a glare her way when she'd asked about battle tactics and war strategy. Percy had taken her questions and replied with an equal amount of seriousness.

Lying in bed, in her darkened bedroom, she admitted to herself that she was glad she was not left to search for Charity all on her own. If she had to have someone accompany her, she could have done much worse than Lord Percy.

In the light of day, her admission was not sitting so comfortably. Would he truly do all he could to see Charity restored into society's highest echelons? Grace knew she would be a fool to blindly follow his lead. She would proceed as though she were the only one with a vested interest in Charity's safe return.

She began after breakfast by asking her mother if she could visit Lady Lark Fitzroy.

Lady Tilbury was ensconced in her sitting room, answering letters and replying to invitations. She detested being interrupted, a fact Grace was capitalising upon. Grace eased into the room and wandered about, lifting books from the shelves to flip through them, before stopping to tweak a flower arrangement. She created just enough noise to break her mother's concentration without being obvious that was her intention.

"Please stop rearranging the flowers, especially since they look worse when you are done. Have you no letters to which you might pen replies?"

"No, Mama. It is a grey day and I find myself uninterested in reading or playing the pianoforte. I fear I am at risk of the doldrums, without Charity here to cheer me up. Might I pay a visit to Lady Lark?"

"We have a full day of calls in the diary," her mother

replied. "I'm expecting several young men who've shown an interest in getting to know you better. We can visit the Fitzroys later in the week."

"I had something more informal in mind. I am sure the news of Charity distresses Lady Lark, especially since she disappeared from the Fitzroy home. I thought to invite her for a walk or a visit to Madame Moreau's to see the new stock of French lace. I can take Elsie with me. She made friends with one of their maids." Grace noted her mother's gaze softening. "We will be back before luncheon, Mama."

"Very well," Lady Tilbury replied. "If you go by Madame Moreau's, please ask whether my new hat has arrived."

Grace promised to check and then hurried from the room. Elsie was waiting in Grace's bedroom with their wraps, hats, and gloves. The women eyed the clouds looming on the horizon and asked the footman to call for the carriage.

At the Fitzroy house, Grace had no trouble getting inside. The butler took her card and came back within minutes with an invitation from Lady Lark to join her in the conservatory. With the butler's permission, Grace sent Elsie to the kitchen for a chinwag before following him to Lady Lark.

Grace had not been in this part of the house before. The conservatory was an octagonal shaped room at the rear of the house, with glass windows and ceiling held aloft by a white iron frame. The iron lines twisted and swirled, creating fanciful views of the cloudy sky. Potted plants with thick green fronds lined the walls, while flowering hoyas perfumed the air with their rich scent.

Lark sat on a cushioned bench, with a book resting beside her. Her pale blonde hair and rosy lips echoed the white and pink hoya blossoms, but the curious glint in her eyes hinted she was no delicate flower.

"Lady Grace, what a surprise," she remarked, moving the book to make space for Grace to join her.

"But not unwelcome, I hope," Grace replied. "I thought to check on you after the events of your ball, and to offer my sympathies on the passing of your housemaid."

"That is very kind of you," a woman's voice said from behind. Grace spun around and found Lady Fitzroy was also in the room. The dowager wore an apron over her gown and had a pair of gardening gloves on her hands. She was examining the soil of a ficus. Tucked away as she was, Grace had walked past her without noticing.

"I beg your pardon, Lady Fitzroy," Grace said, dipping into a curtsy. "I did not see you there."

Lady Fitzroy waved aside her concern. "I get so caught up in my plants, I often forget other people are around. Please, have a seat. I'll ring for tea."

Grace took the place beside Lark while Lady Fitzroy removed her gloves and apron. A footman arrived in short order with a tea tray. He shifted tables and chairs until they had a cosy nook near the far side of the room. As exposed as the room was, it was surprisingly warm. Lady Fitzroy explained she had steam pipes running through the columns to keep the plants from dying during the colder winter months.

"Now, where were we? You mentioned our ball. Pity how it ended, but we all know the travails of finding reliable help. Mrs Godfrey wanted to dismiss the girl, but I bid her to wait until after the event, fearing we'd struggle to replace her in time. This is the thanks I get. The servant helped herself to the guest champagne and toppled over the railing, ruining our night." Lady Fitzroy shook her head, as though still unable to believe it. "That said, I presume the event was not a total loss for you, Lady Grace. I noted you taking a turn on the dance floor with Lord Percy."

Grace felt her cheeks grow pink. She wanted to turn the conversation far away from any discussion of herself and his lordship, but she held firm against the inclination. Handled correctly, she could use it to turn the conversation toward her missing friend. She cast her gaze downward and feigned disappointment. "He asked Lord Fitzroy to provide an introduction, but I fear it was not my attention he sought so much as insight into Lady Charity."

"Ahh, yes. Another person who thought to take advantage of my generosity," Lady Fitzroy replied.

"Mama!" Lark exclaimed, sending her mother a startled glance.

"*Not* Lady Charity," Lady Fitzroy rushed to add. "I was referencing whoever kidnapped her, of course. Taken from right beneath our noses, while all the London ton was focused elsewhere."

Grace nodded her agreement and sipped her tea. She slit her eyes into a sly gaze and leaned forward. "Who do you think it might have been? Your servants must have seen something."

"Unfortunately, most of the servants were well occupied with our other guests," Lady Fitzroy answered dourly. "To our everlasting chagrin, it would appear."

"My mama has been quite upset," Lark confided in a soft voice. "She had put in so much work on this ball and my debut, hoping to attract some more of the better prospects. But Lady Charity is the only name on everyone's lips."

"Not for a reason I suggest you copy," her mother warned. "My money is on one of her suitors. They nipped at her heels like dogs desperate for attention. Perhaps she fluttered her lashes at them one too many times."

Grace was certain Charity had done nothing of the sort, but she kept that opinion to herself. She wasn't there to defend Charity's name, but to find out who might have taken her. Lady

Fitzroy was talking. Grace did not want to do anything that might cause her to hold her tongue.

Lark spoke up. "Did you see Lord Dunstan? I happened to be nearby when he requested a turn on the floor with Lady Charity. He did not take the news well that her dances had all been claimed."

Lady Fitzroy pulled a face. "If he approaches you, I suggest you use the same tactic. He does not meet with my approval."

"Yet, he is invited to all the events," Grace ventured.

"His family name is well respected, even if he fails to rise to its legacy. I'm sure he'll make a match before the season ends, but it will not be with my daughter. Someone with fewer prospects will no doubt find a way to stomach him." Lady Fitzroy flicked her eyes in Grace's direction.

Grace shoved a biscuit into her mouth to keep from retorting.

"He may not have a need for a wife, if he has done what I suspect." Lark lowered her voice. "I spotted him following Lady Charity into the garden shortly before we learned of the maid's death. If he does not court someone soon, perhaps it is because he has hidden away the diamond?"

15

T he morning sun cast a hopeful glow across the sky, but clouds on the horizon threatened a change. Astride Arion in the sunshine as he waited in Hyde Park, Roland felt more himself than he had in weeks. Perhaps his grandfather had been right, he thought wryly to himself. He had been away too long. Grown uncivilised. London proper and society felt stifling, and only here among the trees did he feel like he could truly breathe.

"Percy!" The hail came from his right and behind.

Roland turned his horse in a tight circle to greet Lord Fitzroy. "*Pip*," he replied as Fitzroy drew alongside, but he gave Fitzroy a pleasant smile so the man would know it was in jest. "How are you this morning?"

Fitzroy shot Roland an irritated look at the use of the nickname. "Will you torment me with that forever? I think I must have been addled when I accepted an invitation to spend the morning riding with a scoundrel. Tell me, do you charge others for the privilege of your company, or might enduring your presence be considered philanthropy?"

Grinning, Roland didn't answer. He wheeled his horse

again and leaned forward, signalling the horse silently into a canter with body language alone. Then a gallop. With a curse, he heard Fitzroy slap the reins of his own mount to catch up. And for a few minutes, there was no talk. No thoughts of the past or the future. There was only now — the sun, the breeze, and the green trees dappling them and the grounds with spots of sunlight. He took deep lungfuls of the damp air and closed his eyes as they chased one another and gave their horses a good run.

Fitzroy pulled his horse up slightly, finally, but kept a brisk trot going as he followed one of the paths that cut back through the park again. "Why did you call upon me, Percy?" he asked as Roland drew alongside again.

"Ah," Roland said, gathering his thoughts. How to begin? "Well, I wanted to convey proper regrets for the death of your maid and what happened at the ball. You had put up a splendid evening until that moment. Also, I wanted to apologise for ordering your household about somewhat."

Lord Fitzroy nodded his head, his light blonde locks shining in the light. "You do not have to apologise for taking command in the surprise of the moment, as it was well meant. Otherwise, your words are appreciated. We have been working to compensate the family, and my mother and I have been planning a small service for the poor girl."

"How has Lady Fitzroy been these last few days?"

"My mother has been quite upset. She has had to put a hold on several events planned for the upcoming days," Fitzroy said dryly. "I daresay that has affected her more than the girl's death. She has... well." Fitzroy cut himself off, mindful of propriety. "Let us say I am considering moving back into my townhouse for a spell, to be away from the thick of things—and speculations regarding Lady Charity's disappearance, of course. Even without the maid's death, Charity eloping from our very grounds has blackened our names in the eyes of the ton."

"Sometimes the opinions of the gentry make little sense to me," Roland admitted. "Even if she had eloped, I do not understand why that should reflect upon you. With the matter of the ransom demand, it appears unlikely that is the case."

Fitzroy snorted. "Why, it reflects poorly on our ability to hold a respectable event, of course! The ransom demand is laughable, and we both know the amount is no accident. Lady Charity and her beau mean to distract us while they get away. The atmosphere at our ball—the entertainment, it may have driven the poor lady to such rash or wanton thoughts she could not help but be seized with such notions."

"Perish the thought," Roland said with the faintest trace of sarcasm, and Fitzroy responded with a small smile.

"Not to mention, Lady Charity's last dance of the evening was in my arms. Mayhap I had said somewhat—perhaps I danced too closely and fired a young lady's wild desire for *romance*. In all, our oversight was inadequate to the task, and we must be to blame, especially if it turns out in the end she eloped with someone wholly inappropriate." These words were bitter.

"You think, then, that she eloped with a guest?" Roland asked.

Fitzroy shrugged. "I must. It is the only possibility of reducing our scandal, to find out that there was a love match that happened that night. I hope they do not take overlong to reveal themselves."

"Here is to hoping, then," Roland said, planning his next careful set of questions. "Do you have any suspicions as to who it might have been? Were there other guests who departed early that we know of who might have stolen off with Lady Charity?"

"The Tilbury family departed early, but I believe you were already aware of them," Fitzroy said. "The Tilbury lad, Felix, would be a fit candidate for suspicion, I think, for he is rather charming despite his youth."

"Ah, but I was at dinner with the Tilbury family just last evening, and Felix was accounted for."

"Truly?" Fitzroy said, his eyebrows climbing. "You sly *dog*. Did you and Lady Grace spark something unexpected between yourselves, then?"

"'Unexpected' would be the word for it. Like a match to a cannon," he said drolly, thinking of Grace's outburst at him the previous evening in defence of Charity's character. He did not bother correcting Fitzroy's other misapprehensions, figuring that such might serve them later.

Fitzroy laughed then and clapped Percy on the arm. "Then would you be forfeiting your wager, after all?"

"Yes. I am reminded now of the other reason for my invitation for this morning's ride," Roland said, feigning a sour look on his face as he fished a small purse from his coat. He tossed it to Fitzroy, who caught it in one hand. The jingling of coins made it clear what it held, and Fitzroy did not bother even opening the purse before he stuck it inside his pocket. "No matter what the outcome with the ladies Grace or Charity, it would seem that engaging the diamond is not in the cards for me this year."

"I shall stand you a drink at White's in celebration," Fitzroy said, being a magnanimous winner, his thoughts growing distant. "Back to gossip then... If Felix is innocent, hmm. Who may have absconded with Lady Charity?"

"Mayhap it was yourself, in order to win my spare change to pay for your party?" Roland said lightly. "All those gold decorations must have cost a pretty penny."

Fitzroy did not take offence at Roland's words, hearing the jest as it was meant. "It did cross my mind to sabotage your efforts," he admitted. "But I was rather of the mind to convince her that it would be far more romantic to accept a gentleman's proposal at Midsummer."

"You do not consider yourself one of Lady Charity's many hopeful suitors, then?"

"As half the men of the marriage mart do? Of course. But as Lord Henry so aptly put it, it would be difficult to contend with a... suitor of your breeding." Fitzroy flashed Roland a smile that was both pleasant and somewhat feral. "Even if I should fare a better chance vying for her hand than he would. In any event, she was a lovely girl, but I am not *that* eager to marry... not so much that I would win her by actually ruining a lady's reputation. Faugh."

Roland nodded his agreement and did not speak. They rode in silence for a few more minutes.

"I asked my butler who else from the guest list departed early," Fitzroy finally volunteered. "You would not be the first to speculate on who may have eloped with Lady Chastity, after all. I hear there are a few wagers on it, actually... if you were thinking."

"I have wagered enough for one season, I expect," Roland said, affecting a very small show of ill temper for his loss again. "But who then is being favoured as the responsible party?"

"Well, Felix was high among the possible rogues. But the other notable departure was Lord Barbour."

"Lord Barbour!" exclaimed Roland. "He is already married, and has been so for many years. Why would he fall under suspicion?"

Fitzroy lay a finger aside of his nose. "Not as you might suspect. Lord Barbour left at the same time the majority of the guests did. What was notable about his departure was the fact that he left the party in a hired coach, and not with his usual carriage and driver."

"It seems like a rather improbable course of action to lend it to a young debutante alone. What would be his reasoning?"

"Percy, you are of such a dull wit when it comes to the feminine heart," Fitzroy flapped his hand at Roland. "Lord Barbour is known for his poetry. Many consider him to be the very epitome of romance, and the love for his wife is—well, scandalously legendary. If anyone were to assist a young girl elope to achieve a hopeless romance, Lord Barbour would be the man."

Roland thought about that for a moment, as it did not seem so improbable in that context. If Lady Charity had been using Lord Barbour's conveyance to meet with—or abscond—with someone else, it was still possible she could have eloped. Although it was looking increasingly unlikely, in that circumstance, that she would have done so with one of Fitzroy's guests.

"What, if you suppose, Lady Charity *didn't* plan to elope?" was Roland's next, rather blunt query.

Fitzroy did not seem disconcerted in the least. "Well, then consider the fact that Lord Barbour was also present and well active in you placing your wager. In fact, he placed a rather large one of his own on the outcome. I do not know for certain *what* outcome he bet upon, Percy, but what if he placed a rather large sum on your failure?"

16

Grace was well and truly frustrated. When Lark mentioned Lord Dunstan's questionable behaviour, she'd wanted nothing more but to leap from her seat and track him down. But young ladies of her standing could hardly pay a call on an unmarried man. Even if she could, Grace had used the excuse of inviting Lark to the modiste as a way of getting out of the house early in the day. Now there was nothing for it but to see the event through.

With Elsie in tow, she and Lark rode to Madame Moreau's. The dressmaker delighted in showing her wealthy clients her newest stock. It was nearly time for luncheon when Grace was able to get clear. With her mother's new hat sitting in a wrapped box on Elsie's lap, Grace mulled over her next steps during the carriage ride home.

Finding Lord Dunstan wasn't the challenge. The man faithfully attended the major society events. He'd no doubt be present at the Regent's ball in two days' time. But two days was far too long for Grace to wait. Every moment that passed put Charity at greater risk of ruin, assuming it wasn't already too late.

Her mind was in such a flutter, she did not notice the carriage came to a stop until the footman opened the door and offered her a hand. She climbed down the carriage steps, taking care not to step on her skirt, and turned when someone called her name.

"Hello, sister," Felix said as he came around the coach. "Back from Madame Moreau's I see. How you can spend so many hours admiring bits of frippery remains a mystery to me."

"Much the same way you men spend so much time discussing the fall of Beau Brummell's cravat, I imagine," Grace replied. "Yours is coming loose, by the by."

Felix's hand rose to his neckline, just as she'd intended. There was nothing wrong with his cravat, but his rush to check it underscored her point. "*Touché*, my lady. Come, let us call a truce and go inside before we're late to the table."

Grace took the arm her brother offered and walked into the house. His willingness to lend a hand reminded her he might serve an additional purpose. "Have you any plans for the afternoon, dear brother?"

"Nothing firm. I thought I might attend a lecture at the Royal Society. They have a chap speaking about a new method to refine sugar. We have some investments in the trade, and Father has been harping on me to show a greater interest in such matters."

"Do you expect it to be a popular topic?"

Felix shrugged. "As much as anything else. Why do you ask?"

"Might I come along with you?" Grace caught sight of her brother's frown and rushed to add, "Mother wants me to accompany her for her afternoon calls. All anyone wants to discuss is Charity's absence. I cannot take another afternoon of question after question. Please say you will take me along."

Grace's conscience twinged at taking advantage of her

brother's soft heart, but the ends justified the means. She'd have a far better chance of bumping into Lord Dunstan at a talk than in some stuffy drawing room. As expected, her brother acquiesced to her request with only a little grumbling. "If you do not mind, let us allow Mama to believe this was your idea. She will be cross with me, otherwise."

"Fine, but you are now in my debt. When the time comes for me to settle down, I expect you to shower praise on my shoulders for all the debutantes to hear."

Grace would have done so anyway, but she kept that information to herself. Over dessert, Felix floated the suggestion that Grace accompany him to the afternoon event. Lady Tilbury offered a token protest, but her desire to keep her only son happy won out in the end.

"We will still have time to pay a call or two before you go. Felix, you may collect your sister from Lady Marlborough's home. Do not be late and do not leave her unaccompanied at any point. Do you understand?"

Felix swore to keep her by his side from the moment he collected her until she was safely back home after the lecture. As promised, Grace found him waiting in his phaeton at the appointed time. She batted her lashes and pleaded innocent when he questioned whether she had ulterior motives for joining him.

"Is there anyone specific you hope to see?" he asked as they rode toward Somerset House. "A certain Earl?"

Grace had been so focused on finding Lord Dunstan, she had not given Lord Percy a second thought. At her brother's teasing, she was of two minds. It would be useful to have a quiet word with Lord Percy, to update him on what she'd learned. But what would he do with such information? She could not imagine him standing aside while she posed the questions.

No, it was better for both if he was not there. She would, of course, share anything she discovered. Later.

"I have shown no preference for any suitors, as you well know. Even if I did, given the events of the past few days, such things have been the farthest from my mind. I am going for the same reason as you. To learn," she added.

Felix turned off the Strand into the courtyard of Somerset House. The Palladian edifice held a place of pride in the city of London as the home of various public offices and societies. The Royal Society shared the North Wing with the Royal Academy.

Grace walked through the vestibule, admiring the busts of Michelangelo and Newton. Why had she waited so long before venturing here? In these halls, the mind and the spirit of adventure outweighed the contents of one's bank account. She had only to turn up to learn about some far-flung corner of the world, and what it might offer. A man who appreciated such things was more likely to visit here than waste time in a ballroom. With that in mind, she followed Felix into the lecture hall.

There were mostly men in attendance, but Grace noted more than a few women among the group. Some were spinsters known for their bluestocking tendencies, others the wives of prominent intellectuals. Grace was likely the only woman there who was still in the market for a husband, for she rarely saw these women at the high society events. She committed their names to memory with the intent of learning more about them once all else was said and done.

Perhaps it was her status as an outlier which drew so much attention. Any hope she had of passing unnoticed fled when a nearby man caught sight of her face and approached with a wide grin. He had bushy eyebrows and thick lips, which he smacked in satisfaction.

"Lord Felix, well met, and I see you have brought your delightful sister along as your guest," the man said.

"Afternoon, Lord Clarence. I suppose you are angling for an introduction. Grace, meet Lord Clarence."

Grace offered her hand, as was expected.

"How delightful to see you, Lady Grace. What brings you here today?"

"Why, the lecture, of course," Grace replied. "And you, my lord? Have you a particular interest in cane production?"

"Calling it an interest is a vast understatement," Felix said. "Lord Clarence owns several of the largest plantations in the West Indies."

"They are trifling, I assure you," Lord Clarence said, his voice conveying the very opposite. "And far too boring to interest you, Lady Grace. Tell me, how are you finding the season? Do you prefer the busy city life or your country estate?"

Grace did not roll her eyes, but it was a near thing. Even here, in this bastion of learning, men refused to acknowledge that she, too, had a mind. She pasted a bright smile upon her face and replied, "I prefer to spend my days in the libraries and museums, my lord. Hours upon hours of reading, studying, and growing my knowledge. I find it hugely helpful in forming opinions of my own."

Lord Clarence blinked several times, too caught off guard by her response to reply straightaway. "How, err, lovely for you. If you will excuse me, I see someone I know."

Grace bobbed her head and took great care to avoid her brother's heated glare. She skimmed the room and spotted Lord Dunstan's mutton-chop sideburns not far away. She trusted Felix to keep up as she bustled through the crowd as quickly as was seemly.

"Lord Dunstan, I did not expect to see you here," she called in a clear voice.

Lord Dunstan turned at a woman's voice calling his name. His brow scrunched in confusion, which abated little when he caught sight of Grace.

Better confusion than guilt, Grace thought to herself. She and Lord Dunstan were far from fast friends, and he was right to wonder why she was so eager to see him again. But Grace had already prepared herself for such a possibility.

With an innocent grin, she feigned delight at being in his company. "It is nice to see a familiar face amongst such a large and varied group," she explained. "I fear I am in over my head, but I trust *you* and my brother will help me understand."

Lord Dunstan gave a stiff bow in reply to her simpering, but his face lightened with pleasure. "Of course, Lady Grace. It is lovely to see you again."

"I was not aware you two had been introduced," Felix said, coming up from behind.

"We were, courtesy of Lady Charity," Grace supplied. She beamed at Lord Dunstan while subtly elbowing her brother. "Lord Dunstan often visited the Cresswells while I was staying as their guest. Given the events of the past few days, I had not yet had the chance to further my acquaintance with Lord Dunstan."

Lord Dunstan blinked, almost as if waking from a dream at the reminder of Lady Charity. "Oh yes, that poor girl! Have you had any word about Lady Charity?"

Grace shook her head, not needing to pretend her sorrow. "I am at a loss. I cannot imagine where she is. It is all I can do to keep from fearing the worst. If only I'd gone into the garden with her that night. I might have seen something."

"Or you could have been a victim, as well," Felix countered. But he was looking at Grace strangely, as if he had realised she was about something.

Grace ignored him. "It was so busy that night. Someone

must have seen something. What of you, Lord Dunstan? I noticed you exiting to the gardens soon after Charity. Did you see where she went?"

Grace watched his face for any signs of anything—guilt, anger, satisfaction. How might the man feel if he had kidnapped the queen's diamond from a busy event?

Lord Dunstan lowered his eyes and shoulders as he slowly shook his head. "It is my biggest regret that I was so close and yet saw nothing to indicate Lady Charity was at risk. I offered to fetch her wrap, but she waved me off and said she needed the cool air. Someone called my name, and I turned my back. When I glanced into the gardens again, she was gone. That was the last I saw of her, I swear."

His desolation was writ large in the lines of his body. This was not a man crumbling under the weight of guilt, but of despair. Lark Fitzroy had spoken truly when she said Lord Dunstan desired the diamond above all. But apparently, even he had his limits.

17

Roland felt a small twinge of guilt about dropping in so unexpectedly on Lord Barbour. They were not especially close friends, after all, and Roland was hard pressed to think of an excuse for his visit that would not come off as nearly an accusation. Perhaps he could ask the gentleman for an opinion about new art to decorate his London home.

He was more guilt stricken to find an event happening at the Barbour household—and in full swing, it appeared. But the footman took his coat and hat as if his arrival was not untoward in the least, and bid him wait.

"Lord Roland! What a delightful surprise." Roland turned to see Lady Barbour, dressed in a high-waisted silk evening dress of a pale blue, with a light shawl over her shoulders. She was an elegant woman in her late thirties, her hair only beginning to show the beginning threads of grey. Roland had not seen her in years, not since the days when his parents hosted hunting parties at their country house. Though he had been much younger then, it seemed Lady Barbour remembered him.

Roland accorded her a small bow. "You look lovely this

evening, Lady Barbour. I apologise for my unexpected visit; I did not realise you were entertaining. I will visit your husband another time."

"Oh, nonsense!" Lady Barbour laughed gaily. "I'm hosting a salon with some members of the literary and academic world. You are quite welcome to join us!"

Stiffening, Roland tried to imagine how he might politely refuse, for this did not sound at all like an event in which he wished to take part. But before he could frame a reply, the lady took his arm. "I think," Lady Barbour murmured to him, "you might prove very stimulating to have in conversation!"

Effectively trapped, he allowed himself to be led into the parlour where three men and one other woman sat conversing. One of the men, fortunately, was Lord Barbour himself. A discreet footman offered him a goblet of wine as he sat, and he took it as if it were a lifeline.

"Roland!" Barbour cried in welcome. "How wonderful to see you here. We have just been discussing a few new novels released this year. Have you read *Pride and Prejudice*?"

The guests had stopped their chatter, looking rather expectantly at Lady Barbour and Roland.

"Forgive me, Barbour, I have not had much time to catch up on reading," Roland replied regretfully.

The man on the couch beside him coughed into his hand, covering up a smile.

"Ah, yes, a rather common plight of the military man on the field, I imagine," Barbour returned with good humour. "I would like you to meet our guests. Lord Roland Percy, I present to you Lady Wetherby, a scholar and an advocate for women's education. Montford, here, is a philosophy student studying some of the newer works in German idealism, and beside you is Austen, a banker and a good friend of ours. He is the one who introduced us to the book of discussion."

"It is a shame you have not yet had a chance to read it. It is a fine work," Lady Wetherby told Roland. "Perhaps you should find the time to enjoy it this summer."

Roland met her gaze. She was considerably older than Lady Barbour, possibly in her fifties, and she had the soft, steely look of a kindly grandmother who could smell childhood nonsense a league away and brooked no tolerance for it. "I shall keep that in mind, Lady Wetherby. My library has been neglected lately."

Montford piped up. "Is it truly fine work, though, Lady Wetherby? Critically thinking, might your opinions be influenced by suspicions of the nature of the writer?"

"I do not deny that there is ever that possibility, Lord Montford," the older woman said evenly. "You must agree, however, that such connections, forged through influence and perceptions, bind us to one another. This is the very nature of sympathy. It is the foundation upon which one human is able to relate to one another, and the ability to draw upon such skillfully may be a mark of a true artist."

That quickly, this conversation bid to make his head swim, and he had only barely touched his wine. "Suspicions?" Roland asked, looking to Lady Barbour for guidance.

She smiled at Roland. "There is much conversation in literary circles that the author of Austen's new book is likely a woman, as this book was published 'by the author of Sense and Sensibility.'"

"And if it is so, how it is a terrible shame that a woman, in this age following enlightenment, fears to put her own name to a book," Lady Wetherby added.

"I suspect Mr Austen could admit to knowing more about who the author may be," Lady Barbour said, running her finger over the side of her glass, "since he seems to find the gossip so amusing and absolutely refuses to participate in speculation. He finds it more entertaining to let curiosity run wild."

Austen smiled a private smile, one rather like a cat that had caught himself a canary. "My Lady Barbour gives me more credit in wit and connections than perhaps I deserve. But surely you would agree that if one knew the truth, it would deprive a great many people of the entertainment to be had in these speculations."

"Let us get a soldier's opinion on the matter!" boomed Barbour gleefully. "Percy, as you have not yet read the book, I cannot ask you whether you have an opinion on the author. I can ask, however, what do you think about women involving themselves in literature and art?"

When all eyes fell upon him waiting for reply, Roland took a deep drink of his wine. "If I must be perfectly candid with you, Lord Barbour—I do not think of it."

That caused Barbour to hide a laugh with a cough, and the philosopher to eye him in veiled approval. The women seated with them raised their voices in protest, and he raised his hands in supplication. "To be clear, good ladies, I have not educated myself overmuch in the fields of arts at all, and have few thoughts on literature and art produced by either men or women."

Lady Barbour laughed at him openly then, leaning in towards her husband. But it was gently meant, and Roland did not take any offence. "Dear lad, you cannot neglect to take at least a base education on such a thing. However else do you plan to win a lady's heart this season?"

Roland's eyes shot to Lord Barbour's, but fortunately the Lord did not see fit to embarrass Roland by repeating his words that first evening at the gentleman's club. That only the lady's hand needed to be won.

"It is true," Barbour said instead, resting his hand upon his wife's, "that reading poetry to a lovely lady can be… remarkably effective in getting her to agree to your proposal."

The look that Lord and Lady Barbour shared was so intense and private, he felt as though he was a peeper, and he took another deep sip of his wine. Looking around as he did so, he noticed that the other guests also avoided looking directly at this display, but Lady Wetherby did have a rather fond, small smile on her lips as she glanced away.

How curious. What must it be like to actually love someone that intensely? It seemed so very strange to have such a close connection with anyone—that one might have a partner with which to navigate the currents of life together.

Montford, whose sour face indicated that he appeared to be a rather prudish individual despite his relative youth, finally coughed to break up the tableau.

"Montford," said Austen, "since we find ourselves on the subject, tell me. How do idealists feel about love?"

"Perhaps to Lady Wetherby's earlier point of sympathy, Hegel believes love is the recognition of oneself in another," Montford said, sounding rather reluctant to impart this information. "Kant, however, felt that there were different kinds of love. One based only on feelings and inclinations, which he called pathological, and he determined that it cannot have moral value. Practical love," he continued, warming to this subject, "is a duty to another, a deliberate, moral action since it is an act of will. Only this deliberate love can result in true moral worth. He said as much in his works, the Doctrine of Right and the Doctrine of Virtue."

"How fascinating," Lady Barbour said politely, though it was clear she was in disagreement. "Can one have both practical and pathological love in a relationship?"

"Yes," Montford said, spreading his hands in defeat on the subject. "He did not feel that pathological love necessarily invalidated the moral worth of actions made of practical love."

"Well, there you have it then," Mr Austen concluded

brightly, as if he might be holding back a laugh of his own. "Clearly, while we must engage in the duties of love to be morally good, there is no reason not to seek out this... this pathological love as well."

Lady Barbour looked towards Roland again, clearly inquiring with her politely raised eyebrows what he might think of the matter. "All of your arguments have considerable merit," he temporised, feeling like a drowning man in this company. "I am fortunate to have your willingness to bring my poor officer's education up to date on these loftier ideas. I shall be happy to add whatever books of poetry you think I need to my shelves, Lady Barbour."

"Whatever you should pick, I think it should not be Byron," the lady said slyly, lifting her glass to her lips. "Perhaps you might pick up some verses or two from my husband."

Barbour smiled at his wife again, but it was brief and tolerant of her jest. "I am sure your education was just fine and proper, Percy. What did you study, mostly?"

"Strategy and history, for the most part," Roland admitted. "As I joined the military rather early, not much time was spent in the manner of philosophy, politics and social progress, to the detriment of your conversations, I am sorry to say."

"Pish posh. Do not be sorry!" Lady Barbour assured him. "It is good to have fresh perspectives and voices outside of our common circles. This is how we grow. Oh! I must have another salon soon, and then I will invite Lord Kingsley. He has been quite enamoured with Antoine-Henri Jomini, although... well, you can understand it's quite difficult to get his works right now."

With the Napoleonic wars still on, Roland could well imagine. "Indeed? That sounds like a most stimulating conversation. I would be grateful to receive such an invitation, my lady. I did not plan to interrupt your evening plans tonight; I only sought to have a word with your husband. Might I borrow his ear for a moment?"

"Of course, Roland, of course," Barbour said cheerfully, escorting Roland out of the parlour and into a study down the hall. "What is on your mind?"

His original plan, to be discreet and which was poorly laid at best, crumbled. In the end, Roland decided on a blunter course of action. "Barbour, given the conversation tonight, I am sure you find it no great surprise that some consider you rather expert in the matter of romantic gesture."

"Oh?" Barbour drawled, his eyebrows climbing high on his forehead. "And are you seeking more explicit advice, Percy?"

"No! Of course not, Barbour," Roland said, colour rising in his cheeks. "No, I came to inquire about a different matter. You have heard of the disappearance of the queen's diamond, I am certain. Yes?" Barbour nodded, his face losing all trace of humour. "I have come to ask you if perhaps a certain young lady sought your aid in eloping."

"My aid! To elope!" Barbour sounded genuinely shocked. "Well, no. Why ever would you suppose such a thing?"

"You did not arrive with Lady Barbour on the night of the Fitzroy ball." Roland counted on his fingers. "Second, when asked about unusual events of the evening, the butler was reminded to note that you left in a hired carriage, which brought questions as to the whereabouts of your usual conveyance. Thirdly, some suggest that you may have placed a rather large wager of your own on the circumstances of my marrying the diamond, which might have compelled you to aid Lady Charity if she had made an... unorthodox request."

Roland did not expect Barbour to respond to his deductions with a belly laugh. "Oh, Roland. My sweet wife is right; we must have you over again—with other company, to be sure."

Roland rubbed his temple in frustration, realising this was a dead end and feeling a fool.

"My love was not feeling well that evening, which is why she did not attend," Barbour explained kindly. "To your second concern... I hit a nasty rut on the way to the Fitzroy place. It cracked one of the carriage wheels. As I was rather close, and the evening was fine, I sent my driver off for repairs and planned to hire a conveyance at any rate. I can give you the name of the place, if you would like to confirm my man took it straightaway there."

"And the last?" he had to ask, but he did not truly wish to know, for he was coming to like Lord Barbour.

That brought a brilliant smile back to the man's face. "I did, in fact, lay a rather large wager upon you, Percy. But it was not about whether you would marry the diamond. It was whether you—and whoever you did end up finding to accept your engagement—would find love along the way. Whyever else did you think my lady was suggesting you might need the help of poetry?"

18

Roland had made his excuses to leave shortly after that revelation from Lord Barbour, but in retrospect, perhaps that had not been the wisest course of action. While the conversation in the salon had been dizzying and high-minded, at least it had been diverting. He did not care, however, for the path his thoughts took on the way back to his house.

Finding love! *Zounds*. What possibly could have possessed Barbour to make such a wager? The gentry making love matches was the exception, far from the rule. If Roland could simply stand living in the same house as his future wife, that would make his marriage a wild success in comparison with many—including his own parents.

At home that evening, he had nothing to do but pace. An entire day, wasted, chasing the vaguest of suspicions and rumours, and with naught to show for it. Not even an idea of how or where to proceed next. He wondered if Grace had had more luck on her end with the female Fitzroys. He hoped it was so, because he did not care for this feeling of being at a loss.

But...

"Thorne," he grumbled to his man, "truly, we are blockheads. How is it we failed to arrange a method of correspondence with Lady Grace? How else were we supposed to reconnoitre with one another regarding the intelligence gathered?"

Since Roland was busier with pacing than sitting, Thorne had somewhat uncharacteristically appropriated a spot on the couch to wait out his employer's frustration. He would never have done so in the presence of another person, but Roland despised standing on ceremony when it was just the two of them alone with one another.

"Do you want an honest answer?" Thorne asked mildly, amused.

Roland gritted his teeth. "No." He knew the answer. He had expected to find the information himself, and had not expected Grace's search to bear any fruit. If it was pointless, what purpose would there have been in arranging a meeting with the lady? "I must write to her to meet. Now."

"You will not." Thorne's mild refusal pulled Roland's pacing up short, and he turned to look at him. "Despite your growing reputation for being nigh a barbarian in the ton, it would be irregular in the extreme to write the lady tonight. You may write to her tomorrow."

"Tomorrow!" Roland had the most ridiculous urge to pull at his hair. "If this was the military, it would be so easy. I could just send a coded letter and be done with it, and she could send one back, no matter the time. But Lady Grace does not understand ciphers, and so..."

"Since we do not have a method of passing letters discreetly, cipher or no, you must meet," Thorne replied calmly. "Write her tomorrow and request her company."

"And further the suspicion that we are courting?" Roland shot back.

Thorne refused to let Roland's mood irk him. "If needs must. Did you have such a terrible time at the Tilbury dinner?"

"No," Roland said, cooling off slightly. He did not wish to pretend to court Lady Grace, but she also did not deserve his behaving so badly. And neither did Thorne, for that matter. "Fine. If needs must," he agreed, pausing to collect his wits. "Perhaps I may pay her a call in the morning."

"Absolutely not, Sir Barbarian. Even if you could contrive an excuse, her mama would hang on your every word, and you would be unable to talk, anyway."

The urge to pull his hair rose again. "I love London. I do. The dealings of the ton are so much more wonderful than being a military man."

His sarcasm was so blatant, Thorne couldn't help but grin at his master's frustration, but at least he took pity on him. "Write a letter to send in the morning," Thorne suggested. "If you invite her to the park, we can take the phaeton out."

Roland had quite forgotten they had discovered the sporty little open carriage tucked away in the back of the coach house, gathering dust. Since Roland preferred to ride astride, and he had not hired or brought any other staff, the coach house was empty otherwise. The phaeton—likely his father's—still sat beneath its sheets.

"That is an excellent thought," Roland acknowledged. The little carriage was open enough that they could be in plain view of everyone without the need of close chaperoning. And as it only had seats for the driver and two passengers... Lady Grace's mama would have to be excluded by necessity. "Yes, I think that might do. Although I must press you into service then as the driver."

Rubbing his hands together in anticipation at the thought of driving the challenging but speedy little conveyance, Thorne did not actually look displeased at all. "I shall attempt to keep my disappointment in check."

"And the carriage upright! I hope your skills are up to the task," Roland teased, but he sat down at his writing desk in a much better humour, feeling the need to take action. Perhaps he could not yet send the letter, but nothing was stopping him from writing it.

Lady Grace, he wrote.

I keep a fond memory of our meeting at the palace, and the hospitality I enjoyed with your family. I wish to thank you again for the opportunity to meet your family.

The day we spent apart, I spent whiling away my hours. I was quite unable to derive satisfaction. The endeavours seemed quite empty, and I find myself wishing I were in your presence once again, to hear your thoughts and opinions on the smallest things.

I suppose instead I must distract myself from these thoughts by taking a ride at Hyde Park to enjoy the air on this fine day, for otherwise I find myself disinclined to leave my rooms.

Lord Percy

Thorne looked over his shoulder as he signed his name with his usual flourish. "Very well done, my lord. Reading this, I would almost think you rather like the girl."

Roland waved his hand at Thorne irritably. "I should have never taught you to read. This truly is my penance for doing you a service."

Thorne grinned to himself and let his prickly employer be.

The footman came into the parlour bearing a note on his tray. Lady Tilbury motioned him forward, but it was toward Grace that he walked.

"For you, my lady."

Grace's hand did not shake as she reached for the note, but it was a near thing. She was accustomed to receiving quickly penned notes from Charity, but that could not be the case today. She half feared it was from the queen, demanding an explanation of her search efforts. But the handwriting inside was distinctly male.

"Well, who has sent you a message?" her mother asked. "What does it say?"

"It is from Lord Percy, Mama."

"A love note?" Her mother gasped and clutched a hand to her breast. While Lady Tilbury would welcome such overtures from a high-ranking suitor, they would only be allowed with Lord Tilbury's permission for a proper courtship.

"Of course not," Grace rushed to reply, keeping her tone cool. She passed the note to her mother. "He thanked us for dinner and commented on the fine weather."

Her mother skimmed the page and then glanced up, her eyes shining. "Have you gone mad? He did more than that, dear girl."

"What do you mean?" Grace asked, looking flustered. Surely her mother had not caught onto their plan.

"He is the heir to a dukedom! Your father and I never dreamed you could aspire to such heights, but here he is, sending you such lovely notes. And surely you are not so naïve as to misunderstand his suggestion. He will be in the park this afternoon and would like to see you there."

Grace feigned ignorance. "Are you sure, Mama? He made his preference for Charity clear."

"Charity is not here. As sad as that is, we must all move on. Do not question me, young lady. I am wise in the ways of courtship. This is the first step and you must not make a hash of it. We shall go for a ride through the park and you will see that I am correct. I have been remiss in educating you about the stages of a proper courtship. This is an excellent opportunity to remedy my failing."

Grace had obviously understood his subtext—it was barely hidden, after all—but had opted to let her mother raise it first. It would not do for Grace to seem too eager. She had made her intentions for the season clear to her parents — that she was keen to get to know her suitors before making any sort of commitment. If her mother feared her at risk of falling under the Duke of Northumberland's spell and damaging her reputation in the process, she would never let Grace out of her sight.

With Elsie's assistance, Grace dressed with care in a high-waisted walking dress with long sleeves in a deep emerald green. French lace lined the neck, protecting her modesty. A spencer jacket in the same shade completed the look. Before she left, Elsie passed her a pair of tan, kid-leather gloves.

Her mother nodded in approval of Grace's choice of clothing, adding that the shade of green made Grace's brown hair appear to be a richer colour. "We should ask Madame Moreau to fashion you a gown in deep green silk."

As Lord Percy had promised, the day was indeed fine, with a bright sun hanging in the cloudless sky. The warm air brought a shade of rose to the women's faces. They took the landau to the park, with the hood folded down to keep the women on display. The driver kept a steady hand on the reins as he guided the team onto Rotten Row.

Lines of carriages stretched before and behind them, as the men and women of the ton joined the parade through Hyde Park. Lady Tilbury waved at passing acquaintances, raising her arm to display the new emerald bracelet on her wrist. Grace kept a pleasant smile on her face while allowing her mind to wander.

Had Lord Percy learned something from Lord Fitzroy? His words left her uncertain whether he had any luck. Or perhaps he had a new lead to share. Despite the queen's threats and Percy's promises, Grace still held a shred of doubt about his commitment to finding Charity. She, meanwhile, had proceeded apace, chasing their only lead. She relished seeing his reaction when she informed him of her progress. That her questioning of Lord Dunstan had come to naught was irrelevant. Bit by bit, she would chase every lead they uncovered.

A booming hale pulled Grace from her reverie. Coming from the other direction, she spotted Lord Percy riding in a black phaeton pulled by a pair of matching horses. Lady Tilbury tensed as he drew near, and all but sighed in relief when he stopped beside their rig.

"Good afternoon, Lady Tilbury and Lady Grace. It is a fine day for a ride, is it not?" he asked, oozing charm.

Lady Tilbury simpered a reply and tossed her head, no doubt checking whether anyone else was noticing Lord Percy's attention. "It is, indeed. You were so kind as to draw the matter to our attention in your gracious thank you note."

"I had hoped you might interpret it as such. I enjoyed supper very much, especially the opportunity to better become acquainted with your children, Lady Tilbury. If I might be so bold, would you permit me to escort Lady Grace for a turn? I promise we will not leave your sight."

Grace's emotions warred at his invitation. It was a clever way to arrange for a quiet word, but in the open carriage, riding through Rotten Row, she would be as on display as she'd been during the set they'd danced together. But at least this time, no fancy footwork was required.

"You may, if you will turn around and ride in front of us. Grantham, please help Lady Grace climb into Lord Percy's carriage."

19

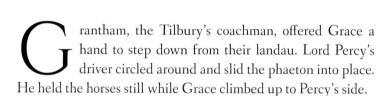

Grantham, the Tilbury's coachman, offered Grace a hand to step down from their landau. Lord Percy's driver circled around and slid the phaeton into place. He held the horses still while Grace climbed up to Percy's side.

Grace took care to keep an acceptable distance between them. The driver of the phaeton snapped the reins smartly, and the little carriage leapt forwards, rocking both back in their seats. Grace made a small exclamation at the rough start, but settled quickly. She noted that Percy had fired a disgruntled look at the back of his driver's head, but he otherwise made no comment, and they sat there in silence for a long minute.

Finally, the driver lifted his hand to his mouth and coughed into it, which broke the spell of silence.

"Forgive my driver," Lord Percy finally said. "He claimed to be a skilled man of all trades, but seems to be rather new at this task. It is good to see you again, Lady Grace. Are you having a pleasant day?"

Grace openly stared at him. "Given your penchant for directness, Lord Percy, and the heavy-handedness of your letter practically demanding that we meet, I am surprised you are spending time on such inanities."

"Very well, let us skip past them. I recalled yesterday that neither one of us had been wise enough to establish a means by which we could inform the other of our progress in looking for Lady Charity. Thus, it became of paramount importance that we meet face to face."

"Yes, I suppose there are only so many times we can bump into one another on my doorstep or at the palace. However, your effusive sentimentality had my mama hearing wedding bells. Even reminding her of your interest in Lady Charity made no dent in her enthusiasm—she is well prepared to give up the search for my friend in the hopes your eyes have turned my way." Grace turned her head away and fell silent.

Roland noted her distress and felt a small pang of sympathy for women. Lady Charity had been snuffed from the memories of the ton like a candle. Grace likely felt she was one of only a few people who cared if she ever was found. He admired that Grace was willing to persevere in the search despite such social adversity, even if it meant entering into a faux courtship.

When he was ready to move on with his search for a bride, he would have to tread carefully, at risk of leaving Grace with the appearance to be a cast-off, unworthy of holding his attention. As Thorne liked to remind him, he was no longer on the field of battle, where a brave charge made one a hero. Already, Roland and others suffered from his ill-thought wager. He could not make a similar mistake again.

Grace took a deep breath and resumed their conversation. "We must come up with a better way to communicate moving forward — one which doesn't take place under the collective gaze of high society. But first, let us share what we have learned so far. Did you speak with Lord Fitzroy as agreed?"

"I did. He had little to offer. He said his family has been

quite upset since the incident. As for him, he is of the firm belief that Lady Charity eloped. I had to push hard to get him to consider other explanations."

"I shall never understand why people are so quick to leap to that conclusion, given a complete lack of evidence to support it."

"It is because it is a simpler, and safer solution; the ton dislikes being reminded about the darker facts of life outside of the world of fancy balls and park rides. I did, however, dig for anything of use. Pip—I mean, Lord Fitzroy—noted that Lord Barbour left in a hired conveyance. I took it upon myself to follow up on this information and pay Barbour a visit, but he had a perfectly reasonable explanation for his behaviour. What of your efforts? Did Lady Lark cast any light on the matter?"

"She reminded me that Lord Dunstan was particularly enamoured by Charity's charms and had dogged her footsteps all night. Like you, I saw a chance to cross paths with Dunstan and questioned him."

Percy reared back in mild surprise. "Did you? Where did you find him?"

"There is life beyond balls and park rides, my lord. I chanced into Lord Dunstan at a lecture at the Royal Society and I asked him about his whereabouts at the time of her disappearance. He does not have her."

"How did you determine whether he might have Lady Charity? I hope you were not so direct as to ask him straight out if he had taken your friend."

Grace sniffed in disdain before replying in a tone drier than the ground. "I *am* capable of subtlety. He expressed only sadness over Charity's absence. And before you suggest he might have been lying, I will add that every thought the man has plays out on his face... to his detriment, most of the time."

Roland looked mildly sceptical, but let it go. "So, we are back where we started." Roland glanced around, searching for inspiration. "I confess, I was rather hoping you had better luck than I did, for I am not sure where next to look for a clue."

Grace was not sure either. She looked out of the carriage again, examining the faces of the people around them. So many of them were familiar, and yet, how much did they really know about any of them and what they might be like behind closed doors or inside their own thoughts?

"Perhaps we are thinking about this in the wrong direction," Grace finally murmured. "We are looking so far only at the lords and ladies, wondering about their motivations. But it would be difficult—perhaps even impossible—for a lord or lady to take a person on their own without being seen. There must be somewhat more to Charity's disappearance that we are not considering."

Roland nodded. "That is a fair point. Assuming that the lady was capable, she would have struggled—made some sound, surely."

"Unless she had been dosed with something, and was unable," Grace was quick to point out.

"In that case, then, she would likely need to be carried—an awkward enough task to carry a woman alone through the gardens or out of the house without servants or guests seeing anything."

"If that is the case, that would mean... servants must be involved—with or without their lord or lady's knowledge. Could that be it?" Grace shifted to face Percy. "Would that not then still put the likelihood of the perpetrator in the Fitzroy household? Is that why the maid died? Was she somehow involved? The Fitzroys were quick to point us away from them. What if there is a reason for their behaviour? If no one saw Charity leave, maybe she is still there."

"I cannot imagine how she could be," Roland muttered. "We combed the estate from top to bottom. I even put my man here, Thorne, to work searching through the back halls and servants' quarters, suspecting that perhaps they could conceal her. Incidentally—I trust him with my life. If ever you cannot reach me, you can trust any message to Thorne."

From the driver's bench, Thorne tipped his hat, but did not otherwise turn around or speak.

Grace studied the driver's back, wondering what else Thorne did for Lord Percy. But now wasn't the time for such questions. She was allowing herself to get off track. "If it were the Fitzroys—Why would they do such a thing?"

"That Lord Fitzroy could be capable of such an act of malice would surprise me, for I rather find myself liking him," Roland said, thinking. "Mischief... well, that is another matter altogether. Could he have wanted to win the bet so badly that he would have done such a thing in jest? I find it hard to believe, and yet..."

"Is it wrong of me to hope that is the truth?" Grace asked. "The maid's death is a tragedy, and I would much rather think it an accident. Mischief can be forgiven, and Charity restored with no damage to her person. But if Lord Fitzroy spirited her away... perhaps by one of his servants... and it was not at the estate... where would he take her? Was there somewhere on the grounds that went unchecked?"

Percy grew silent as he pondered that possibility. "Somewhere else? It would have to be another property, because I do not see how they could keep her concealed on the premises. Wealthy as they are, they surely own other abodes in London. In fact, now that I think on it, Pip made mention of a townhouse."

"We must check it!"

"We?" Now it was Percy's turn to quirk his brow. "How would you explain your absence? Or are you planning to bring your lady mother along?"

"Leave that part to me. Can you get the address?"

"I believe I can find it. I need to speak with my business manager, anyway. I can ask him if he is familiar with the Fitzroy holdings."

"Excellent. Have Thorne send a note to my maid. Her name is Elsie, and she can be trusted as well. I will instruct her to step out for a breath of air early tomorrow afternoon. Say half past two? Is that time enough for you?"

"It will have to be," Percy replied. "But Lady Grace, I must ask again. Are you sure it is wise to take such a risk with your own reputation? Despite appearances, I have no wish to find us dragged to the altar."

Grace pulled a face at that image. She was being reckless, but yet she could not stop herself from hurtling headfirst into the search. Yet, it was not the desire for adventure alone that compelled her to continue. How to explain her dedication to Lord Percy?

She resorted to terminology he would understand. She inclined her head in Thorne's direction. "You seem to know Thorne well. Did he accompany you in battle?"

"Yes. He was my batman, among other things," Roland replied. "Obviously, seldom my driver."

"If something happened to him — if he were captured on the field, or went missing, would you abandon your search for him?"

"If there was a chance I could make a difference, of course I would not." Roland said.

Grace could not swear it, but it nearly seemed that his face grew lighter by a shade. She suspected Thorne was more important to him than he let on. More important than a servant ought to be. Her estimation of the man raised at this sign of his willingness to ignore class lines.

"Why do you ask?" Roland asked her, pulling her back to the present.

"Charity is not just my dearest friend here. She was my *only* friend. In the days leading up to our court presentation, we imagined together how the season would progress. I pledged to help her vet her suitors in her search for a suitable match. If I abandon her now, what does that say about me?"

Roland flattened his lips into a grimace, but he nodded in understanding. "I will send word. Now, let us speak of the weather while we finish our loop so that you may have an honest reply to your mama when she asks what we discussed."

20

Roland's business manager replied speedily to his inquiry, word arriving within an hour of his note to the man. The Fitzroys were within possession of not just one, but two houses besides the estate, although one was rented, and had been so for quite some time.

Well, that was of no matter. Peregrine's townhouse, located between Covent Garden and the Seven Dials, was convenient for him to bring his mistresses from the theatre. However, it was also a more plausible hiding place for a young debutante.

That was assuming Fitzroy was guilty of such a prank.

Roland did not like this overmuch. Even less, he liked the idea of inviting Grace and her maid to such a rough area of London after dark. Covent Garden in the evening hours could be rather debaucherous for a young lady, if not dangerous. Neal Street was barely on the edge of a respectable neighbourhood.

"You are thinking of going without her," Thorne said, less question and more statement.

"You seem to be taking residence in the space of my thoughts, Thorne," he replied lightly, toying with the quill.

"Asking the ladies to accompany us to the townhouse seems rather foolhardy and dangerous at this moment."

"Elsie should be familiar with the market," he reminded Roland. "She will know how to keep the lady safe. Besides, I rather think Lady Grace will be vexed with you if you send no word."

"As you say," he relented, and quickly, he wrote a single line on a piece of foolscap. Just the address and a time, unaddressed, to prevent the possibility of it ending up in her mother's hands. He rather hoped that they would be unable to meet them at the townhouse, anyway.

Half an hour after sunset. Neal Street.

"Tell her the house number in person." He gave the scrap to Thorne, who read it before folding it and putting it in his pocket. Roland knew he had committed it to memory. He had done so at the front lines with much longer correspondence. Thorne always made sure messages got through.

Thorne nodded to his master. "I will deliver this to the hands of the lady's maid."

Covent Garden was, predictably, beginning to grow boisterous near the pubs, but the crowd had not yet swelled with the after-hours men, nor had it devolved into rowdy. Although it did, Roland noted, stink of piss in a few places.

He and Thorne were riding side by side in a hired hackney, posing as two servants out for a night of entertainment. Roland had borrowed some of Thorne's clothes for this excursion, glad that they were so near in size, and had taken the man's hat as well, pulling it low over his eyes lest he be recognised by someone.

In the lamplight, Thorne's eyes shone with anticipation, and

Roland smiled, recognising the rising feeling of excitement within himself as well. This London frippery and intrigue was not anything a military man should want to endure overmuch. He missed this... this sense of purpose. Action. While it was somewhat less satisfying to invade Fitzroy's townhouse instead of, say, France, it was still better than being at a ball.

Roland bid the hackney stop at Seven Dials. From there, they would walk.

He and Thorne casually backtracked from the boundaries of the slums, creeping back towards their destination with care. Soon enough, they found Fitzroy's townhouse, a modest three-story affair of brick with iron railings decorating the well-proportioned windows. A classic portico marked the front entrance, with white painted pilasters framing the door. A line of similar homes flanked Fitzroy's townhouse. They all had clean-swept doorsteps and washed windows. This was a step up from the slums, but shy of the more fashionable homes closer to Covent Garden.

Thorne motioned for Roland to follow. They walked along the pavement, giving every appearance of indifference to their surroundings. When they reached a narrow alley between two houses, Thorne directed Roland to turn into it. They followed it to the dirt path that edged the rear gardens of the townhomes. There, they turned again, counting lots until they arrived at the rear of Fitzroy's place.

A wooden fence lined the narrow garden. Thorne gave the gate a tug and was surprised when it swung open without a sound. "Hinges are well-oiled."

They took care to check the garden for any sign of people before slipping up the path to the back of the house. Tall glass doors, covered by curtains, likely led to a study or dining room. The men ignored them, choosing instead to walk towards the side of the house, where they found a set of plain concrete stairs leading down to the kitchen. There, they found the servants' door and artfully picked the lock.

"One day, you are going to have to tell me where you picked up that skill," Roland muttered. It was an old jest between them. Roland knew the answer—or at least knew well enough. Thorne hadn't always been employed by the Percy household, and given some of Thorne's skills, Roland suspected that Thorne's early boyhood had probably not been far dissimilar from that of some of the pickpocketing waifs that plagued the market after dark. It was a rough life for such boys, and many of them did not grow up to adulthood.

Door unlocked, they waited for some sort of sign the house might be inhabited—a called inquiry, footsteps, any movement. The house was silent.

"I suppose now we wait," Thorne said reluctantly, for the ladies had not yet arrived.

"Wait for what?" came a cheeky query from the shadows behind them.

Both men spun, finding Elsie and Grace coming up the path, swathed in dark cloaks. It was Elsie, Roland was surprised to note, who had spoken. His estimations of the woman he thought had been just a timid, tittering maid rose a few degrees.

"Lady Grace," Roland greeted her softly, unable to wholly forget his manners.

"*Hush.* You shouldn't be calling me lady anything here!" she replied with a wave of her fingers. Like he had, she had clearly borrowed a maid's clothing, but on her the fit was ill; the owner was a couple fingers taller and had a fuller figure.

"Let us go inside before we are noticed or overheard," Thorne reminded them, and they trundled through the servants' entrance into a cramped mudroom. They found a couple of candles in plain holders, and Roland lit one and passed it to the girls.

Everyone was silent, listening, but the house was deadly still, and it had a mouldering, unused smell about it. Roland's hopes of finding anything here fell immediately; he rather doubted Fitzroy had been here in weeks—if even at all this season. Still, he soldiered on, taking charge. "Thorne—cover this exit until we clear the next floor. Ladies, go together and search the bedrooms on the topmost floor. I'll check this level and the one above."

"But—" hissed Grace.

Elsie, however, shushed her and tugged on her mistress' arm, pulling her upstairs, leading the way with soft candlelight. Roland followed behind them, stopping on the first floor as they continued on to the second. He lit the other candle and made a sweep of the level, which was quick. There were only two rooms—a decent sized parlour and a study.

As he descended back to the main level, a muffled ringing of metal striking upon brick rang up from below. Seeing Roland nearly back, Thorne cursed and immediately dashed down the stair to the basement. Sharing his thoughts nearly, Roland headed into the main level, both to check the front entry, and checking to see if there was another main staircase leading down.

The ground level was clear, and as the townhouse was rather small, the staircase Thorne had taken down had been the only one leading down. The kitchen was clearly below, and the servant's entry on the side had been practically designed, opening rather neatly into the dining area. There was a commotion happening below, loud enough that it was attracting the attention of Elsie and Grace.

"Stay up there," he commanded them. Seeing that there was no one else around, he felt safe enough leaving the girls and heading below to make sure that Thorne wasn't overwhelmed.

Rushing downstairs, he was surprised to find Thorne was

wrangling with not one, but two youngsters fighting to be free of him. Immediately, he moved forward to grab the nearest. "Hold, hold!" he cried, trying to soothe them.

"Careful, you grabbed the spitfire," Thorne warned him, wrapping both hands now solidly but gently around the upper arms of the other. "I caught them trying to shimmy up the coal chute."

The spitfire, as Thorne called the waif, immediately tried to bite Roland's restraining arm. Roland thanked all that was holy that he was wearing a rather thick, rough spun woollen coat, for the teeth did little more than pinch.

"Stop it," he said, shaking the child briefly. "We are not going to hurt you. Ouch!"

Thorne's child pulled briefly and ineffectually at his restraints, but a child of eight or nine had little hope of breaking free from Thorne's grasp and he quickly desisted. Roland's, however, was fiery indeed, and after taking a mouthful of wool, proceeded to kick him in the shins.

"Trade you," Thorne muttered, and he pushed the docile one to Roland, reaching out with both hands to sweep the other child off their feet. Suspended in the air, one of Thorne's arms wrapped around their chest holding their wrists, his other around their skinny legs like he was carrying a bundle of sticks, the child flopped a bit like a beached fish.

"Let him go," the young one—a boy in Roland's grasp said. "We were just lookin' for a place to stay out of the cold. We'll go away if you let us go!"

"You are not in trouble; we are not going to hurt you," Roland repeated. "We were just here looking for something. If your friend settles down, we can talk."

"You're thieves," the boy said, his eyes growing bigger in his coal-grimed face. His colleague, still dangling in Thorne's grasp, grew still, as if sensing a threat.

"No, we are not. We are looking for a young woman. How long have the two of you been here? Has anyone else been nearby?"

"No one," the boy finally replied after a long pause. "We been sleeping here a ten-day. An' we watched the place for longer than that, to be sure it was empty."

That tallied with Roland's thoughts, and he sighed. "Tell your friend not to bite us again, and Thorne will put him down."

The boy didn't ask. "He won't," he promised. "As long as you don' hurt me."

Thorne put the other child down, and the two of them clung to one another. Now that they were standing side by side, he could see a familial resemblance as they both stared at him, uncertain what would happen next. Siblings, for certain.

"No parents?" Thorne asked softly, and both children transferred their wide-eyed suspicion to him.

"Died," the second child finally said shortly. Thorne cocked his head at the spitfire child, and gave a meaningful glance at Roland, who pretended to ignore it.

"What is going on?" Grace's voice floated down the stairs, preceding their entry into the basement. She and Elsie sized up the situation quickly. "Oh!"

"Orphans?" Elsie guessed, and Thorne nodded.

"Orphaned! How awful!" Grace said, covering her mouth with both hands.

"La— Grace," Roland said, stumbling as he almost automatically gave away her title, tearing her attention away from the filthy children. "Did you find anything of import upstairs?"

Grace shook her head ruefully. "Nothing. Everything is covered in sheets and dust. No one has been here in a while."

The hellion's face turned calculating. "*You're* no thieves.

We can tell you're fancy, you know. You're probably some lady. Oh, you are going to be in so much trouble for being out after dark! If you let us go, we won' tell nobody."

A wry grin twisted Thorne's face, and he crossed his arms over his chest, feigning nonchalance. "Even if you knew who she was, nobody'd believe you, sprouts." Then he reached over and plucked Roland's purse out of the brat's pocket, tossing it back to his employer.

With an internal sigh, he tucked it back inside his belt pouch. "We should leave before we are all discovered."

"But what are we going to do with these children?" Grace said. "Somehow, we must take them with us. Elsie, do you suppose we could—?"

Elsie was shaking her head. "No, miss. You can't take these two back with us. Not to your father's house, even if you could trust them to be silent and behaved. Which you can't..." Her censure came through as she looked down at the kids with a pitying but knowing look.

Grace spun towards Roland, her eyes already full of entreaty. She was going to ask him to take the waifs; he knew it.

"We'll take them with us," came the response—but not from the source Grace expected.

She spun, her cloak twisting in the dust, as she gaped at Thorne for answering in his master's stead. She looked back at Roland to see how he was going to take this surprising claim, but Roland was smiling a trifle wryly, as if he expected this.

"We will take them with us," he agreed, echoing Thorne.

"See here. You can't just decide that my brother and me will go with you." Thin arms crossed in defiance over the old sack that was serving as a shirt.

"Oh, aye, you have somewhere nicer to be?" Thorne drawled. "You'd rather be filching food and sleeping in coal dust rather than do honest work like washing and looking after horses?" he asked, plucking at the child's filthy hair.

"We know how to look after horses," the mousy boy hissed to his sibling, looking hopeful.

The other child still looked mulish, but hunger appeared to be taking the fire out of them. If these waifs knew how to look after horses at their age, they had likely not been orphaned for very long. The odds of them learning to survive on stealing through the winter were low, and Roland and Thorne reckoned both knew it.

"Thorne, take them back with you and get them fed—and washed," he said. "If they run off again, at least they will do so on a full belly."

"Of course," Thorne agreed. But both men knew that by the time they had been fed twice, these wild children would be domesticated.

21

With the departure of Thorne and the children, Elsie, Grace and Roland were left standing in the kitchen of the empty townhouse. Desperation compelled Grace to search the room again for any hint of recent occupancy. All she saw were empty counters shadowed with a faint haze of dust. Her spirits plummeted. Once again, they were at a dead end in their investigation.

Grace's mind spun in circles, hunting for new ideas of where Charity might be. Already, they had eliminated possibilities. Charity had not eloped. Checks into those who had bet against Lord Percy had come up clean. Her second most ardent suitor, Lord Dunstan, was as bereft and confused as everyone else.

Elsie must have sensed her mistress's distress, for she reached out a hand to squeeze Grace's arm. "I'm ever so sorry we did not find Lady Charity."

Grace gave her maid a gentle smile of thanks, grateful to at least have her presence there in support. The upper class set preferred to pretend their servants did not exist unless needed, but Grace had never fallen prey to that haughty way of thinking. If not for the accident of birth, she and Elsie could have been in each other's shoes.

Grace's stomach lurched. What if that was the answer? Had a servant acted out of jealousy and kidnapped Charity? She voiced her question to Percy.

"It is a reasonable guess, but I do not believe that to be the case," he replied after a moment of thought.

"Why not? We already agreed that if Charity's kidnapper is a member of the ton, they'd have required the aid of their servants to carry her out. Is it not possible that the servants acted alone? I am not casting aspersions," she hurried to add, casting a glance at Elsie. "Good and bad people exist at all levels of society."

"They do, indeed. In my experience, a thick layer of gilt can hide even the worst of evil. But we are getting off track. Answer me this, Lady Grace. How many servants did your family bring along to the Fitzroy ball?"

"Two. Elsie and Grantham, our carriage driver. Mama's lady's maid remained at home."

"Excellent." He looked to Elsie. "You spent most of the night in the company of the other servants. Would you say the other guests brought along a similar contingent of help?"

"Yes, my lord," Elsie answered, bobbing her head. "We lady's maids stayed in the parlour. Grantham said he was looking forward to playing a few hands of cards while he waited. The men had more freedom since they were off outside on their own."

"Men always have more freedom," Grace grumbled under her breath.

"The drivers can move more freely, but remember that they were left in the cold, while the maids stayed warm upstairs. But we are getting off track. I cannot see any way for a single person, man or woman, to have absconded with Lady Charity without being seen. If this were a military operation, I'd send at least four men to do the task. One each to guard the front and back, one to carry the girl, and one to head off any problems that might crop up." Roland shifted his gaze back and forth between Grace and Elsie. "Would four carriage drivers from four different households come together to kidnap the season's star debutante?"

When he put it that way, Grace had to admit he was correct. The story was too far-fetched to beggar belief.

Lord Percy was still talking. "If we are searching for a group of servants, they'd have to be part of the Fitzroy household. That night, as far as I know, all the servants were accounted for. I drafted them to help us check the house and grounds. I can ask Fitzroy, but I doubt he has had four people leave their service in the days since. The Fitzroys certainly saw no gain from Lady Charity's departure. If anything, their reputation took a hit."

"There's also the matter of the ransom," Elsie said in a quiet voice. Her cheeks flushed pink in embarrassment from speaking out of turn. Grace encouraged her to explain. "Servants don't have a lot of coin. If they took her ladyship, they'd want a lot more than a few pounds and some foreign mark."

"We are back to the upper class." Percy grimaced and wiped his hand over his face. "We must think on this again, starting with the age-old question. *Cui bono?*"

"Who benefits?" Grace blurted. She scowled at Percy when he reared back in surprise. "I am not uneducated, my lord."

"Forgive me, my lady. Last I checked, most women did not study ancient Latin as part of their upbringing. Since you understand the question, you may assist me with an answer. The Fitzroys have not gained from Charity's disappearance. You and I have not benefited. We have excluded the servants and the suitors. Who remains?" he stared off into space, contemplating the question.

Grace needed no such time. She had already heard tongues wagging about how her own star was on the rise with Charity out of the picture. Grace cared little for the title of Diamond of the season, but many other girls disagreed.

Yet, the act screamed of desperation. How many debutantes had funds enough for only a single season? Who was edging close to a lifetime left on the shelf? With Charity holding the men's attention, the other women risked not making a match. It took no great leap to believe a young woman at wits' end might do something to get Charity out of the way.

"Perhaps it is not the menfolk who wanted to stop your suit," she said.

Percy lowered his head to meet her eyes. "The debutantes? You believe a woman may be behind this?"

"We would be fools to ignore the possibility," she answered. "Charity was in no rush to express a preference among her many suitors. As such, the men clung to her side in the hopes they might rise to the top. You, yourself, among them, Lord Percy. How many other debutantes have you danced with this season?"

"One."

Grace scrunched her brow. His attention to Lady Charity had been singular.

Percy coughed into his hand. "You, Lady Grace. Or have you so quickly forgotten our time on the ballroom floor?"

Grace waved him off. "That hardly counts, seeing as you only asked for a dance because Lord Fitzroy obligated you to do so. And because you wanted to pepper me for information about my friend. Nonetheless, you have proven my point. With Charity gone, the men will look elsewhere."

"I still cannot imagine how an innocent debutante would arrange the logistics required, but since I have no better suggestion, we will investigate this possibility. Have you any suggestions of where to begin? Perhaps you can make a round of calls to ask."

"It will take me days to visit everyone, assuming I can even manage such a feat with my mama at my side. Time is of the essence. We must take on this task together, beginning tomorrow night at Regent's ball. You will have to break your unwritten rule and ask women to hold you a dance. See if they will let slip any negative word about our diamond."

Percy curled his lip but did not say no. "And you? Will you watch from the edge of the floor with a heartbroken expression on your face? I am meant to be courting you, or have you forgotten?"

"I have not, though I have *tried* many times to put the thought from my head. Unlike you, I am in no rush to complete my time at the marriage mart. One wonders why the urgency. Have you some dark side to your personality you seek to hide?"

Lord Percy clenched his jaw. Grace had struck a nerve, but she did not know what to make of it.

"I would like to think my personality is not in question here. Come, we are wasting time with pointless remarks." He pulled his watch from his pocket and consulted the time. "It grows late. You must get home before the streets are unsafe."

Grace rocked back at his haughty tone. Whatever ease they'd found in their communication was gone, and her thoughtless remark was to blame. She wanted to apologise, but feared that might only make things worse. Instead, she resorted to her tactic of keeping her gaze low and agreeing with whatever was said.

"Come, Elsie. We can hire a hackney near Covent Garden."

He held up a hand. "Wait. You did not come in your carriage?"

"How would I explain my request to Grantham? 'Please, sir, can you drop us in the Seven Dials? Also, do not mention it to my parents.'" Grace huffed. "As I said earlier, men have all the freedom. Elsie and I have enough coin to get back to Mayfair. You need not worry on our behalf."

"I will not worry because I will escort you home," Percy replied.

"*Escort us?*" Grace's voice nearly grew shrill. "If I am seen stepping out of a carriage bearing yourself and no suitable chaperone, we might as well post the wedding banns!"

"What if someone sees you in Covent Garden?" he put his hands on his hips and loomed over her. "How will you explain being out of your house, dressed as a maid on her half day off? You will have no fear of any wedding banns, now or in the future, when your reputation lies in tatters."

"Excuse me, my lady," Elsie said in an even, no nonsense tone. "He could drop us one street over, and we can enter through the alley. No one will give us a second glance that far from your home."

"Finally, a voice of reason," Percy sighed, adding his agreement.

Grace matched his stance. "Please, do not take credit. Your plan was as flawed as my own."

The trio left the way they came. Roland waved to stop a passing hackney and handed the women up into the carriage. He followed them in, chose the bench opposite, and pulled the curtains on the windows to block the outside.

Grace opened her mouth and watched her breath puff in the cold spring night air. She shifted closer to Elsie, wanting her warmth as much as to get away from Percy's long legs. Her gaze longed to study him, but she forced it away. The man thought enough of himself as it was. Besides, the manner of his dress and strength of his form made no difference to her. His highhanded ways precluded him from her consideration. Her future husband, whoever he might be, would treat her with respect due to an equal.

And so, they covered the short distance between the edge of London's slums to the glories of Mayfair in silence. When the carriage stopped at the appointed place, Grace climbed down the step and walked off without ever looking back.

But the memory of Roland Percy, sprawled across the stained bench of the hired hackney, his brow creased in thought, remained.

22

The Regent's ball, held at Carlton House, was a high point of the social season. Hosted by the Prince Regent, the event was the very epitome of elegance and exclusivity. Or so Roland had been told by Thorne between gasps, as the man had nearly been laughing too hard at him to help with the waterfall of his cravat.

Barbarian, Thorne might call him, but even Roland dared not stray from a strict adherence to dress code and conduct. He had reminded himself of this repeatedly as he had dressed for the occasion in his finest silk tailcoat and fitted black silk trousers. He had suffered the indignity of allowing Thorne to knot his cravat into the elaborate waterfall popular amongst the Prince Regent's set. The result, which left him attired like a ridiculous popinjay, had sent Thorne into fits.

Needless to say, Roland went to his stables, already in a bit of a mood.

As he shoved open the wooden door to get his horse, he regretted his temper immediately. He had quite forgotten that Thorne had bedded the two urchins there the night before. As they had expected, the promise of easy food had kept them from vanishing back into the streets.

Like rats, the two children scurried immediately for the shadows. But they were still there; he could feel their eyes upon him. And it seemed that the mouse had not lied after all. His thoroughbred had been well groomed and sat properly saddled in his stall, waiting to depart. Thorne's chestnut gelding, in the stall next door, looked similarly groomed and content, though his beast hadn't been saddled.

Checking the buckles, Roland spoke to the dark corners. "My apologies for startling you. Thank you for caring for my horse."

"What's 'is name?" came a small voice from behind a mound of straw.

Roland waited, rubbing the dark velvet muzzle of his horse until the mouse's head popped up where he could see it. The boy's face was still gaunt, and a bit smudged, but he had clearly made some use of the bath and one of the sets of clothing Thorne had picked up from a secondhand clothing stall. They were somewhat overlarge, but for now, they'd do.

"This is Arion," he told the lad. "Thorne's beast is just 'Horse.' What about you? What are your names?"

"Me, sir?" the boy said, suddenly remembering Roland's station. "I'm Wes. That's Will," he added, gesturing at the pile of straw where the hellcat child was apparently still hiding out of sight.

"Will, is it?" Roland murmured softly and nodded, mounting his steed. "I need to be off. Good evening, the both of you; I will see you when I return."

In the crisp evening air, the soft glow of gas lamps cast a warm, flickering light on the cobblestone streets of London. As Roland drew nearer, the rhythmic clip-clop of horse-drawn carriages echoed in the distance, signalling the arrival of other esteemed guests.

Carlton House's classical architectural features came into view, displaying a grandeur that befitted its location on Pall Mall. Tall, Corinthian columns supported the entrance, and a line of uniformed guards stood at attention, ensuring that only those with a coveted invitation gained entry.

As he drew nearer, Roland discerned the murmur of lively conversation and the strains of a minuet drifting through the tall windows. The entrance was abuzz with liveried footmen, impeccably dressed gentlemen, and elegantly attired ladies, their fashionable gowns and bejewelled figures catching the eye.

He was a few minutes later than he had planned, but according to his pocket watch, he arrived at nearly half past ten. Grace, according to the correspondence she had sent back via Elsie, had planned to arrive somewhat before, and he wondered if she had yet had much luck. But likely not; the night was very young. After making his way through the entrance, Roland set towards the dance floor to see what he could make of things and choose his targets.

The ballroom was far busier than Roland had expected, and for a moment, he was at a loss. But gradually, things fell into order. There was a cluster of young ladies standing at the edge of the floor, clearly holding court—of a sort. The blonde girl in the centre of the knot of gowns had been a fawning thing, and he recalled how she had tried to get him to dance with her at a ball very early in the season.

That evening, he had avoided falling into her trap, but tonight was different. The young woman came from a fine family name, one that spoke of past honours to hide their current sparsity of funds. Her father's mismanagement of funds explained why she was in her third season. Few men could afford to wed for love and beauty instead of the promise of a dowry. It was no wonder she had made such a bold play for Roland's attention.

She, however, being in her third season might possess a wealth of a different sort that the fledgeling debutantes had not amassed. Lady Elizabeth was a canny young woman, and Roland would bet his own title that she had a network of gossip that bid to compete with that of anyone else in the ton.

"Lady Elizabeth," he greeted her, and the cluster of her friends tittered and batted their eyes at him. Roland ignored them. "It is good to see you here. How has the season been treating you?"

"Lord Percy!" the young woman pressed her fingers to her chest, drawing attention to her bosom, of course. "The season has been rather exciting so far this year, I confess, much more than last year. Of course, all that pales in comparison to this moment, since I believe this is the first time I've seen you at Carlton House!"

Lady Elizabeth's simpering tone grated upon his nerves, but needs must. "Indeed, Lady Elizabeth. This is my first visit. Do you regularly come to these events?"

"Every chance I can," the girl responded with a coy smile.

"Perhaps then you would like to dance with me? You can tell me everything a new visitor should know," Roland said, according her a small bow and an extended hand.

One of Lady Elizabeth's friends let out a small squeal of delight, but the lady kept her face cool and triumphant as she accepted his hand and let him lead her towards the floor.

"I love these events," Lady Elizabeth told him gaily, fluttering her lashes. "The best of the ton are brought together and then one may easily see what is going on. Who is in love? Who is out of love? Who is out of favour? All that sort of thing."

Roland smiled benignly at her from across the line, waiting for their next turn to reply. When the dance led them together again, he said, "I bow to your expertise, Lady Elizabeth. For I am rather not one to notice such things. Possibly to my detriment, because I trust there has been much to gossip about this season!"

She pouted so very slightly that he made little overture to her, but only slightly, because he guessed rightly—Lady Elizabeth did love to gossip. "Oh yes, it has been very entertaining," the girl chattered. Each time they came together, she filled his ears with inanity as she pointed out faces near them with her chin. Lord Winthrop's son was rumoured to have amassed quite a debt from gambling at the horse races. Lady Katharine had broken off an arrangement of marriage, and everyone was speculating whether it was love or scandal at fault. Though he tried to feign interest, it was hard to focus on such trivial things.

Toward the end of the set, she caught his attention rather abruptly. "Lord Percy, with all due respect to current fashions, don't you find Lady Grace's choice of dress colour rather... bold for the season? It is certainly a statement, yet there's no denying it draws the eye."

"Lady... Grace?" he stammered somewhat ungracefully, discomposed. "I have not seen her tonight to form an opinion on it."

Lady Elizabeth glanced about, her tone speculative. "I saw her earlier. Perhaps she has gone to take air."

"Perhaps," he murmured, resolving to seek Grace out.

"There is much speculation about you and Lady Grace. Are you courting her?"

"Courting—not exactly," Roland said, caught off guard by the inquiry. He was saved from further dissembling by a change in partner. This was not at all how he had anticipated the conversation would go. He had hoped Lady Elizabeth would be gossiping about Lady Charity, not his current prospects. When

Lady Elizabeth again reached his side, he had an explanation ready. "Lady Grace has been most distressed by the disappearance of her friend."

"Not courting! Then, I daresay, the season remains full of possibilities for you, Lord Percy." The young woman tilted her head back, exposing an expanse of creamy skin, clearly implying that she would be thrilled to be considered one of those possibilities.

Roland did not reply straight away, distracted. Since Lady Elizabeth had made mention of her, he had been scanning the floor for the face of that particular lady—one he did not see.

He refocused on his dance partner and took a more direct approach with the only opening provided. "Perhaps, Lady Elizabeth. Although I must confess, part of me is deeply troubled by Lady Charity's sudden disappearance. Tell me, do you share the common view that she might have eloped, or do you sense other forces at play? Your perspective would be most valued."

Lady Elizabeth's eyes widened slightly at his words, a flicker of surprise crossing her delicate brows. "Other forces, Lord Percy? I must admit, that thought hadn't crossed my mind. Yes, perhaps there have been whispers of envy towards Lady Charity. Being named the diamond of the season is no small accolade, after all. But to suggest that such envy could lead to... other forces at play? Pray, what exactly do you imply?"

Roland clenched his jaw slightly, thinking before responding. "Apologies, Lady Elizabeth. It's no secret that Lady Charity's many blessings have set many tongues wagging, and I am sure you have heard not all are in favour. I only wonder... have you observed any particular instances of envy that could have escalated beyond mere whispers?"

"Escalated...?" For a heartbeat, the lady nearly looked shocked, and then she forced a small laugh. "Oh, Lord Percy!

161

Mayhap you have been too long listening to the gossip mills churn with tales of elopements and dramatic exits. If I may be so bold, speculation about what—what matches or otherwise Lady Charity has made is beneath us. I think we ought to focus on the present company and the delightful opportunities it offers. Do you not agree?"

Judging by the slightly strained and bemused look on Lady Elizabeth's face, Roland was not sure that even his dance partner agreed about the delight to be found in the present company. But he acquiesced and smiled politely and spoke no more of Charity—or anything else. He could not, for the life of him, think of any charming thing to say to rekindle conversation at all.

The silence stretched between them as they finished the dance. As the musicians put on the final flourish, Roland halted and gave her a small bow. "Thank you, Lady Elizabeth, for your company."

Belatedly, he realised that he should have, perhaps, attempted to be gentlemanly and flirtatious with this lady. She was, after all, one of a handful of possible suitable alternatives to the lady diamond. But truly, if he were honest with himself, he was not sorry that he did not make the effort.

Lady Elizabeth smiled politely at him, but it did not reach her eyes. "Lord Percy," she breathed. "It was an experience." She floated off to rejoin her friends, and Roland watched her back as she left.

With a small exhale through his nose, he scanned the place again, looking at the many debutantes. Though his first attempt had been disastrous, he should have been looking for another to inquire regarding Lady Charity.

Instead... he looked for Grace.

There, in the back, near the refreshments—was that a familiar shade of chestnut hair? A posture he recognised?

He made his way to where the lady stood politely, talking to another face he knew. With Lady Charity absent, Lord Dunstan had found himself able to appreciate Lady Grace's charms. As there was a break in the music, he caught just the tail end of Lord Dunstan's query as he approached from behind them.

"—I would be honoured, Lady Grace, to escort you to the balcony if you wish to catch a breath of fresh air. It is lovely outside, though of course it pales in comparison to your gentle beauty."

Roland nearly rolled his eyes at the man's heavy-handed gallantry, abruptly vexed that he was flirting with Lady Grace. Lord Dunstan would presume he could flirt with her? "Good evening, Lady Tilbury, Lady Grace. My apologies, Lord Dunstan. Lady Grace will have to accept your invitation at another time," he interjected before anyone could reply. "You see, she already promised the honour of a dance to me."

23

Preparing to attend Prinny's ball was a trying experience for Grace. Her mama had ordered a new gown, one with a slightly more fitted bodice and a square neckline. Intricate floral embroidery overlaid the bodice, stopping above the satin skirt in a deep emerald green.

It was a lovely colour, but Grace had tugged at the long and sheer sleeves, wishing she could cover her arms in white silk gloves. Elsie had taken her to task, reminding her she'd be grateful for the lighter weight fabric once she started to dance. At that, Grace had raised an eyebrow and swished her skirt, revealing the subtle train at the bottom.

"Dancing? How am I to dance in *this*?" she'd asked in all seriousness. Elsie promised to be there to repair any damage done, just like last time. She'd meant the words to be a soothing balm, but they hung in the air, just as the Fitzroy maid had done in the seconds before her fall to her death.

In the carriage ride over, her mama had prattled on about who might be in attendance. She listed several suitors worthy of Grace's time, should any ask to dance. Grace only half listened.

She'd been occupied with another list, this one of debutantes most likely to resent Charity's success.

The Tilburys had arrived at Carlton House a few minutes after ten in the evening, late enough to make a proper entrance, but still early enough to avoid the crush. Lady Tilbury surveyed the room with the experience of a general surveying the field before battle.

"Your new gown was an excellent choice this evening," Lady Tilbury murmured. "The other girls are faded flowers compared to your jewel-like presence. It is a shame the queen is not here yet to see you."

For once, her mother had not exaggerated. Gowns in the palest shades of rose, ivory, lemon, and grass coloured the ballroom floor. Grace was decidedly against the fashion in these emerald tones. There would be no hiding in this place; her dress would be the centre of many conversations that evening.

The very thought of it made her heartsick. The only jewel in her mind should be the missing diamond, and Grace had no wish to take her place. She did not aspire to lead the gentleman of the ton along a merry chase until she gave in and married the most eligible bachelor.

...But perhaps, for one evening, she could put aside her disinterest in courting and step into Charity's shoes, at least long enough to perform the duty that she needed to. For her.

With a newfound confidence, Grace latched arms with her mother, and together they entered the ballroom. Her mother made for a group of middle-age women in the centre of the room —the women who ruled the infamous Almack's Assembly with an iron fist.

The patronesses of Almack's might not be royalty, but during the Season, they were without equal. Each April, they met to determine which members of high society were worthy of admission to the Assembly rooms. Wryly, Grace recalled how at the beginning of the season, she and Charity had both fretted over the possibility they might be overlooked. When the vouchers had arrived, their sighs of relief had been so long that a footman came in to check on them.

Lady Tilbury and Lady Grace bobbed curtsies. As long as Grace remained unengaged, it was worth a few moment's of their time to pay their respects to these powerful women.

"Good evening, Your Grace," Lady Tilbury said to the Duchess of Dorset. "It is fine weather we are having, is it not?"

The duchess lifted her quizzing glass and scrutinised the pair. Her gaze lingered overlong on Grace, causing her to fear she'd made a dreadful faux pas. "We have had cloudy days, but I see at least one person benefiting from the heat of the sun. Take care you do not get scorched, young lady."

Grace nodded her head in understanding, despite having no clue what the woman meant. Her mother made haste to leave the women as soon as was appropriate.

"The duchess referred to Lord Percy's interest in you. It seems your star is on the rise, my dear. Did he mention anything about his plans when you rode around the park?"

Grace shrugged her shoulders, unsure which answer would make her mother happy. He had made his plans clear, but that was not because he was interested in courting her. It was best for everyone if she feigned being unaware.

Such behaviour, however, was easier said than done. Circulating amongst the women, she attempted to inquire discreetly about Charity with several groups, but it seemed every woman who crossed Grace's path quickly wished to turn the conversation to his lordship. Had Lord Percy come to call? Had he spoken with her father? Every word from Grace's mouth became an on dit for someone else.

As her poor luck would have it, the only person truly uninterested in discussing Lord Percy or Charity was Lord

Dunstan. He approached Grace while she stood with her mother, clearly resolved to speak with her.

"Good evening, Lady Tilbury and Lady Grace." He gave a curt bow in their direction. "I am much pleased to cross paths with you again, Lady Grace."

"Again?" Lady Tilbury cast a sharp glance at her daughter.

"Yes, we both attended the lecture at the Royal Society. It was the most fascinating discourse, was it not? Perhaps you would like to exchange thoughts about it during the next set? It would be a delightful opportunity to learn more about you, and, I confess, to enjoy your company for a while longer."

Grace regretted her pointed flirting that day at the lecture a hundred times over. She had no wish to spend a set in Lord Dunstan's arms, and certainly not discussing the lecture to which she had paid little attention. In desperation, she turned to her mother, assuming she would understand Grace's predicament.

Her mother did not. The woman was tickled pink to discover a second eligible bachelor sought her daughter's affections. "It is so difficult to carry on a conversation during a dance. Why not step out on the balcony? Within sight of the doorway, of course."

"I would be honoured, Lady Grace, to escort you to the balcony if you wish to catch a breath of fresh air. It is quite lovely outside, though of course it pales in comparison to your own gentle beauty."

"She will have to accept your invitation at another time, Lord Dunstan," a man's voice said, cutting into the conversation before she could reply. "You see, Lady Grace already promised me this dance."

Grace froze in place at the man's announcement. Slowly, she turned, certain her ears deceived her. They had not. Before her stood none other than Lord Percy.

Though her eyes had sought him out several times over the hour since she arrived, she still found herself unprepared to speak with him. Moreover, he had not asked her to save any dance. She could not imagine what he was about.

Somewhat of her confusion must have shown upon her face, for he swooped in to fill the awkward gap her silence had created.

"Lady Grace, am I incorrect? I believe we agreed to dance the waltz." His eyes widened ever so slightly, encouraging her to agree.

Lady Tilbury cocked her head to the side and studied her daughter, wondering how she had missed the pair conversing.

Grace was not about to admit that no such thing had occurred. She had been so intent on questioning the ladies watching from the side that she had avoided any man who seemed interested in inviting her to dance a set. Yet, she could hardly reveal such behaviour now, if for no other reason than that her mother would leave her ears ringing.

"You did indeed ask me to save this set, Lord Percy. If you will please excuse us," Grace said. She nodded a goodbye to Lord Dunstan and her mother, all the while keeping a polite smile firmly fixed up on her face.

The first notes of the violin floated into the air, setting a merry pace for the Viennese tune. Lord Percy raised his arms and offered Grace his hand. She baulked at the sight, the ramifications of her decision coming home to roost.

"The waltz? Of all dances?" she whispered in a harsh voice.

"Why ever not? We can hardly carry on a conversation while switching from one partner to another, Lady Grace." Roland wiggled the upturned fingers of his extended right hand in encouragement.

Grace forced her feet to move herself closer to him to take it, and he tugged her towards the dance floor. Turning towards her, he placed her right hand in his left and drew her in, settling his other hand at her back. Each touch burned like fire, even through her glove and gown.

"You may touch me, you know," he said, his tone sounding nearly like a laugh.

"W-what?" she stammered, shocked.

"Your left hand, Lady Grace. It is customary, Lady Grace, for your hand to find a resting place upon my shoulder," he prompted, and she looked down at her one limb held aloft as though she did not know what to do with it. Hurriedly, she set it down on his arm.

Her nerves had nothing to do with him, she assured herself. The waltz was barely acceptable in high society, and it only played here with the Prince Regent's encouragement. The music and steps demanded Grace stick close to Roland, his cheek only inches from her own. She stiffened her back and shoulders, fighting the flowing three-part beats of the music.

This near, there was no way for Grace to look down at her feet. The waltz demanded no intricate step pattern. Perhaps this is why it had been a favourite of hers. With a pang of grief, she remembered that it had been Charity's favourite as well.

It was like a spell that cast upon the thought of her name, tugging Grace's thoughts away from the present, her mind slipping down the corridor of memory. On the quiet evenings before their debut, before they had been permitted to attend the grand events, the pair had pretended to be partners upon the ballroom floor. Charity would curtsy, leaving Grace to play the man. They had hummed the tune while spinning around Charity's bedroom, whirling, not stopping until they fell into a giggling heap upon Charity's bed.

With their cheeks flushed and breath ragged, they had stared up at the ceiling, seeing not the moulding and cornice decorations, but the shadowed faces of their future suitors.

Charity seemed to have always had some specific man in mind. For Grace, any images were nebulous at best.

With a sick twist in her belly, she thought to herself that this moment was meant to be Charity's, not hers. Charity should have been the one to dance here with the handsome Earl Percy. To be the belle of the floor.

Grace's feet stumbled as she lost the rhythm of the beats. Her motion pushed her off-centre. Lord Percy's steady arms drew her closer to keep her safe and balanced.

"Grace," he murmured in her ear, rousing her to the moment.

The sound of her given name on Roland's lips shocked her to her core, but it seemed that was his intention. Had he called her name before, and she had not heard? She swivelled her head, gaze clashing with his.

"Grace, what is wrong? Did somewhat happen? Did you learn something tonight?"

Learn? Her railing mind resisted her attempts to pull it back on track. She turned away, her wild eyes seeking an exit. Dozens of faces stared—glared at her from the side of the floor. Debutantes and mothers alike. Did they question why the heir of Northumberland saw fit to grant her, a no one, his time? Their mouths twisted. Grace was sure she could hear their snide remarks.

"Grace!" Roland clenched his hand around hers, tightening his grasp on her fingers. "Are you all right? You look unwell. Do you feel faint?"

"No, it is not that. I—I have never been very good at dancing," Grace mumbled, feeling blood rush to her face in a flush. It was not entirely untrue, even if it did not explain her current unease. "I am afraid I will embarrass the both of us in front of the ton."

He smiled. For once, the gesture reached his eyes and

170

transformed his expression. Grace marvelled at the change, wondering if she had ever truly seen him smile before. "Thorne has told me that my dancing is barely proficient, but he admitted I should not cause my partner disgrace. Let the music and the feel of my hands lead you. Trust in the dance, and in me."

Grace followed his instructions, tilting her head until his face filled her view. This close, his dark eyes revealed themselves to be the deep brown of her morning cup of chocolate. They softened, melting her resistance. Tension bled from her shoulders, back, and arms as she relinquished control. Roland took the lead, his hands guiding her until her feet once again moved in time to the music.

She opened her mouth to thank him, but caught herself before a word slipped out. She had held his name on the tip of her tongue — a name he had not given her leave to use. Roland. When had she made the switch to thinking of him as Roland and not Lord Percy?

Realising it, she struggled to rebuild the walls between them. She was Lady Grace. He was Lord Percy. Together, their only task was to find Charity. Nothing else could come of it. For once she was found, it would be Charity whom he would ask to court. To marry him. When they found Charity, Grace would once again return to her search for adventure...nevermind that these few days with him had offered her more than she had ever had before.

Despite her attempts to regain her composure, her tongue still felt thick. She cleared her throat to banish the tightness. "Thank you for your patience, Lord Percy. Everyone was staring at us, and though I have practised, I have not yet had the chance to dance the waltz at a ball."

His lips lost the soft curve of good humour, as though her cooler tone reminded him of the weight of propriety. "I would suggest that you pay them no mind, Lady Grace. What the assembly thinks they know about you and I together is of little consequence to either of us." Almost defiantly, he extended his hand to guide her into a twirl in front of the watchful eyes of the ton.

Despite her resolve to keep her feelings in check, it felt as though he had spun her many more times than a single twirl. Like she had consumed too much punch. She was dizzy from his nearness, and for a single moment she thought that perhaps, if it was like this, mayhap getting acquainted with other gentlemen at the balls would not be such a terrible thing after all.

Nearly cheek to cheek, he whispered, "Tell me. Did you find anything? Speak to anyone suspicious?"

The question cooled her blood instantly. Ah, yes. He was only pretending. He was pretending, and she would be a foolish girl to have forgotten again that there was no more to it than the business of finding Charity.

"Lady Grace, did you hear me? This dance will not last forever," Roland warned. "If we are to compare notes, we must do so now."

"Many spoke only of you, my lord," Grace said in all honesty. "Our newfound friendship has not gone unnoticed."

"That was to be expected. What of Lady Charity? Any vitriol of which I should be aware?"

"I heard a few whispers suggesting we were all benefitting without Lady Charity's presence, but those girls were also quick to add that they felt terrible about whatever happened to her. I sensed no real rancour—more like satisfaction that the way was clear for others to rise to the top."

"My, the kittens do have claws. Anything else?"

"The only other name I heard mentioned was Lady Cresswell's. It seems she was the incomparable of her season, and thus none were surprised by the queen's selection of Charity. The people pitied Lady Cresswell for what has happened. Whatever shine she brought to the family may not withstand the current tarnish. Charity's younger sister Phoebe will have to work hard to rise above what happened to Charity."

Lord Percy contemplated her answer. "Unless we can restore Charity back to her family. I, too, made little headway. Let us continue with our conversations and see if we cannot pry loose something of value."

Lord Percy remained silent for the remainder of their time on the floor. Grace was grateful for the reprieve. They bobbed around the floor in time with the violins, one couple amidst a sea of others. For a moment in time, Grace forgot who she was with, and why.

The melody's end brought reality crashing back. Grace pulled her hand free, and Lord Percy took a large step away. He bowed with the utmost propriety and thanked her for the dance.

His dark eyes flashed with unspoken words—reminders of how much rode upon their shoulders should they fail in their endeavour.

24

When he returned to the townhouse in the early hours of the next day following the Regent's ball, Wes had been the one to wake up to collect Roland's horse, bleary-eyed and with a few flecks of straw in his hair. Roland patted the sprout's head paternally, and crept inside, wishing fervently for nothing more than to fall into bed.

Alas, it was not to be. Thorne was waiting for him inside, feet propped on the hearth. It could only mean one thing: there was bad news.

"Thorne," he greeted the man as Thorne woke up from his dozing. "I do not suppose you have been waiting up to tell me the joyful news that my grandfather has passed and we are freed from the burden of family."

"No, quite the opposite. I took a small sojourn after your departure and discovered activity happening at the estate house. Your grandfather sent people ahead to reopen it."

"So the old man is on his way... or soon will be." The pit of his stomach dropped several inches, and he tightened his jaw reflexively, willing his face to bear no sign.

But Thorne, damn the man, knew him too well. "If I did not

know you better, I would be fooled into thinking this was of no consequence to you, but I think that's not so. You're worried about his reaction to discovering you are not yet engaged," Thorne surmised. "I cannot imagine why, Roland. Yes, your grandfather threatened your purse, but after all these years together, surely you cannot imagine that my loyalty is bought only by a steady pay."

"Of course not," he snapped, and immediately regretted his tone. "No... I know it is not. I know you would stand beside me even if I were penniless and disgraced. I will never doubt it." Roland did not mention, however, that there were plans that only his money could support. Not to mention duties and responsibilities, which now numbered among them an addition of orphaned children sleeping in his stable.

Thorne's brows drew down over his piercing blue eyes, and Roland looked away, into the fireplace where the fire had burned down to a few smouldering coals. He did not like when Thorne looked at him in this manner; it felt as though he was rifling through his very soul.

"You worry for the waifs, then? I will make sure that they're given the knowledge to better survive should they run, at least for now. I think they'll stay, though, unless we give them reason to flee. If they don't stay, they would have to consider some alternatives..."

"Because the young 'Will' is a girl pretending to be a boy," Roland finished. "Her disguise did not hold well when she spoke, and I would suppose it holds worse now that she is clean."

"Aye," Thorne smiled briefly. "She pretends still, although she is smart enough to stay out of sight. I haven't had the heart to inform her I know her ruse."

"It would only scare them," Roland agreed. "We will create an environment where hopefully she feels no need to continue the pretence for safety's sake. Honesty shall be met with protection, not punishment."

With a nod, Thorne clasped his hands behind his back. "Yes. Then perhaps we can put her to work within the house as better befitting a girl, ending her charade."

"As long as my grandfather permits us to stay in it, at any rate," Roland said rather dryly. "This property is entailed."

Lifting his eyebrows, Thorne thought that over. "You said he threatened your allowance. I did not realise that he threatened your title."

He hadn't. He had threatened something worse. "At ease, Thorne. My title is safe enough, however my grandfather made it clear that he holds the power to rescind most of the privileges I currently enjoy in a number of ways. A distant, six-year-old third cousin, I am informed, is the next in line if I fail to bear my own heir!"

Thorne stared hard at the back of Roland's head, knowing that the privileges that Roland 'enjoyed' were precious few. Yes, the deceased Thaddius Percy's London townhouse was owned by the duke. Roland had put no monies towards making it his own. If he thought on it, his master had been rather extraordinarily frugal, buying the minimum required to attend the events of the season, with very little in the way of extravagance. Thorne had simply thought it was Roland's personality; Roland had never expressed to care overmuch for fine clothes or things. As they had both been considering a return to military service once this pesky matter of securing a wife was complete, not being a spendthrift in such things had seemed to be nothing more than common sense. Clearly, there was somewhat more to the matter.

In fact, there was a great deal more to the matter. Yet Thorne also knew that despite their unusually close familiarity, he had no right to ask some things.

"Then if your marriage and begetting is such a matter of import, we must do what we can to ensure you meet your grandfather's demands. You must consider contingencies, Roland. It would be prudent to be considering them at any rate. There remains time before the season's end for you to marry."

Worrying his fingers over the edge of the mantle, Roland paused. "Is there enough time? She has been absent for over four days now, and we still have found no sign of the missing Diamond."

There was a long silence. "Roland, it grieves me to point it out thusly, but you must entertain the notion of courtship beyond the diamond. The young lady may indeed be truly lost."

The first image that sprung to mind was of Grace. How determined she had been, how angry, and fearful... how devastated her face threatened to be that evening when she told Roland in the parlour of her home that he could not cast Charity off. As if it had threatened her entire world.

He closed the hand sitting on the mantle into a fist. "I am not prepared to relinquish hope for the diamond just yet. There are a few more days until the ransom is due."

Roland turned then and noted with a flicker of amusement a most unusual sight: Thorne, typically the composed and merry one, now looked as if he were the one wrestling with despair and the urge to tear at his hair. Somehow, this reversal of roles lightened his soul—just a little.

"But, Roland, the queen—" Thorne began.

"I know. The queen does not want the ransom paid. She did not want anyone to think that the Crown approves of any such games. If necessary, I will bear the cost myself to ensure her safe return, making clear the arrangement is of my doing and not the queen's or her family's."

"Fine. It is a fine, kind deed you propose. But the deadline looms large on the horizon. The young lady has been missing for four days already. What if the ton is correct? What if she is ruined? You know that even if she was left truly untouched, without a vouchsafe, they will assume her virtue is tarnished. What then? Would you marry her still?"

Pausing, Roland considered this. "Truthfully, my friend? I do not know."

"No. You do know. I believe you would, if you came to believe it was the right thing to do. Roland, you must consider the implications!" Thorne said firmly, coming close enough to set his hands on Roland's shoulders. "Your heart is sufficiently tender to entertain such a notion, but if you think The Breaker will be angry at your lack of courtship progress now, I can only imagine what may happen if Lady Charity's virtue has been compromised when she is recovered and you decide to wed her anyway."

"You speak of matters well known to me, Thorne, but I refuse to let my grandfather's sense of approval wholly govern my sense of right and wrong without the slightest hesitation or consideration."

Thorne's hands tightened their grip. "I know you, and I know how deep that sense of... of impulsive nobility runs. I worry you will break yourself over the impossible task of atoning for your family's sins. Of a surety, no one in the ton would appreciate or sympathise with your need to obey this instinct."

Roland turned away again, breaking free of Thorne's grasp with a wave of his hand. "You worry without cause, and I shall not borrow trouble before its arrival. You know already what I believe of my grandfather's thoughts. Well, I hold the ton's opinion in no regard whatsoever."

"Truly?" Thorne asked softly.

Blood rushed to Roland's head in a fury as he was reminded again of that benighted wager and already how far he had been driven to protect his honour over that. As quickly as his anger rose, though, he let it release with a sigh. "A statement truer now than it was before, mayhap. I rather liked things more," he said slowly, "and found a certain comfort in the pursuit of a marriage of convenience, when there was no need to account for the lady's personal plight."

When his man made no reply to this, Roland came to a decision. "What we do will depend on what comes. You say I must think. Fine, I will think on things—tomorrow. Should Lady Charity indeed find herself compromised beyond salvage of her reputation, then... then we shall then take whatever measures necessary, even if it requires seeking another alliance. But at the very least, I will sleep better knowing I have done what has been in my power to see her restored to the people who love her, and that is what truly matters."

Thorne made a sound of agreement. "I should hope her family's relief at her safe return should outweigh the tarnish on her name. They may have to navigate the repercussions to her standing, but at least they will be able to do so."

"If her family does not feel that relief, then to hell with them," Roland said bluntly, shocking the man as he headed to the stairs. "At the least, I know Lady Grace will feel it and be grateful, nonetheless."

25

Rain sluiced down the windows of the Tilbury carriage as it jumbled its way along London's uneven cobblestone streets. The cushioned, velvet-upholstered seats protected Grace from the worst of the bumps. She focused her attention on the world outside, still amazed at how little an impact the weather had on the population. Out in the country, on a day like today, people would huddle around fireplaces, or find tasks to do indoors. Not so in London. Men, women, and even children clogged the pavement, hurrying from one place to another, all the while praying their oiled cloaks kept off the worst of the damp.

Grace's gaze dropped lower, entranced by the muddy swirls etching curved lines between the cobblestones. Dark thoughts followed a similar path through Grace's mind. Another day had dawned without Charity's return. She and Lord Percy were making little headway in their search. Though Grace was loath to admit it, holding out hope became ever more difficult.

Not that Grace contemplated giving up, but her past dreams of seeing Charity once again walking into events at her side thinned until the light of day forced reality into view. Like it or not, a debutante's value hinged on her carefully guarded innocence. An absence of this length would put Charity's virtue in question, at best. At worst, she'd be shunned by the ton. Lady Tilbury would ensure Grace followed suit. No matter Grace's opinion on the matter, her friendship with Charity would be at its end.

While storm clouds clogged Grace's mind, pouring icy cold water upon her hopes, Lady Tilbury saw only the hint of blue in the distance. She reached over and took Grace's hand in hers, and gave it a squeeze.

"Darling girl, I realise this is hard for you—it is for all of us—but you must not let Charity's mishap ruin your outlook on the season. I promise, all will be well. You will see."

Grace shifted away from the window to study her mother's face. Silver threads wove through her chestnut hair, reminding Grace of her mother's years of experience. "Truly, Mama? You think she is safe?"

Lady Tilbury's brow wrinkled in confusion. "Lady Charity? How would I know that, when I am as in the dark as everyone else? I meant for *you*, Grace. I would have never wished Charity any harm, but even you cannot deny that you are flourishing without her to cast you in the shadows. Lord Percy, Lord Dunstan," her mother said, ticking names off her fingers. "I saw the way they looked at you last night. Others will soon come to recognise what a gem you are... who knows? Perhaps even the queen, herself. She called you into her chambers once. If her diamond is gone, she may very well select another."

Grace shivered in horror at the images her mother's words provoked. Her, the diamond? Even if she were worthy of such a compliment, it was not an honour she sought. How could she hold her head high, knowing the true cost of her gain?

It was a pointless concern, given that her connection with Lord Percy was nothing more than a facade. Soon enough, the truth would come out. Everyone would learn Lord Percy's only interest in Grace was getting her help to bring home Charity. As for Lord Dunstan, the man flitted to and fro, like a butterfly drawn to every passing flower. If Grace had not spoken to him at the lecture, she doubted he would even remember her name.

Her mother mistook Grace's silence for nerves. She squeezed her daughter's hand again. "Embrace this chance, Grace, for the good of us all. Marrying above your station benefits not just you, but also Felix. As the brother-in-law of a Duke, all of society's doors will open to him."

Grace nodded her head. What other choice did she have? Her mother would not hear any words to the contrary, no matter how hard she tried. Grace was better off putting her efforts into solving the mystery of who had Charity.

The carriage drew to a stop in front of the neoclassical facade of Buckingham House, Queen Charlotte's home in London. A line of carriages proceeded theirs, each pausing before the grand entrance to disgorge its passengers. Footmen stood at the ready with umbrellas in hand to protect the upper-class men and women from the elements.

Lady Tilbury descended first and waited for Grace to follow. A cold, damp wind swept through the courtyard, but Lady Tilbury did not waver. Her proud back stayed straight, her head upright in a perfect posture. The only concession to the weather were the leather boots on her feet.

Inside, the footman guided the pair to the first in the line of drawing rooms. Afternoon tea awaited, offered in steaming cups of bone china decorated with blooming flowers and vines, along with their choice from tables laden with cakes and scones.

"I do not see the queen anywhere," Lady Tilbury said after surveying the room. "Let us help ourselves to tea and set off to see and be seen."

Emphasis was very much on the latter. Everywhere they

went, eyes followed. For once, Grace did not welcome the attention. Despite her intention to speak with more of the debutantes, the urge to hide from scrutiny clawed at Grace's throat.

When she could take it no more, she stopped her mother and asked, "Do I have a spot of chocolate on my face? Everyone keeps staring at us."

"I would have told you well before now if you did. People are staring because they are finally seeing what Lord Percy has recognised. You shall be the incomparable. I promise." Lady Tilbury stopped a passing footman and deposited her empty cup onto his tray. Without asking, she took Grace's only half-drunk tea and handed it away as well. "Square your shoulders, dear. I see the queen. We must go pay our respects."

Somehow, Grace put one foot in front of the other, although her legs trembled with each pass. Her long skirt swished in time with her steps, hiding the evidence of her fear. Her brittle smile threatened to shatter. The queen would almost certainly demand an update, and Grace knew not what to tell her.

Queen Charlotte stood in a circle of admirers, basking in their well-deserved compliments. She shone like a beacon of prosperity and abundance in her ivory muslin gown decorated in pale pink rose blooms and delicate traceries of green. The floral theme continued in her bejewelled pendant and rose gold earrings. A towering bouffant wig in pure white rose above her head, making her impossible to miss. It, too, bore blossoms in pink, yellow, and lavender.

Lady Tilbury dropped into a curtsy, and Grace followed suit. She lowered her gaze, silently praying that the queen would let her pass unremarked. She should have said the words aloud.

Charlotte's mouth shifted into a sly smile. She gave the women permission to rise. "Lady Grace, I was hoping you would attend. We must have a word. In private," she added, daring Lady Tilbury to protest.

Lady Tilbury smiled like a cat sitting on a canary. She nudged her daughter forward. "How generous of you, Your Majesty, to dispense your advice to my dearest child. Go along, Grace. I will await you here."

The queen's coterie of advisors and ladies-in-waiting cleared the way for Charlotte to lead Grace into a nearby room. The queen's aide opened the door for them to enter and barred the way to any who thought to follow.

This room was less opulent than the formal drawing rooms in which the tea party carried on. Book-lined shelves filled the walls on both ends of the room. Grace spotted a telescope standing near a window. She had heard tell of the queen's support for the intellectuals, but had given them little credence. Here, however, lay the truth. This room, with its comfortable furnishings and peaceful atmosphere, was where Charlotte ceased being queen and embraced the simplicity of life beyond the throne.

The knot in Grace's shoulders loosened and she drew her first deep breath since she had arrived at Buckingham House. In doing so, she made a terrible mistake.

Queen Charlotte raised a hand, her numerous rings flashing in the light of the candlelit chandeliers, and jabbed a finger toward Grace. "Lord Cresswell sends me daily notes to ask permission to pay the ransom. He cannot grasp that this is not about money, but about my position. I will have no one believe I approve of such antics. Therefore, I demand an update. What progress have you made in finding my diamond?"

Grace rocked back on her heel and stuttered, "We are searching, Your Majesty, as thoroughly as we can. Lord Percy and I are taking advantage of every chance to question possible kidnappers."

Charlotte waited, but Grace said no more. "And? Have you narrowed the list of likely candidates? Well, who are they?"

"I, well…"

"Do not hold your tongue around me! If there is even a hint of involvement, I will see the person punished." Charlotte paused to allow Grace time to speak. The silence lengthened, itself more telling than words. The queen drew herself up. "You have no names, do you? Five days you have had to search and you have nothing to show for it."

"We are doing our best," Grace whispered, barely loud enough to be heard.

"What you are doing is leading us all on a wild goose chase, founded upon pure fiction and speculation about the death of a drunken maid. It may be that there is no one to blame because Lady Charity disappeared of her own accord. She is a fool, and I am not so blind as to be unwilling to admit I made a mistake in bestowing my favour upon her."

Loyalty compelled Grace to speak out of turn. "No, Your Majesty, you made no mistake."

"You dare contradict me?" Charlotte raised her hands in disbelief and looked at her aide. He tittered at Grace's faux pas.

Blood drained from Grace's head, leaving her dizzy with fear. She froze, unsure which course of action would cause the least offence.

Queen Charlotte speared Grace with a dagger-sharp gaze. "So, you are not completely mad. Brave, loyal, perhaps even defiant. These are traits I admire—ones I seek for the incomparable of the season."

Grace shook her head, wanting the queen to stop. Black threatened the edge of her vision until she reminded herself to breathe before she passed out.

"You do not seek this honour. You *fear* it. Good. Let it incentivise you to work harder. Bring Lady Charity home

185

within the next two days, or her position in society is forfeit, even if her father makes good on the ransom. I have already said that if someone thinks to deprive me of my favourite, I will elevate another. Either way, I will see the wager won and my diamond wed Lord Percy. Perhaps that diamond will be you." She spun around and swept from the room, leaving Grace standing with her mouth agape.

The aide cleared his throat and nodded toward the exit. Grace closed her mouth and sucked air through her nose, begging her stomach to settle. Without conscious thought, she walked back to the drawing room. Despite her promises, her mother was nowhere to be found.

Grace did not stand alone for long. Lady Elizabeth, two years her senior, sidled up to Grace. She glanced left and right, checking who was within earshot.

Seeing no one else was paying attention, Lady Elizabeth murmured. "I see the rumours are true. With Lady Charity gone, you are being favoured to replace her in the queen's eyes."

Grace blinked and shook her head. Barely a minute had passed since Queen Charlotte issued her threat. She grabbed a hold of Elizabeth's hand and dragged her to a nearby vacant alcove. "People believe this?"

"How could they miss your private conference? The room has been a-twitter since Queen Charlotte took you aside. Methinks Lord Percy was the first of us to see your depths. Is that why he's after you?" Lady Elizabeth shook her head and gave Grace a woeful smile. "You must take care, Lady Grace. His only aim is to win that silly bet of his. Do not mistake his interest for proper sentiment. Before her disappearance, he only had eyes for Lady Charity. Do you know, he asked me to dance at Prinny's ball the other night, and the only thing he wanted to discuss during our dance was Lady Charity? Even with her gone, I fear he has not moved on."

Grace could not stand by and let Lady Elizabeth blacken Roland's name, not when she knew the truth of the matter. "I am certain he is concerned, as am I. As, I hope, we all are."

Lady Elizabeth patted Grace's arm and feigned sympathy. "I have only your best interests at heart, Lady Grace. That is why I asked him about you, in between his queries regarding Lady Charity. He made it clear he was merely being sympathetic to you in your time of need. In your shoes, I would want someone to tell me. Do not let him fool you."

"I—"

"No need to thank me for my honesty. It is the least I can do. And on that note, I must take my leave. I see Lady Lark across the room. Her mother had been so certain that Lady Lark was going to be this season's incomparable, but the diamond has slipped out of her grasp now twice."

Lady Elizabeth left without a backward glance. Grace shuffled backwards until she reached the wall. For the first time since her arrival, no one was looking her way. She closed her eyes for a moment, picturing herself anywhere but here. No one could deny Lady Charity's right to the exalted status of favourite of the queen. If Grace did not find Charity before the ransom deadline, Lady Elizabeth and Lady Lark would not be the only ones enraged to lose their chance at being the diamond a second time, especially if the empty honour went to Grace.

26

Roland's arrival at Buckingham House went surprisingly unremarked. Glancing about, he realised that instead of the normal conversational clusters one would expect at a tea party, people had formed rather tight knots. The secretive, gleeful looks on their faces and the hushed sound of their voices could mean only one thing: there was gossip afoot.

He didn't care about whatever fresh scandal had set the ton's tongues to wagging. *Let the busybodies talk*, he thought to himself. There was other urgent business to attend.

Straightening his clothes as he surveyed the room, he began looking for the queen. Though he had gone to bed after talking with Thorne, sleep had eluded him. Thorne was right; he must ensure that he figured out contingencies. The first fallback plan had to be if he and Grace were unable to locate the missing Diamond in time. He had to convince the queen to let him pay the ransom in a way that did not contradict her word. Surely, he could make the queen see reason if he could convince her she would save face.

"Lord Percy!" a happy exclamation pulled him from his thoughts, and he blinked, looking down to see Grace's mama beside him. "Good day to you. Did you enjoy Prinny's ball last night?"

"Lady Tilbury. I did." Roland cast about desperately for anything to say to the woman. An image of a very nervous Grace in his arms during the waltz sprung into his head. "Your daughter looked lovely last night. I must commend you on the choice of the colour of her dress. Green suits her very well."

"I am so glad you agree! I know such a bold colour is not exactly the height of fashion right now, but perhaps we can make it de rigueur once again because it seems such a shame not to use such lovely shades."

"Quite, my lady," he agreed rather absently, already lost on the subject. "Have you perchance seen Queen Charlotte? I... I have yet to pay my respects to Her Majesty."

Whatever response Roland had expected from Lady Tilbury, it had not been that his query would practically make the woman glow with some secret happiness. "Oh, yes, she is in the next room," Lady Tilbury indicated with a graceful wave of her fingers, her voice going soft and breathless. "She pulled aside my daughter for a private word! I cannot imagine—well, yes, I can... I hope she can see how Grace is shining now that she is no longer standing in the shade of another. It is such a tremendous honour..."

Tension gripped Roland's belly. The queen had had a private word with Grace? Had there been some news then? Could it possibly be that someone had found Charity? Suddenly, Roland was desperate to find Grace instead.

He made some excuse—he did not know what—and left Lady Tilbury standing there as he stalked through the party, looking for Grace. He knew her well enough by now that he was certain she would enjoy the quiet of the periphery some place and not in the thick of the gossiping members.

He passed through room after room filled with people until

he reached the last in the line. Seeing the open doors and relative emptiness of this smallest drawing room, he stepped inside. There were many nooks, crannies and alcoves which one could find some peace in here, and certain of his deductions, he strode forward.

Grace was there—he found her hidden in one such alcove. Despite her back turned to the open room, he would recognize her posture and the shade of her hair anywhere, even among a crowd. "Lady Grace," he called to her softly so as not to startle her badly. "Everyone is abuzz about your meeting with the queen. Has there been news?"

Grace turned abruptly, her face stricken, her voice nowhere to be found.

"I can see something is amiss," Roland said, stepping into the alcove to block her somewhat from the view of any passerby. Looking about himself, he took her gently by the arms and backed her up against the wall in the shadow of a large statue. Even once he got her there, he was reluctant to release her entirely. The poor girl looked as faint and uncertain as she had in the middle of the waltz. "Grace," he said her name again, holding her shoulders firmly as he hoped to call her to herself. "Are you all right? Is there news of Charity?"

"No." The shake of her head was almost violent, and he wasn't sure which question she was answering. Mayhap both.

Lowering his voice slightly, he tried again. "You were speaking with the queen?"

"Yes."

When she made a soft sound of protest, he realised his grip had tightened. He let his hands slide down to cup her elbows loosely, reluctant to let her go entirely. Roland paused, trying to guess what must have upset her. "Has there been... has something been found of Charity that suggests an unhappier ending?"

The way Grace stared at him, he understood immediately that he had somehow said exactly the wrong thing. "Lady Elizabeth was right," she blurted harshly. "All you can think of is *her*, and now your stupid wager is going to ruin both of our lives."

Confused, Roland released her and stepped back. "Grace... whatever are you talking about? You must explain. I do not understand what has happened. I conceded the wager to Lord Fitzroy and paid him back days ago."

She barked a nearly soundless laugh. "This is not about money or concessions, *Lord Percy*." The emphasis on his title made an epithet of it. "You may make wagers and mistakes and the damage to your honour, your very worth—" she broke off, trying to compose herself. "The damage you do to yourself is nothing compared to the damage you do to others."

Roland's eyes grew round in concern, and he stepped towards her again. "Grace—"

"*Do not call me that!*" she hissed. "Or do you want me to call you 'Roland,' and for us to remove all doubt in advance of the queen's determination?"

He lowered his head, thinking. "Lady Grace, clearly you are upset and something terrible has happened, but I cannot follow the reasoning or know what transpired. Help me understand. Please."

His entreaty reached her, and Grace's anger abruptly broke and turned to despair. She lowered her head and refused to meet his gaze. In a voice thick with emotion, she said, "Mayhap you were content to lose the wager, my lord, knowing your honour would recover. The queen, however, is not. She will do what is required to ensure that she will win, including bestowing such honours upon me. She has threatened to name me as her own diamond of the season and announce our engagement to the ton."

Roland's jaw dropped in surprise, although in retrospect, perhaps it was not so surprising after all. "Unless... we find Lady Charity?"

Grace folded her arms over her stomach. "If it is still an option, Lord Percy. The time for it is even shorter than you suspect because the queen has all but given up on our ability to find her. In fairness... so have I." Her voice broke and she heaved a breath to stem the onslaught of tears. "We have nothing to go on... no leads... I cannot imagine that we are going to ever find her... ever see her again. In two days' time, I will be shoved into Charity's place whether I like it or not, and then you and I will be as good as engaged by the queen's own word."

He rested his hand on her arm. "We will find her, even if we cannot make it by the deadline. I swear it."

"To what end?" her voice grew bitter. "Even if you get her back, she will be ruined. Anything not stripped from her by shame, I will have taken from her." Grace gestured at him. "She will never forgive me."

He spoke to her as he would a frightened child. "Do not let your hope be stolen from you, Grace. We still have some time. I will do what I can to fix this and see your friend restored in every way."

She stared at him again, this time in frank disbelief. "The queen will never accept such an outcome."

"We will not know until we try. In truth, I came here to speak with Queen Charlotte about the matter of the ransom itself. I believe that by offering to pay, we can work out a solution that allows her to save face.

Grace's cheeks flamed with anger again. "Save face? Are you not listening to what I say? The queen was adamant that the ransom will not be paid. *Ever.* Nothing you say will change her mind."

Roland grasped Grace's arms. "I will make her listen

somehow. Perhaps I will go to Prinny—he will make his mother see reason."

Grace shook free of his hold. "See! You do not understand what it means to be a woman at all. Even if you pay the ransom and Charity comes home, the queen will shun her. All of society will shun her."

The harsh words battered Roland's intentions. His mind spun, searching for any alternative in which everyone won, and no one's virtue was impugned. One thought rose to the top. He latched onto it. "They cannot shun her if she is the wife of a duke. I could marry her to salvage that reputation."

A grim set to her lips met this. "And what of me?" Grace whispered, her face hardening to stone. "If we do not find her before the queen decrees us engaged, will you break that engagement announced by her? You would ruin *me* in the process? I am not fond of this situation either. You have constantly reminded me you are determined to marry Lady Charity, and she is determined to marry you. For that I am sorry, but I can see no way out of it. It seems inevitable; I shall lose my dearest friend—and you and I will be stuck in a loveless marriage where we will come to hate one another."

Roland's throat thickened with some emotion. Was this regret? Hopelessness? He was uncertain. But Grace's words about a loveless marriage, full of hate—it was like a dagger through his heart. Surely that could never be true. Would it? Grace had not been the object of his pursuit, but... if it happened... if the worst case that Grace envisioned came to pass... he could not imagine the two of them together without a certain respect and understanding.

Surely there would at least be that. Wouldn't there?

Breathing slowly through his nose to slow his racing heart, Roland put his mind to work, seeking a solution. "Grace," he whispered to her, hoping she would hear and be calmed. "I know I am not... the perfect gentleman. I have been a soldier far too long, mayhap. Still, I have learned that even when things seem their most desperate, one must continue to fight. If you do not keep fighting... if you give up that hope... you will have given your enemy the victory long before they win it. If you give up hope, you cannot see an option to turn the battle if it presents itself."

"Well, *Roland*," she said in a flinty voice, "If you speak of turns, there is one remaining possibility. The queen cannot make us wed if you are not here. Leave London if you do not want to marry me. You can find a suitable wife elsewhere, or return in a year or two's time. If you leave right now, there is the possibility of you saving both of us."

Roland did not care for the way she said his name. Not in the least. "Unfortunately, that is not an option."

"Why not?" Grace gripped her gown, uncaring about the wrinkles in the fabric. "It is by far the simplest solution. They will name another diamond next year, and the one after. You will find someone else as beautiful and enchanting as Charity, a match with far fewer strings and gossip attached."

Roland's mouth tightened. "Ask anything of me, Lady Grace, but I cannot agree to this. I cannot leave London. I cannot go seeking a wife on the continent or in a year's time."

"Of course you can! Men are free to come and go—to marry whomever they please."

"Perhaps you think we are in control of our destiny, but it is not so. Think of your brother; is he so free? Will your parents not have thoughts regarding his choice of a wife? How would they react if he dashed off, leaving not one, but two young women in a lurch?"

Grace squared her shoulders. "They would forgive him, especially if he explained."

She meant the words as a balm, but they cut through

Roland like a blade. Forgiveness was not in the cards. He shook his head. "Well, then your parents are more generous than others. Some things cannot be forgiven. Even if the queen were to forget about my abrupt departure... Well, my grandfather, the duke, will not. It is a complicated story, but I bear many responsibilities, and some of these are contingent upon what transpires this season. People depend on my marriage."

He watched as the last defiant hope faded from her eyes. "So, you will not go away?" Grace said as she tried to turn her head away, but Roland refused to let her hide from him. He slid his fingers around her chin, letting them rest upon her cheek, and he urged her to show her face. To make her tear-filled eyes meet his.

Zounds. He hated to see her cry. And that it appeared she was crying at the thought of being forced to marry him? Well, that only made it a thousand times more terrible.

"If this is the only way you believe you can escape a—a loveless marriage to me, then we cannot give up looking for her. We must continue, as long as we still have some hours to search."

Grace gave a single nod of understanding and then pulled away, disappearing into the crowd of guests.

His mood now most foul, Roland stalked out of the room, preparing to depart. He did not care that others would talk. That he hadn't seen the queen. What was the point of it? Before he could make his way out of the party, however, he found none other than Lord Fitzroy stepping into his way.

"What is the matter, Fitzroy?" he asked testily. "I am not feeling much in the mood for talk."

Fitzroy looked him over, his eyes speculative. But though Roland was wearing his heart upon his sleeve, Fitzroy did not ask what had happened. "One can tell. I am sorry to approach you at such a moment, but this reminds me of how negligent I am in my duties as the head of the family.

Taking another breath, some of Roland's anger left him, but he could not muster curiosity. "Duties?" he inquired politely.

Sucking in a breath of his own, Fitzroy nodded. "I understand you have been waiting, hoping to see Lady Charity restored. Since most believe that is unlikely to happen now, it will seem passing strange if you do not pay attention to some of the other ladies. My mother has rather baldly asked why I have not introduced you to my sister."

Roland's temper surged again, but he held onto it. "Unfortunately, I have obligations at the moment, Fitzroy. Now is not a good time."

He waved his hand in dismissal. "Just as well. They are in line to greet the queen and curry favour. She is hoping Lark will rise in prominence now—well," he stopped before uttering the words on his lips that Roland could hear clearly, nonetheless. Unaware of Roland's wandering thoughts, Fitzroy continued, "Tonight, perhaps? Surely you are coming to Vauxhall; everyone shall be there. I hate to be the person who presses you into a dance with a lady twice..." Fitzroy trailed off, a mischievous grin lifting his lips. "But perhaps you could find a moment for a dance with Lark to soothe my mama."

Unable to think of a good reason to refuse to dance with Lady Lark out of hand, Roland nodded curtly and left.

27

L ater that evening, Grace sat still despite the pulling and tugging of Elsie arranging her hair. She had thought herself long immune to the pain associated with proper coiffure, but tonight each tangle made her snarl.

"Sorry, my lady," Elsie murmured. "It's just that I want you to look ever so lovely for Lord Percy. Surely, he will be there tonight."

"Not you, too," Grace moaned, shaking her head to force Elsie to step back. "You, if anyone, should know why he speaks with me. It has naught to do with the style of my hair or the décolletage I display. He wants to see Charity returned safely, as do I."

She expected Elsie to give up, but the girl lifted the comb and smoothed the sides of Grace's hair into place. In a low tone, she muttered, "It isn't why he speaks to you that caught my attention, but how he looks at you when he does. But if you insist otherwise, who am I to say you are wrong?"

Grace lifted her gaze and met Elsie's eyes in the mirror. London had changed them both, it seemed. As an upper floor maid, Elsie would never have been so brave to speak her piece.

Grace could chastise her for her boldness, but she lacked the desire to do so. With Charity gone, Elsie was the closest thing she had to a friend. Did it matter if they came from very different classes? Thorne and Roland were close, and for them, the gulf was just as wide. Elsie had shown nothing but loyalty from the moment the Fitzroy maid stumbled from the room and fell over the balcony.

It was on the tip of Grace's tongue to tell Elsie about the queen's threat when her bedroom door opened and her mother came inside.

Inspired by the fireworks display planned for later that night, Lady Tilbury had chosen a gown with a bold red satin slip, with short full sleeves and a wide border of lace trimming the bottom. Diamonds and rubies winked from her neck and ears. She closed the door carefully and walked over to survey her daughter.

"You should wear your new gown in that lovely shade of lawn green. Lord Percy himself said the colour is becoming on you, and we would not want to disappoint."

Grace stiffened, her cheeks flooding with colour. Without a word, Elsie set the comb aside and hurried from the room.

"Mama, you must not get your hopes up about Lord Percy."

"Fiddle, Grace. You do not need to be coy with me. Lord Percy has been dancing attendance upon you ever since our paths crossed at Buckingham House. While you may not have been his first choice, you cannot deny he is enamoured of you now."

But Grace could deny, and therein lay the problem. He had no more moved on than Grace had forgotten Charity. Although Grace desperately hoped he was right, and they would find a way out of their predicament, she was too realistic to blind herself to the alternative.

Despite this past week, Roland Percy was still a veritable

stranger. She knew nothing of him. Nothing of his plans. If they married, would he drop her in some property and forget her? Would he force her to spend her days at his whim? Would he allow her any freedom?

Did it matter if he did? For the end would be the same. He seemed to be an honourable man, and that would mean he was just as trapped as she was. Perhaps she was too harsh in saying they would hate one another, for he seemed a decent man. She could not imagine he would be deliberately cruel. Not at the beginning, at any rate. If he went into their marriage with regrets... Well, regret had a peculiar way of turning into resentment.

Grace had to put on a brave face, but such a mask lay beyond her grasp. Her mother's expression turned joyous as she pictured Grace as a duchess. Until now, Grace had been content to allow her mother the fantasy. But with it so close to becoming real, she had to confess Roland's supposed interest in her was nothing more than a facade. She spun around and grabbed her mother's wrists.

"Mama, listen to me. It was no accident we met Lord Percy at the queen's residence. Queen Charlotte demanded he find out what happened to Charity. I promised to help. That is all this has been—a series of discussions about who might have taken the woman he truly cares about and Queen Charlotte values above all. He has no intention to wed me, nor I to him."

Her mother's face creased with concern, but she soon enough shook off her worry. "Have you found Charity? Found any hint of where she might be?"

"No," Grace whispered.

Her mother's face went through a quick and complicated set of changes. Sadness. Pity. Resolution. "Then it makes no difference. We must all accept that Charity is gone. You are here, and Lord Percy is getting to know you better. He has looked at no other woman. Keep a tight hold on him, and you will see. Soon, he will grow fond of you. How could he not? When all is said and done, he will discover he is served just as well by making a future with you. Believe me, marriages have been founded on much less stable ground."

Grace fought the urge to shake her mother. Shouting, screaming, throwing a tantrum — she had tried them all as a child desperate for attention in a busy household. The attention had been upon her brother Felix in his role as heir, and Mercy, their firstborn child. Grace ranked as a distant third. Her mother had even forgotten about Grace's debut, so caught up was she in the forthcoming birth of her first grandchild. That was why Grace had accompanied the Cresswell family to London and spent her first weeks of the season at Charity's side.

Seeing Grace wed to Lord Percy would be her mother's dream as much as it was Grace's nightmare. Grace would be set for life and no longer a nagging thought in the back of her parents' minds.

Grace found the courage to try again. This was far too important to simply roll over and bare her throat. "Mama, Lord Percy loves Charity. He has gone above and beyond in his search. Would you have me marry a man in love with another woman?"

"A woman who is gone?" Lady Tilbury twisted her arms free of Grace's loose grasp and latched onto Grace's hands. She pulled her daughter to standing, her eyes roving over Grace from head to toe. "Grace, you may not believe me, but you are no consolation prize. You are fair of face and form, well-educated, and caring. You have everything a man could hope for in a wife. No one marries for love, dear, no matter what the fairy tales say."

Grace pulled back from that statement. "I am no fool, Mama, but as you say, I am caring. And as such, how can I abandon the search for Charity if there are pathways left unexplored? Surely even you admit that friends are important. I would not be me if I gave up now."

Lady Tilbury dropped Grace's hands. She rubbed her forehead, consternation writ across her pinched lips. "What would you have me do or say, dear? If I had known Charity would go missing from the Fitzroy garden, I would never have let her out of my sight. But I did not know. None of us. Not me, you, her parents, our hosts, or even Lord Percy, who you claim is in love with her."

"Someone took her," Grace insisted. "You are acquainted with everyone of quality in London. Perhaps you have heard some whisper, some hint?"

"Of a crime? And kept it to myself? I am not so desperate to see you rise I would ignore a missing girl!"

"Then help me figure out the puzzle, Mama! Please, for a moment, put yourself in my shoes. Someone wanted Charity for themselves, or they wanted her gone so they could take what is hers. Guess, if you must. I will take any advice you can offer."

"If I do, will you cease with this nonsense and do as I say?"

Grace had no intention of giving up so easily, but she was perfectly willing to lie now to achieve her ends. "Yes, I will."

Lady Tilbury heaved a great sigh and then motioned for Grace to follow her to the pair of wingback chairs near the fireplace. She perched on the edge of the seat, taking care not to wrinkle her gown, and then rested her hands in her lap. "You say the queen gave you permission to investigate this matter? Is this why you attended that lecture with your brother?"

Grace nodded.

"I suppose I should be thankful you are not becoming a bluestocking. Did you go in order to speak with the men who danced their attention around Charity?"

"Yes," Grace admitted, having no reason to keep that a

secret. "I spoke with Lord Dunstan, as I understood he was one of the last to see Charity. Whatever happens between me and Lord Percy, please do not get any ideas about Lord Dunstan. I would choose ruination over wedding him."

Grace's mother gasped in outrage. "I will have no talk of that, young lady! What of Lord Percy? Did he do the same as you?"

"Yes." Grace saw an opportunity to drop her mother's estimation of Lord Percy by a few notches. "Have you heard of Lord Percy's wager?"

"I overheard Felix discussing it with your father. While I cannot and will not condone such an ill-mannered bet, your father made a good point. Lord Percy received an excellent education, but spent the last decade among the common soldiers instead of abroad polishing his social skills. He is rough around the edges, clearly in need of a woman to smooth those."

Grace dropped her arms to her side and slid her hands under her skirts. Out of sight, she clenched them until the pain caused her to keep quiet. Was there nothing a man could do wrong? She and the other debutantes had only to bat their lashes at a rake and risk blackening their reputations.

Lady Tilbury turned a blind eye to Grace's silent suffering. "Where were we? If you and Lord Percy have spoken with the suitors, and believe none of them took Charity, then I have no further suggestions to offer. Perhaps it was a servant, or a carriage driver, or a passing vagrant who snuck onto the property. I hardly see how you or Lord Percy could evaluate every possibility."

"But Queen Charlotte asked us—"

Lady Tilbury cut her daughter off. "Queen Charlotte is consistent in her love of only one person—her husband. As for the rest of us, we are but passing fancies there to help her while away the time. Fear not. She will soon forget your failure, and in time, Charity herself. Find another way to honour your friend. I am happy to discuss that with you further, but not now, not when we are due at Vauxhall Gardens. I will ring for Elsie so she can help you into your gown."

Grace's stomach rebelled at the thought of draping herself in expensive fabrics and traipsing around the garden's delights. She scrunched her eyes closed and swayed in her chair. "I am sorry, Mama, but this conversation has set my temples pounding. Might I be excused?"

"Absolutely not! Lord and Lady Lancaster invited us to dine at their table. If you don't show, the numbers will be off. I have got just the thing." Lady Tilbury rose from her chair and hurried to the hall. She called for the footman posted to the top of the staircase. "Fetch a tincture of henbane from Mrs Griffin."

The footman returned minutes later bearing a tray with a glass of water and the bottle of liquid courtesy of the housekeeper. He set it on the table between the chairs and took his leave. Lady Tilbury pulled the stopper from the bottle and measured a single drop into the glass. She urged Grace to drink it all.

"Put this into your pocket and bring it along in case you have need again. But you must be mindful of it. Do not take too much, as it might leave you dizzy, confused, and disoriented. We cannot have you getting lost in the gardens."

Grace eyed the glass with a nervous expression, given that she did not truly suffer from a headache. "Are you certain this will not cause any ill effects?"

Lady Tilbury nudged the doctored glass of water closer to Grace. "I have it on excellent authority that this is an effective treatment. Instead of attending lectures with Felix, join me for the next meeting of the Horticultural Society. Marian Fitzroy is quite the expert on the properties of plants! It was fascinating to see how fine a line there is between a poison and a medicine.

Even the queen attended her last talk on medicinals. Marian sent us all home with these tinctures. Did you know foxglove may treat weaknesses of the heart?"

Grace choked on the water sliding down her throat. Her mother reached over to help her, but Grace waved her off. "I am fine, truly. You caught me off guard with the mention of Lady Fitzroy. I was aware of her interest in plants, but did not know she was so knowledgeable about the topic."

"Oh yes, her gardens have the most astonishing variety. Some physicians acquire herbs from her, even. It would do you no harm to get better acquainted with her," Lady Tilbury suggested. "She has found a balance between the womanly arts and her pursuit of knowledge. I believe you would get along well with her and her daughter. We should have them over for supper."

At that moment, Grace could imagine no worse than sharing a table with a woman who might have poisoned the drink that led to the death of that poor maid. But if Lady Tilbury was willing to impart information, Grace would be foolish to ignore this opportunity.

"While we are on the topic of Lady Fitzroy, what else should I know? I do not want to make a faux pas in our first conversation."

"Avoid discussion of her marriage," Lady Tilbury warned. "Lord Robin Fitzroy—Peregrine's father, that is—was much older."

"Why did she marry him? Did she not have other choices? Or did she simply hope to be a widow?"

Lady Tilbury shifted closer and lowered her voice, a sure sign she was about to impart some juicy tidbit. "I am not prone to gossip, but this is water under the bridge now. When it came time for Marian to make her debut, she was widely expected to be the great beauty of the season. For all the little season, men flocked around her, desperate to curry favour. But all that changed after her presentation at court. She executed her part to perfection, and Queen Charlotte smiled upon her bowed head. And then, in walked Charity's mother. You have seen Lady Vanessa, and can certainly imagine how glorious she was at the height of her youth. The queen fairly swooned at the sight of her, and immediately declared her the favourite of the season."

"I understand how this might have left Lady Fitzroy with a foul taste in her mouth, but how did that lead to her marrying an old man?"

Lady Tilbury lowered her voice even further, despite them being alone in Grace's bedroom. "Lord Cresswell was the catch of the season and had been dancing attendance around Marian in the days leading up to her official debut. Like the queen, when he laid eyes upon Vanessa, he did an about face and never looked back. I do not believe Marian has ever quite forgiven Vanessa for stealing her beau, though I cannot imagine why. She married well enough in the end, and as a widow is now free to do whatever she pleases."

Free to do whatever she pleases? How far would Lady Fitzroy go? Those words echoed in Grace's head as she climbed into the family carriage for the ride to Vauxhall.

28

Roland had planned to mope at home that evening, but Thorne had forced his hand into attending Vauxhall after all. "I think you should inflict your charming scowl on the gentry," he had drawled, and tossed a cravat at Roland's head. "Go be merry with all the ton."

Catching it, Roland snarled, "I am not in the mood to go dance and flirt with women tonight."

But he had lost that argument with Thorne, who had counted on his fingers all the reasons he should go, including that he had left the queen's tea party so precipitously, and the fact that Thorne himself was growing tired of his brooding.

"Fine, I will go," Roland had finally growled in surrender. "But I shall not be a merry man!"

The entertainments at Vauxhall Gardens were open to all—as long as they could afford the entry token. After paying the fee, Roland made his way inside, marvelling at the size of the crowd and the fact that anyone could locate one another in such a bustling place. With any luck, perhaps he would not find the Fitzroy family at all. Still, it became clear as he strolled through the gardens, there clearly were lines of demarcation. The supper boxes were full of faces he recognised—and who recognised him. Bowing to the inevitable, he joined Lady Fitzroy and her daughter.

"Lord Percy, I am so glad you made it tonight," Lady Fitzroy said, resting her hand lightly on his arm. "It is wonderful to see you in a less formal setting where you might be more comfortable."

"Quite, Lady Fitzroy," he said, tactfully withdrawing his arm from her reach after a moment. "Is Lord Fitzroy here as well? I saw him earlier at the queen's tea."

"He is about—getting us drinks," she said with a dismissive wave of her hand. "Lord Percy, allow me to introduce my daughter, Lark. We had such a pleasing conversation with the queen today at tea. I rather hope this favour will reflect on Lark for the rest of the season!"

Transferring his attention to the young lady beside her mama, Roland appraised the girl. She seemed even younger, somehow, than Grace and Lady Charity had. Perhaps it was the stamp of her mother's features, including the same bright blonde hair she shared with her brother. Or her wide, guileless hazel eyes. Smiling demurely at Roland, Lark extended her hand for him to bow over.

Lady Fitzroy's smile widened in satisfaction in a way that was nearly predatory, like a wolf preparing to pounce on a lamb. "Mayhap..." she said, dropping her voice fondly as she touched her daughter's shoulder, "she might finally even recognise you as the diamond you are."

Roland's hand, automatically stretching out to take Lark's extended one, hesitated for the briefest instant before completing the gesture. Lady Lark—or her mother, more likely—was hoping to seize the prize and take Charity's place?

Savage mirth tightened his belly. Lady Fitzroy and her daughter did not know that the title of Diamond was all but promised to someone else, and it had been promised as a threat, no less. As his hand closed upon Lady Lark's, however, and he completed his bow over it, his mind galloped ahead.

Lady Fitzroy was hoping her daughter would be recognised as a diamond of the first water. It struck him, then, that in the discussions of the suspects—jealous men, perhaps servants, perhaps debutantes—he and Grace had never once examined the possibility of one of the mothers. If Lady Fitzroy had been manoeuvring towards this end, she might not have been the only one.

Grace. He needed to find Grace at once, he realised with painful intensity.

Both Lady Lark and Lady Fitzroy were looking curiously at him. Abruptly, he noticed he had not yet let go of her hand, and he smiled weakly at them as he released her. "Apologies, Lady Lark. Your name reminded me of a poem, and my mind instantly leapt a continent away as I tried to recall the name."

It was more prettily said than he would normally have managed, and Roland knew Thorne would crow about finally rubbing some charm off upon Lord Barbarian. To be sure, both women looked pleased at the thought Lady Lark would remind him of poetry. Doubtless, it was romantic or some such.

Roland couldn't bear to think of such things right now; an urgency bordering upon panic seized him and he struggled to keep the emotion from rising to his face. There were thousands in Vauxhall. Where could he find Grace? How? And how could he get out of this conversation to go looking for her?

As he prayed to the heavens for any distraction, Lord Fitzroy, blessedly, chose that very instant to return with a glass of punch for both his mother and his sister. "Lord Percy, you look much better than you did this afternoon," Fitzroy greeted him.

"Yes, I... I had come into some bad news," he explained,

meeting Fitzroy's gaze. It was not precisely a lie. "It is being addressed."

Fitzroy looked briefly and genuinely concerned for Roland's sake, and Roland studied the man's expression. "That is good to hear. I see you met my sister already," he continued, raising an eyebrow at his mama. Then Fitzroy's eyes returned to Roland's. "We shall hope to see you later at the dance?"

His words were casual, with no special intonation. He and Peregrine were not exactly friends, but perhaps... it felt as though they were laying the foundations of a better relationship between them. Regarding intentions for his sister, it did not seem like there was an ounce of calculation or condemnation in him. Fitzroy, it seemed, either had no horse in that race, or he was a better liar than Roland was.

"Yes, of course," Roland said, grasping the excuse to be away. "I shall look forward to it. Ladies," he said, nodding to them, and then he departed as though the soles of his boots were afire.

He did not see any of the Tilbury family in the supper boxes or the clusters of aristocrats. She was not nearby the concert, listening to the music, or watching the dancers on the floor. He could not find her on the Grand Walk or watching the performers. Desperate, he considered the possibility that she may have paid the fee to enter one of the more elite areas. Just as he concluded that was where he must search next and hurried that way, he spotted her. There—on the other side of the crowd that lay between them. She was looking directly at him, her brows drawn together in worry.

He pressed through to reach her, begging pardons along the way, and finally the last few bodies parted, leaving him free to approach. Surrounded as they were by listening ears, he carefully chose his words. "Lady Grace," he said, his voice rough. "I hoped our paths might cross."

"And I you," she countered, her face still looking strained. She dropped her voice to barely more than a whisper. "We overlooked someone on our list of suspects."

"The debutantes' mothers," he said, finishing her thought. Grace looked surprised that he had come to this conclusion, but before he could say more, she cut him off.

"We cannot have this conversation here," she told him nervously, and she flicked a glance toward the hedge maze entrance a short distance away. "Take the first two lefts and meet me in a few minutes."

She stepped away quickly. Roland wanted to tear his hair out in frustration at the need to conceal themselves, but he conceded she was right; the thick of the crowd was no place to have a conversation. He waited the bare minimum he could before he nearly raced after her, finding her where she had said. It proved to be a darkened dead end, half-hidden by a tall hedge.

"I just had an encounter with Lady Lark and Lady Fitzroy," he explained, "and it is apparent she plans to use this unfortunate incident to elevate her daughter." Finally, giving in to the frustrated urge to do so, he ran his hand through his hair as he recalled the words. "She said that perhaps the queen might finally even recognise Lady Lark as a diamond. If she only knew—"

Shock stiffened Grace's body, and her hands tightened painfully on Roland's. "She said that? Lady Fitzroy?"

"Yes? More or less. She may be the most blatant, but how many other mamas did the same..." but his voice trailed off. Grace's face grew deathly white, and she swayed on her feet. He hoped she was not about to faint, because she had not released his hands. "Grace? What is the matter?"

"Speculation aside, only you and I know the queen has threatened me with the honour of the title," she reminded him.

"Yet, Elizabeth—Lady Elizabeth said something about Lady Fitzroy having lost the diamond twice. I paid it no heed. At that moment, I thought she meant I was the second diamond's loss, but I cannot be..."

She snatched her hands back, clutching her fists to her stomach as though she were about to be sick. "Roland, you were nearer the mark than you knew. Gossip has it Lady Fitzroy herself was denied the title, years ago, when Charity's mother swanned onto the scene. Lady Cresswell became the queen's new darling..."

"And in the doing, snatched the accolades right from Lady Fitzroy's hands," Roland finished grimly, his mind racing through the implications. "Lady Charity stealing the show from Lady Lark would serve as more salt in the same wound of Lady Cresswell's dealing. It is a motive, surely, but is there aught else that might serve as proof?"

"Oh yes," Grace laughed once, harshly. "I claimed I had a headache earlier and my mama gave me a tincture of henbane in my drink, one which she had courtesy of Lady Fitzroy. She warned me to go cautiously in using it. Do you know why? Lady Fitzroy told her that too much can cause blurred vision, confusion, and incoordination. Sound familiar?"

"Lady Charity's clumsiness, and then the maid's strange behaviour. Are you suggesting?"

Pressing her lips together, Grace nodded firmly. "Lady Fitzroy warned that the line between a poison and a medicine is slim at best." The barest shimmer of moisture showed up in the corners of Grace's eyes and was quickly banished. "Elsie knows something of the common tinctures. She said that too large a dose of henbane could lead to death. What if Charity is dead, and her body was thrown into the river?"

A chill ran down his spine as the parts of the riddle fell into place too neatly to be disregarded. "For her to consider outright murder—!" His breath failed him, and pausing, he envisioned the Fitzroys as he had seen them earlier. Lady Lark, wide-eyed and fawning. Lady Fitzroy, with the self-satisfied look of a cat drinking cream. Lord Fitzroy, unexpectedly compassionate. Nearly a friend...

Then the thought struck him. "Mischief," his voice trailed off. "Murder has consequences that I have to imagine even Lady Fitzroy would baulk at entertaining. I cannot imagine that even the most cold-blooded individual would fail to calculate the risk of committing murder at their own party. But what if it was meant only as mischief? You said your mama cautioned you against using too much. A dizzy, clumsy girl would embarrass herself, and the ton would assume she was foxed."

Hope crept into Grace's eyes, and then the embers cooled again. "She would have her reputation damaged, for certain. But if it was mischief, then where is Charity?"

"Perhaps the maid's accident provided an opportunity for a greater mischief Lady Fitzroy did not originally plan. Where could she be concealed? We searched the estate house top to bottom, and Fitzroy's townhouse." Roland mulled, and then straightened. "Grace. We only checked one of their London houses. The other was rented!"

"Perhaps that was a ruse," Grace breathed.

"Or an accomplice," Roland acknowledged. "I must go home and get Thorne. We must check the other house at once."

"Not without me!" she said so fiercely he was taken aback. "Elsie and I must go with you. You cannot rescue her alone without compromising her virtue."

"Assuming she has any left to compromise," he said reluctantly, and then cursed himself for reminding her of that possibility. "Fine, I will look for you and your maid where we dropped you off the night we looked at the townhouse. Ten o'clock. If you do not show—if you cannot show, I will go anyway with Thorne."

Her jaw set rather mulishly, and Roland wasn't certain whether she was preparing to argue or was attempting to hold back tears. Mayhap it was both. Whichever it was, he laid his palm gently alongside her cheek to forestall it, his thumb grazing her lip. "Grace, all my years away have done nothing but prove to me that the people of the ton cannot judge a person's worth. Not truly. I know you haven't had a chance to see much of it, but there is a bigger world outside of the narrow window they let you see. No matter what remains of Charity's reputation in their eyes, what disapproval she will see, I promise in the end, she will be fine. Your love for her alone will see her through."

And with those shocking words, Roland spun and left her standing there.

29

The feel of Roland's fingers against Grace's cheek lingered after his abrupt departure. Standing there in the shadows, Grace touched her lip where his thumb had grazed across it. Roland Percy had rough edges, indeed.

They had been lucky no one had stumbled upon them. His touch had been so intimate, surely it would have caused an outcry if someone had noticed. Her heart, however, refused to forget. It swelled at the remembrance of that phantom touch. She reflected on the way he had looked at her, again and again. For that moment, she almost wished their connection was not a farce.

She was uncertain how long she stood there. A group of young women lurched around the hedge, giggling at their wrong turn. Grace threw her hands up in frustration, pretending to have made the same error. She let them wander ahead before turning toward the exit to go look for her mother. She had to leave Vauxhall.

Thankfully, Lady Tilbury was where Grace had left her: talking to their host from dinner about finding the best viewing spot for the evening's fireworks display. Grace waited for a gap in the conversation before tapping her mother on the arm. Motioning for her to step aside, in a low voice, she whispered, "Mama, with all the noise and the lights here, my headache is getting worse."

Lady Tilbury searched her daughter's face and frowned when she noted how pale Grace was. "You do not look well. Did you bring the henbane with you? Perhaps you need a little more."

"I added some to my glass of water during dinner and all it has done is make me feel somewhat dizzy."

Those turned out to be the magic words. Lady Tilbury insisted she remain there and then bustled off to find Felix. She returned in short order with the announcement that Felix would escort Grace home.

Felix grumbled the entire way to the garden exit. Apparently, he and some of his friends had plans to meet up with a group of chorus girls from Covent Garden. A dependable brother he might be, but he firmly believed being asked to give up such an opportunity simply for the sake of propriety was too high a price to pay for remaining in his mother's good graces.

"You could not sit on a bench somewhere, waiting for us?" he asked wistfully.

"I am sorry, brother, truly. All I wish to do is go straight to bed." For her part, Grace was equally unhappy with her mother's decision to send Felix home. Time was already of the essence if she wanted to rendezvous with Roland and Thorne.

It would be risky enough to leave the house. The last thing that she needed was for her brother to check in on her after her departure to meet Roland. If he found her room empty, surely he would raise the alarm. When they reached the carriage, Grace offered her brother an escape. "Felix, there is no need for me to ruin your evening as well. Grantham will see me safely home, and then I can ask Elsie to stay in my room tonight.

215

Between the two of them, I will be in safe enough hands. You should stay with your friends."

Felix brightened at the idea of this, but then his face fell again. "Mama will not be happy with me if I leave you alone."

"Well, I will not tell her if you will not," Grace murmured. They had played such games before, in the country estate.

He was half-won over. "Are you certain? I do not want to leave you alone if you feel so poorly."

Grace grasped her brother's hand. "Truly, it is all right. It is likely a headache from too little sleep. I just want to go home and close my eyes."

Felix did not need long to ponder Grace's proposal. He opened the carriage door and helped her climb inside. After instructing her to pull the curtains so that no one would see she was alone, he directed Grantham to drive her straight home and then return so he could collect his mother and father. As for himself, Felix would find his own way home and into the house, leaving Mama none the wiser.

Once home, Grace played the role of an ailing young woman to perfection. She rested a hand on her brow and moaned, complaining about the flickering lights from the candles. She went straight to her room and waited for Elsie to join her.

Elsie arrived bearing a cup of warm milk, no doubt laced with a spoonful of laudanum. Grace took the cup and poured the contents into her chamber pot. "I am fine, Elsie. I simply needed an excuse to take my leave. We must hurry; Lord Percy and Thorne will be waiting for us."

Elsie's eyes were wide with concern, but the forbidding expression upon Grace's face caused her to keep her questions to a minimum. "Where are we going at this hour?"

"We are going to rescue Lady Charity. We know where she

is. Now, do you have any idea how we can get out of the house with no one noticing?"

If Elsie had thought to protest, the words died on her lips. "You know where Lady Charity is?" When Grace nodded, she thought for a moment before answering, "I know how Lord Felix sneaks out. If you are game, we can give that a go... but you will never manage it in that gown."

After sneaking into her brother's room to pilfer some clothes, the women emerged twenty minutes later, clad in raven-black maids' uniforms, with pairs of Felix's breeches worn underneath.

To climb the wall, they had to ruck their skirts up to a height that made Grace blush to think about how much leg was on display if anyone caught them. The breeches would keep the girls from the horrifying possibility of having to do this in their drawers, and once they let their skirts fall back into place, they were invisible beneath.

Grace and Elsie climbed over the stone wall, edging their property without mishap, and threw their cloaks over their heads. They reached the meeting point just as a plain black carriage pulled up, the driver's hat pulled down low to shade his face, and a small child riding on the back of it.

Elsie withdrew into the shadows, but Grace peered closer. The man lifted his hat just enough to reveal that it was Thorne sitting in the driver's seat, and he gave her a smile and a brief nod of encouragement. He knocked on the roof, and Roland threw open the door, urging them to hurry inside.

The women settled on the rear-facing bench. "Are you aware there's a child riding on the back of your carriage?" Grace asked.

Roland raised an eyebrow, but he smiled faintly. "There are two of them," he corrected. "Remember? You wanted me to take them in."

Grace attempted to square the clean-faced boy she'd seen peering around the back of the carriage with the coal-blackened face she had seen at the Fitzroy townhouse. She supposed it was possible it was the same child, but without Roland's explanation, she never would have guessed. However, his words did not fully explain why he had the children out at this hour.

"We do not know what we're going to find when we arrive at the house. We need all the help we can get. The Sprouts are clearly good at getting in and out of places they aren't supposed to be."

"But it might be dangerous," Grace argued.

Roland's brow furrowed. "Grace, I would never put them in a dangerous spot. I will ask the sprouts to act as lookouts and pass messages. Thorne and I will handle anything else."

"The sprouts? Is that what you call them?" Elsie asked, daring to speak up.

"Thorne coined the term. They... well, they are still rather timid, and Thorne and I have been reluctant to press them on their past for fear that they will run away. They gave us their names, though—Wes and Will."

The trio sat in silence for the rest of the ride. Finally, the carriage slowed to a stop. The carriage jostled as Thorne jumped down and he opened the door wide enough to speak. "I stopped far enough away that we would not arouse suspicion. Wes, Will, and I will take care of reconnaissance."

Dressed in rather plain clothes—perhaps borrowed from Thorne—Roland went to take Thorne's place in the driver's seat. Grace switched to the other bench, and she and Elsie scooted close to the window on the street side. She shifted the curtain covering the window to allow them a slit to peer out of it. With that, Grace finally got a good look at the neighbourhood.

The air carried the mixed scents of coal smoke and the foul stench of the Thames. The residences were older, showing signs of wear and neglect. Densely packed, they rose two or three stories high, with facades of exposed brick darkened with soot and age. They were a far cry from the districts Grace had seen thus far. Most of the small windows were dark, but thankfully unshuttered.

The steady clop of horses' hooves and spinning carriage wheels caused Grace to shift away from the window. The gas lamps illuminated a hansom cab as it passed by at a steady clip. Far too soon for comfort, the horses slowed. Worry caused Grace's stomach to churn. What was the likelihood that whoever was in the cab was going to the same house? Although the odds were slim, Grace could not help but fear the worst.

She nudged the curtain covering the back window to look out, but the other cab was too far away for her to see who got out or where they went.

Grace returned to watching the street. A few minutes later, she saw a small, shapeless form rise from the shadows and scurry across the lane. She thought her eyes might have been deceiving her until Roland shifted from his position. She slid across the bench seat and dared to twist the door handle, allowing the door to open wide enough for her to hear Roland's conversation.

Based on the pitch of the voice, it must have been one of the children. "The new man wot turned up, Thorne says he recognised 'im. It's the lady's butler who arrived with some small things. We took a squint at the windows. He's been gabbing with a bruiser inside and a mean-looking bird. Maybe she's a maid?"

"No sign of a young woman? Blonde hair?" Roland asked the boy.

"Naw, but she might be upstairs. There's a light on."

Charity had to be inside. It was the only explanation that made sense. Grace did not wait any longer. "Come along, Elsie."

In a trice, Roland hopped down and pushed the carriage door shut, leaning against it with his weight. "No. You two will stay here."

Grace looked into Roland's face. It was hard to make his eyes out in the gloom, but there was none of the softness there had been earlier this evening. "Let us out at once."

Roland removed his hat and ran his hand through his hair with impatience before shoving it back into place. "Did you not hear? We are outnumbered."

She set her jaw. "There are two men and a woman. Surely you and Thorne can take the men, and Elsie and I can take the maid."

A soft, child-like snort of a laugh escaped the shadows, and Roland allowed a small grin at that. His teeth flashed in the gaslight before vanishing back into the darkness. "I am sure you could," he answered, but plainly he was humouring her. "Still, we should wait and see if the butler leaves first to improve the odds for Thorne and me."

"He's gonna," the child murmured. "The carriage is waiting. Whatever he's up to, he don't plan on taking much time with it."

Relenting, Grace sat back, and Roland removed his hand from the door. "If Charity is there, she is likely safe enough for now," he told Grace. "We will bide awhile and form our plan."

The butler ended up leaving within a quarter hour. By then, they had a rough sketch of a plan, and the sprouts left to throw pebbles at the windows on the far sides of the house.

The bruiser, predictably, came outside to investigate the noise, and both Thorne and Roland set upon him. Grace didn't wait to see the outcome, trusting that the men knew what they were about. She grabbed Elsie's hand and yanked her as they ran for the door of the house.

As she threw the door open, Grace nearly ran straight into

the woman inside. Both ladies screeched briefly in surprise, staring at one another.

"Who're you?" the woman said indignantly. "Get out! Robbers! Robbers!" she shouted, grabbing a heavy cast-iron skillet from where it hung.

Grace frantically looked about to defend herself. As a weapon, the cast-iron was sufficiently menacing. Elsie was quicker on the draw and found a knife that she brandished in defence of her mistress.

The woman looked at the door, clearly wondering why her confederate hadn't arrived at her shouts. Grimly, she wrapped both hands around the handle of the skillet, hoisting it aloft in preparation to swing it at Elsie.

But she hadn't been paying attention to Grace, who had taken one step to the side. Grace saw her opportunity to leap in and shove the woman. With the heavy skillet throwing off her balance, she toppled to the side, striking her head against the wall.

Elsie immediately snatched the skillet away, and Grace put a hand to her mouth, horrified that they might have hurt her. But it was apparent that she wasn't dead, or even unconscious; she moaned softly, dazed.

At that moment, the door crashed open, and Thorne stepped through it, bleeding from a cut above his eye. He looked around, seeing the downed woman and both Elsie and Grace standing there like deer frozen in their tracks. Reaching down, he turned the woman's head to check on her. "She'll live," he told the two of them. "Go. Quickly now, since she made so much noise."

Thorne's words set Grace moving like the opening gates of a horse race. Upstairs she hurtled, finding the room with light shining beneath the crack of the door. She flung it open, Charity's name upon her lips—

But it was empty. Empty?

Bewildered, Grace finally noticed that one window, near a tree, stood open. She raced to the window, seeing a figure clinging to the tree in much the same manner that she had clambered over the wall. "Charity?" she cried.

The figure scrabbled and paused. Roland, hearing Grace's exclamation, jogged into view below her. "Lady Charity? You can let go and drop. I've got you," he said in a low voice. There was a pause, and then Grace watched as the figure fell... and Roland caught her in his arms.

Stiffly, Grace backed from the window and then raced back down the stairs. She nearly tripped as she hit the landing, and fortunately Thorne was there to steady her.

"We have got her. What do we do now?" Grace asked him, feeling like a lost child. All these days they had spent looking for Charity—she had never imagined what would come next.

"Now we must go, before someone comes to investigate," Thorne told her, nodding to Elsie and letting the maid collect the shaking Grace. He ushered them out the front. "Hurry. Get in the carriage."

At the carriage, they met Roland, who had apparently just finished putting Charity inside. "Sprouts," Roland said through gritted teeth, "ride on the back until we get nearer to Grosvenor and then make your way home. You two," he continued, looking at Grace and Elsie dourly, "inside, now."

Elsie stepped into the carriage with alacrity, leaving the spot next to Charity free for Grace. "Where are we taking her?" Grace asked, her voice breaking. "Are we taking her straight home?"

"We cannot," Roland told her, his voice harsh with emotion. "Thorne, take us to the Fitzroy's estate. Lady Fitzroy and her son have much to explain."

30

S itting beside Grace's mousy maid, Roland uncomfortably fidgeted, attempting to ignore the scene across the carriage from them and wishing the carriage wasn't so small. He was angry—angry with a depth he could only recall reaching perhaps twice in his life.

Once Thorne had started the carriage moving smartly, Grace and Charity collapsed into each other's arms in a weeping ball of mumbled words. Finally, Grace seemed to recall herself and the needs of this next mission, and she pulled back from Charity, though she still gripped the young woman's arms.

"What happened?" she asked her friend, her voice pitched high enough that Roland could hear the conversation. "When you disappeared from the ball—I was so afraid!"

"I cannot remember much of what happened," Charity admitted, dropping her eyes. "I had been feeling hot... sick... and I went to take some air. One of the... footmen, I think? Or perhaps it was the butler. He noticed I was looking peaked, and led me to a bench out of the way where I could rest without being seen. And then..." Charity made a grasping motion with her hands, unable to recall clearly. "I was offered another drink?

I am uncertain. Then nothing... nothing until I woke up in a bedroom alone, still in my dress."

He took this moment to rake his eyes over the diamond. The Fitzroy servants had given Charity a change of clothing, even though it appeared to be some servant's cast-off. Charity had tied her long hair back in a knot—the better to facilitate her shimmy down the tree. The circles beneath her eyes and strained emotions of her face were plainly visible, but there appeared to be no bruises or cuts to show she had been otherwise mistreated.

Grace's thoughts aligned with his. "Did they treat you well?"

"Well enough for someone being kidnapped, I suppose," she replied somewhat bitterly. "Whole and untouched, and as good as ruined, nonetheless. I am sorry, Grace. I know so little. They told me nothing. I did not know whose servants those were, even. Every day the woman—the maid, I suppose—dosed my tea with laudanum... after the first sip I tried not to drink it, but she threatened me with worse if I did not. So... so... sometimes I would pour it out wherever I could and then I would pretend to be dosed more than I was. But she would not leave until I had taken a drink, so some things are still unclear."

"That would explain how you had the wherewithal to break the window and climb the tree," Roland concluded with approval. "You waited for the opportunity."

"Yes," Lady Charity said, finally turning to look at Roland straight on for the first time. "There was such a racket, I thought no one would hear if I broke the latch. I did not know it was you. All of you..." her blonde brows drew together in consternation and she turned back to Grace. "Why are you here? And how did you find me?"

Biting his tongue, Roland said nothing. Grace tilted her head in his direction as though his reluctance to explain confused her, but she murmured the story, starting with the maid falling from the balcony and the debacle that followed. His attention wandered in the recounting, but the mention of the queen snagged his attention again. Grace deliberately omitted certain details, he realised with a shock. She said nothing of them pretending to come to know one another. Nothing of the queen's threat to see him and Grace married.

Then again, they had found the diamond. Perhaps Grace thought that if they saw Lady Charity restored, he would be pushed into courting her once more, and Grace would be free of him. She would have no need to worry about them growing to hate one another, after all.

The knife twist that happened in his belly at that thought was swift, but went unacknowledged as Thorne knocked on the carriage roof in nearly the same instant. They were there.

"You must let me do the talking," he told both women, and when Grace lifted her eyebrow in mutiny, he lifted his own in reply. *You already caused trouble once tonight. Do not test me!* After a heartbeat, Grace yielded, folding her arms over her chest.

Elsie took off her hooded cloak and wrapped it around Charity's shoulders, turning her face away from the door as footsteps and a brief hail sounded outside. Then the door opened, and Roland stepped down, shutting it behind him. As he approached the front of the Fitzroy mansion, Thorne took up a position on the ground, clearly guarding the carriage door from any investigation.

The Fitzroy footman glanced from Roland to the carriage—he had seen a glimpse of three skirts sitting within it, though little else—but he did not question why they remained. Turning, he hurried to follow Roland to the heavy front door.

The butler who answered was the self-same one as who had been at the rented house. Roland knew it to be true because he had turned to look at his manservant and had gotten a scowl in response. "Good evening," Roland told the butler, turning back. "I am here to request a meeting with Lord and Lady Fitzroy. I know it is late, but it is of some importance."

The butler could manage a rather mighty disapproving look when he wanted. "My apologies, Lord Percy, but Lady and Lord Fitzroy have retired for the evening and did not wish to be disturbed. Might I take a message or perhaps arrange for you to call at a more suitable hour tomorrow?"

"I am afraid I must insist that they be disturbed," Roland said, doing a credible job of feigning genuine regret. "It is regarding the property on Villiers Street."

The butler stiffened ever so slightly to Roland's watchful eye, proving again he knew exactly what property that was. He attempted to test whether Roland was bluffing anyway. "Was there a specific query you wanted to make about it, Lord Percy?"

He clasped his hands behind his back nonchalantly. "Yes. It regards the young lady who was most recently in occupation. Beyond this information, I can only speak about it directly to Lord or Lady Fitzroy. Surely you understand."

"I see," the butler said a trifle grimly, and he opened the door to invite Roland inside.

With a half turn, Roland gestured to Thorne, and Thorne opened the carriage door. Thorne nodded at Roland, knowing automatically to stay with the carriage—and Elsie still inside.

Grace and Charity emerged with their hoods pulled over their heads and their faces in shadow. He glanced back at the butler to gauge his reaction, but the man had been a butler a long time, and his face was now a mask of inscrutability.

Fitzroy and his mother may have retired, but they hadn't been ready for bed. Fitzroy was still in his evening wear, and judging by the smell of ink and scotch that accompanied

Fitzroy, Roland suspected he had been enjoying a nightcap and indulging in correspondence.

"Percy?" he asked Roland, and the bewilderment in his voice was genuine enough. "What are you doing here at this hour? Who—" he finally was close enough to see the hooded young ladies huddled in Roland's shadow. "What is going on?"

Lady Fitzroy appeared at the top of the main stair in a casual gown, her face a frozen mask of anger. "Lord Percy. I know you are unfamiliar with the finer points of society, but we most stringently adhere to the proper calling hours in this house!"

"12 Villiers Street, Lady Fitzroy," Roland replied simply. "Do you know it?"

"The rented property? What of it?" Fitzroy asked. Roland began to doubt Fitzroy had been aware of his mother's machinations at all.

"Peregrine!" the lady responded, lifting her hand in caution. "You can retire. There is nothing about this you need to burden yourself with. I will handle Lord Percy and his... guests."

"Absolutely not, Mother. If there is an issue, I should be present for it."

The lady paused, staring down at all of them. "Very well. In the parlour." She pointed with one long finger, and stalked out, not waiting for them to ascend the stair.

Roland noted that repairs to the broken banister appeared to be underway. They had removed the broken pieces and roped off the gaping hole. It seemed difficult to believe it had happened less than a week previously.

The parlour's lamps mellowed the Fitzroy's flaxen locks into a sunlit gold and darkened the hue of Lady Fitzroy's blue eyes into a broken bottle green, but they were still as cold as the chips of ice they were in the daylight. She took a breath. "You dare—"

"Yes, Lady Fitzroy. I dare," Roland interrupted her, stepping behind Charity and lifting the lady's hood.

Upon seeing her, Fitzroy's jaw fell open. "Lady Charity?" She only briefly lifted her eyes, meeting Fitzroy's once before sliding away. Finally overcoming his shock and putting the comments together, Fitzroy's face grew stormy. "She has been in the rented house?"

"Yes," Roland murmured. "Lady Fitzroy, we are here to call you to account. If we resolve to keep this out of the courts, you may keep the scandal to a minimum for Lady Charity and your family."

Lady Fitzroy tilted her head, weighing Roland's offer. "No."

Grace spluttered beneath her hood, shoving it back. "*No?* You kidnapped Lady Charity. We entered—"

"Grace!" Roland hissed, trying to stop her.

"—entered your house and found her there! You poisoned your own maid. It is your fault that she is dead," Grace finished, glaring at Roland, who pressed his lips together in resignation. "And you would say '*no*'?"

She smiled widely, then, her teeth glinting like a scythe in the curve of her lips. "I would. You come here and make an accusation of murder and kidnapping. Assuming I somehow doctored a drink, I did not put said glass in the maid's hand, nor force it down her throat. The silly chit would be fine if she had simply done her duty. You cannot lay responsibility for her death at my doorstep. As to kidnapping—while we do own property on Villiers Street, it is long rented to other tenants! Even if you could convince a magistrate that the lady was there, you have no proof of the perpetrator. No proof beyond your word, which sounds, by your own admission, like it may be sullied by the serious crime of housebreaking. And when I explain you committed this *crime*—" there was a delicate emphasis on the words, "because you held Charity all this time, and you were driven by a desire to plant evidence that would implicate my family, how will that appear?"

Grace went pale with anger. The way she rocked back on her heels, Roland knew she was aware she had made a fatal error.

"I see what you are thinking. Lady Grace!" Lady Fitzroy continued, lifting her hand to her cheek in mock surprise. "I ask in turn, what are *you* doing? What propriety is there in a young lady of your standing being found in such compromising company, and at such an hour?" With an elegant turn of her head, Lady Fitzroy returned her gaze to Roland's. "So, my young lord, the answer is no. I shall never confess to such a heinous act, and trying to prove it will merely ruin your own lives in the bargain."

There were times in battle when one knew oneself outmanoeuvred. It was a hard truth to accept that in such situations, any hope of future victory lay in retreat so that one might live to fight another day.

This impasse was so fragile; it might be snapped like a twig at any moment. Roland wrapped his fingers around Grace's wrist, willing her to stand down. He could feel the way her pulse was racing beneath his fingers, and the tension in her arm made him glad he had done so, for he was unsure she would have relented.

Grace was not the only powder keg at risk of blowing, however.

"I, like everyone, believed the ransom pointed at Lord Percy being the culprit. Now I know I am to blame. I told my mother of the wager," Fitzroy groaned. "The very night before the ransom came."

Glancing at the lady's son to gauge his mood, Roland found Fitzroy's face was haggard with pain. Doubtless he was running over his mother's every word, and theirs, trying to find the truth. Roland did not envy the man.

It was Lady Charity, however, who ended up surprising them all. "There is no more to be gained in this. All we can hope to achieve is this uneasy truce where we all hold our tongues for fear of causing our own destruction."

When Lady Fitzroy gave no reply to this except for the barest incline of her head, Lady Charity nodded decisively. "Tell me, Lady Fitzroy," she asked, her voice demure and soft. "Did you plan to murder me eventually, or did you intend to let me go once my virtue was thoroughly ruined?"

The canny dowager was not discomposed in the least. "Shall we speak plainly, then? I despise you—you and your mother both. I hope all that brings you joy turns to ash within your hands. That your beauty fades. That your belly is barren. I wish that you marry a brute and suffer a long, unhappy marriage. It might occur to you that you cannot have such a fate if you are dead."

Roland drew a sharp breath at the brutality of her statement, wondering if Lady Charity would cry or faint, but the young woman smiled. *Smiled*!

"How strange, Lady Fitzroy. I wish you nothing but good health and happiness," she replied, her face even more serene than Lady Fitzroy's had been.

The dowager's upper lip twitched. "How lovely of you, dear. Now, the lot of you—leave, immediately, or else I shall have Edmunds toss you out on your ears."

31

Bile burned the back of Grace's throat. No matter that Lady Fitzroy's threats held solid, Grace could not bear the thought of accepting this loss. The kidnapping had been nary more than a game to her ladyship, but for Charity, a sudden, unexplained reappearance would cast a permanent shadow across her name. As Lady Fitzroy had no doubt intended it to.

It had been a neat trap, and Grace could see no way out of it. Had she kept quiet and allowed Roland to do all the talking, perhaps things would have ended differently, but she had rather doubted it. Lady Fitzroy had well-laid plans, and the only thing that the crimson wash of her fury had altered was stripping her of her anonymity. It would have changed nothing for Roland and Charity; now, she faced the same consequences as they did.

Grace climbed back into Roland's carriage with her lips sealed. Charity did not need more tears, or blathering, or empty promises that all would be fine. Grace could see no way to erase the past week from the collective memory of the ton. Had it been so little time? Grace felt years apart from the girl she had been at the start of the season. Her bright-eyed optimism, even tempered as it was by the weeks before the Fitzroy ball, proved to be no match for the harsh realities of high society.

The carriage shuddered into motion, rocking the passengers from side to side as the iron-rimmed wheels rumbled over the cobblestone drive. Grace's gaze shifted wildly, searching for any source of inspiration about how they might see Lady Fitzroy punished. It landed upon the man sitting across from her, but found no quarter there. His ink black eyes formed bottomless shadows in the dark carriage, and as Roland watched the two of them, she could not imagine what he was thinking.

Charity's delicate fingers coaxed Grace's tightened fist to unlatch. She laced their fingers together and squeezed. "Grace?"

Grace did not turn her head. She could not face Charity. Not yet. How could they have managed to both succeed and fail, so utterly?

Charity squeezed again. "Grace, you said Queen Charlotte tasked you with finding me. Was she truly so upset by my absence?"

Yes... although Grace was loath to explain the whys behind the queen's sentiments. She kept her reply to a single bob of the head.

"Then we must go to her. Straightaway."

"*Now?*" Roland's pitch rose. "The hour, and your dress—"

"Does my choice of clothing matter anymore?" Charity countered wryly. "Does anything? My parents will send me away to our country estate as soon as I set foot in the house. There will be lies, weak explanations, and whispers. If Queen Charlotte cares one whit for me, she will want the truth. I intend to give it to her myself. And to say thank you for sending you all to my aid."

The sharp edge to Charity's outthrust chin must have convinced him she was in earnest. He knocked on the roof of the carriage and called new instructions to Thorne. "Take us to Buckingham House."

Charity leaned back with a rather resigned smile on her face. Grace could not help but stare at her in awe. She had witnessed first-hand her friend's determination to make the best possible match, applying a near scientific method to her marital prospects. Was it so hard to believe that the same Charity would see the logic in speaking with the queen before anyone else could intervene?

Grace's gaze drifted further afield and landed upon Elsie. The woman huddled against the corner, taking great care to keep her dirty skirt from brushing against Roland's trousers. Like Grace, Elsie's face wore an expression bordering on idolatry, kept off the mark only by the tears staining her cheeks. She did not need any explanation to understand that their confrontation had not gone to plan. Lady Fitzroy remained behind, safe in her home, while they rode through the dark streets.

The ride to Buckingham House was blessedly short. A guard called the carriage to a halt and demanded to know who was inside. Roland motioned for the women to remain seated before exiting the carriage. This time, he did not take so much care to hide the other occupants. The guard peered into the depths and saw only three women in skirts. Although it did nothing to answer his questions, it did at least lower his concern.

"We must speak with the queen. Now," Roland told him.

"The queen sees no one without invitation," the guard replied.

"She will see us. If you have doubts, rouse her aide. He will second my assertion. Either way, I have no intention of leaving until you let us inside." Roland widened his stance, adopting a militaristic pose of intractability.

The guard must have heard something of Roland's previous

role as a field commander in his voice, for he moved his hand from the sheath of his sword and rapped on the door. Within moments, a footman opened it wide enough to allow them to speak. More time passed while the footman hurried to do the guard's bidding. The only blessing was that the queen's aide was not yet abed. He was, however, well lubricated from a night of drinking. He stumbled outside, blustering complaints, but drew up short when his eyes landed up Charity's blonde head.

"Egad!" he gasped, momentarily forgetting himself. "Yes, yes, the queen will not want to miss this. Come inside. And for goodness' sake, cover your head. It seems someone is always watching our movements."

Grace and Charity pulled the hoods of their cloaks over their heads and tugged them low to prevent any hair from slipping loose. Dressed as they were, Grace felt there was little risk of recognition.

The footman was already hard at work, lighting the candles in the wall sconces to illuminate their way along the carpeted hall. He led them to the same private parlour where Queen Charlotte had issued her ultimatum. Find Charity or wed Lord Percy. Grace had accomplished the first, but had no confidence she would avoid the second. All she could do was pray.

The footman remained to stand a silent watch while the aide left to get the queen. She must not have been far, as she arrived before Grace had time to think through what she would say.

For once, her luck held, as Queen Charlotte had no interest in hearing from Lady Grace. She strode into the room, wearing a loose-fitting banyan made of embroidered Chinese silk over her gown. There was no sign of her usual elaborate hairpieces, instead she had only a simple white cap covering her silvered hair.

"Lord Percy, Lady Grace, I see you have found my missing

diamond. Now, pray tell, Lady Charity, where you have been for the past week?"

"Staying in a townhouse in London, courtesy of Lady Fitzroy, your highness. It was an unexpected invitation," she added.

"Yes, I imagine it was. Are you certain Lady Fitzroy was your hostess?"

"We have just come from the Fitzroy abode," Roland said, venturing to speak. "We intended to bring her along for this late conference, but she declined the invitation."

Queen Charlotte bristled. "On what grounds?"

"Despite mounting evidence, she claimed to be unaware of Lady Charity's stay in her rental property, and countered that our efforts to rescue her could be interpreted as forced entry." He opened his hands wide and let silence fill in the rest.

"Drat that woman," the queen muttered, or at least that is what Grace thought she said. The queen did not remain at a disadvantage for long. "I suppose you have come to beg me to intervene, or to ask me to have young George send her into exile."

"No, your highness," Charity answered. "I requested Lord Percy accompany me here so that I might assure you of my good health and to thank you. If not for your decision to allow Lord Percy and Lady Grace to search for me, I am certain I would not stand before you now. I do not deserve such kindness, and although I can never repay you, I will be forever at your disposal."

Whatever the queen expected, doubtless, it was not this. She paused a long moment. "That is it? You ask for nothing?" The arched eyebrow on the queen's face expressed heavy scepticism.

"It is not my place," Charity replied. She dropped into a deep curtsy and waited for the queen to bid her to rise.

The queen did not require Charity to wait long. She bid her to arise and then drew herself up to address her guests. "Do you know what a half century upon my throne has taught me?"

Grace gave the faintest shake of her head, never taking her eyes from the queen.

"There is no greater foe than time itself. One need only to survive to play the next round in order to retain the chance to come out on top. I believe you understand this, Lady Charity. This is the reason I chose you above all others, elevated you to the position of the most favoured debutante. Beauty may be inherited, poise learned through practice, but wit comes from within. It cannot be taught, but it can be fostered. Should I let you leave now, I will deprive myself most of all the chance to see what you will become." She relaxed her pose and moved to sit on a nearby chair. "Please, be seated while I think on this issue."

Grace chose the nearest chair that would not require her to turn her back on the queen. Charity and Roland sat on either end of a long sofa. Queen Charlotte glanced off to the side, her gaze softening while her mind worked through the current challenge. Grace breathed shallow breaths, begging her speeding heart to slow.

Impossible to imagine, but Grace believed the queen might find a way through their seemingly insurmountable conundrum. Although the queen held no political power, her grip upon high society was irrefutable. The hand that raised could become the fist that knocked others from their pedestals.

Yet, the queen did not arrive at a solution quickly. To save Charity, all of society must be convinced of her innocence before, during, and after her absence. Lady Fitzroy would not help, perhaps not even if the queen compelled her to do so. All it would take was one slip of the tongue, and the good works would burn away like the fog under the hot sun.

Queen Charlotte turned her head to face the sofa where

Roland and Charity sat. She eyed the pair through narrowed lids. Her gaze sharpened and her mouth formed a vicious smile.

"Lord Percy, I have been remiss in discussing your boorish breach of etiquette to a further extent. One does not make wagers upon the outcome of one's own marriage."

Roland's cheeks flamed in embarrassment, but he did not bend. "For what it is worth, Your Majesty, I have regretted it every day since. I was a great fool, little excuse as that is."

"I am not of mind to allow such a flagrant violation to go unpunished, especially when it pertains to my diamond. Yet, I was minded to offer you a path toward redemption. The only thing that could save you from further judgement was a grandiose gesture."

Grace clutched onto the scratchy wool fabric of her borrowed dress. She did not know what the queen was thinking. Nor did Roland, it seemed.

"Allow me to make myself clearer. What if I had organised a knight's quest, as of old? A mission, to be undertaken at great personal risk, to save the damsel in distress. As the organiser of this challenge, I would vouch for Lady Charity's safety during her absence. And with her return, I can now give my blessing to your engagement."

Grace twisted in her seat, her attention moving from the queen to the pair on the sofa. Hope shone on Charity's face, and Roland looked stunned into disbelief, as if someone had struck him in the head.

"Yes," the queen muttered, happy with herself. She glanced at her aide for confirmation of her genius. The man smiled gaily and clapped his hands. "This is what we will say. Who will dare call me a liar? Not Lady Fitzroy, that is for sure. Your parents can be compelled to agree with this plan, can they not?"

Charity bobbed her head. For his part, Roland held stock still, his impassive face giving no hints at his inner thoughts.

Had Grace not caught his initial reaction, she'd believe him unbothered by the queen's plan.

Queen Charlotte called the footman forward and bade him to prepare a room for Lady Charity and Lady Grace. They would stay the night, and tomorrow the queen would send them home in her carriage.

"Our clothes, your highness," Charity reminded her.

"I am sure we can arrange for fresh clothing, come the morn." Queen Charlotte rose from her chair, causing the other three to leap to their feet. "I trust this is a satisfactory solution for all?"

Grace lost her battle to hold her tongue. "What of Lady Fitzroy? Is she to go unpunished? There is still the matter of her maid's death, even if it was an accident."

Queen Charlotte scowled at Grace for daring to speak up on a matter she had deemed closed. "Have I said she will go unpunished? You have much to learn about high society, Lady Grace. It is a war of sorts, not a single battle with one winner and one loser paying the piper. I have given you all the chance to retreat with your heads held high. How you bring Lady Fitzroy to account remains to be seen. But I have faith that the three of you will find a way. Eventually."

The queen swept from the room without a backward glance.

Epilogue

It was Sunday, and though it was difficult to believe, only a single day had passed since their desperate rescue of Charity in the early hours of Saturday morning. So much had changed, and the canvas of the world no longer felt like it stretched properly across its frame.

Below her fingertips, the wood of the pew at the Chapel Royal at St James's felt worn by time and the pressure of many bodies. She focused on the feel of it, trying to drown out the whispers of the nobles seated around her. For this service was the queen's way of publicly reintroducing Charity back into the ranks of society. By late afternoon the day before, all of society had heard tell of Lord Percy's valiant efforts to win Charity's heart and the queen's blessing in the bargain. Lady Charity was still the diamond; Roland's quest had been both punishment and absolution for his lack of social grace.

All was forgiven.

There was still some rancour and speculation, judging by the whispers that rose and fell within earshot of Grace. Doubtless, they would be short-lived, for the queen was bound and determined to make it known that all was right in the world.

If any should doubt it, she and her family were seated in a position of honour just behind the royal family. Why else would she have made sure to seat Lord Percy so closely to Charity's side?

Across the aisle, at Grace's side, Lady Tilbury held her head high, pretending as though she were pleased with Charity's return. It was a far cry from the day before, when Grace explained how she had ended up as an overnight guest of the queen. Lady Tilbury had looked as though she had swallowed a lemon while Grace explained that although her blossoming relationship with Percy had reached an end, at least she was now in the queen's good graces. While the queen couldn't acknowledge Grace's full part in the diamond's restoration, she had personally extended the invitation for the family to join her at the palace for worship. All there would note their rise in society.

Bitter as the reward was, Lady Tilbury had harrumphed and then retired to her room for the rest of the day. This morning, Lady Tilbury rose with a fierce expression of determination plastered upon her face. Grace and the family would go to church, for it was practically a command performance.

Grace half-wished she were still alone in her room. It would be far simpler to pass the day sitting upon her window seat, watching the world go by, than to bear the collective weight of the ton's attention. It would have been easier than watching Roland sitting beside her best friend, enjoying the fact that now everything was right in the world.

Though she fought the urge, her eyes betrayed her. Her gaze slipped to where Roland sat on the other side of the aisle from her family, next to Charity. He sat ramrod straight, his face blank. As Grace watched him, he turned his head, as though searching for something. Charity leaned closer to him to whisper somewhat in his ear. Nodding slightly, his mouth quirked into some semblance of a smile, and he turned back to face the pulpit.

A gulf yawned between the two of them, larger than it had been before the Fitzroy ball when he asked her to dance. His life would proceed apace, just as he had planned. He would wed at the end of the season, satisfying his obligations. Charity would achieve her aim of marrying into the highest echelons of society.

What of Grace? She did not regret her actions, risky as they had been. In the last ten days, she had experienced far more adventure than she had ever imagined. Desperate and scary as those days had been, they had also shown Grace that she was capable of far more than society would have her believe.

Could she return to the way things had been? For that was what society would expect. Eventually, she would need to accept some man's marriage offer and become his property, in essence. It was not the life she wanted. Yet, she had only met one man who had hinted at a wider world of possibilities for her.

Now, he would wed her dearest friend. Forever in sight, forever out of reach.

Feeling a telling sting in her eyes, she blinked slowly, studying the way her skirt draped over her legs, and when she lifted her gaze, she looked directly into a familiar set of deep brown eyes.

Grace did not know whether Lord Percy had somehow sensed her thoughts, or if it was sheer happenstance that their eyes met across the chapel aisle. While all those around them bowed their heads in prayer, his deep brown eyes did not move from her face. She lowered her lashes, but not so far as to break the moment of connection.

Then, as always, life intervened. The prayer ended, and

heads once again raised. Almost as one, Lord Percy and Lady Grace shifted their eyes in a new direction.

No, Lady Grace decided. That adventure was done, but the season was not over. She and Roland would ensure Lady Fitzroy's crimes would not go unpunished.

~

BONUS SCENES -

After discovering two orphans living in an abandoned home, Thorne made a split-second decision. The kids would stay with him and Roland. Why did he make that decision? And how did the Sprouts react to Roland's Mayfair townhouse? Find out in their bonus scene - THORNE AND THE SPROUTS.

Despite having been kidnapped and drugged, Lady Charity showed remarkable poise in her meeting with Lady Fitzroy and later Queen Charlotte. Curious to know how and why she kept her cool, and what drove her request to visit Buckingham House in the middle of the night? Find out in her bonus scene - CHARITY PREPARES TO FACE THE QUEEN.

Click here to get the **BONUS SCENES** for free: https://lynnmorrison.myflodesk.com/tmd

~

Roland and Grace will be back again in **The Ruby Dagger**, book 2 in **The Crown Jewels Mysteries**.

Deadly intrigue meets royal expectations when murder comes for the crown.

London, 1813. In the gilded corridors of St James's Palace, Lord Percy and Lady Grace face a mystery that could shake the throne itself. A murder and audacious theft of the Prince Regent's new ruby dagger thrusts them back into a web of deception and treachery.

Tarnished by his past behaviour, Lord Percy is focused on regaining favour with the Ton. When the queen demands he deliver the murderer and the stolen gift, he cannot refuse.

Lady Grace sees her chance to prove her value to the crown. She'll do anything to avoid endless weeks of ballrooms and beaus, even if that means being in close quarters with the man pledged to her best friend.

As Lord Percy and Lady Grace wade deeper into London's underbelly, love and loyalty will face the ultimate trial. Especially since this culprit is willing to spill blood.

In a society where everyone has an agenda, and half the ton is suspect, they will need to watch each other's backs. If they cannot unveil the criminal mastermind, this time it will cost them more than their reputations.

Find out in **The Ruby Dagger**. Order your copy now on Amazon.

Historical Notes

The Regency Period officially lasted from 1811 to 1820. Despite its brevity, it has long captured the imagination due to the works of authors like Jane Austen, Mary Shelley, Percy Bysshe Shelley, and Sir Walter Scott. In more modern times, shows such as Bridgerton and Queen Charlotte, the myriad of Pride and Prejudice remakes, and the time-travelling An American in Austen, have guided our ideas of how society functioned, what was and was not acceptable, what people wore, and how the upper class lived.

In writing this story, we did our best to stick to the historical record, beginning with Roland's time at war in Spain, through to Queen Charlotte's support for bluestockings and intellectuals, to Buckingham House not yet being an official palace, and to the societal restrictions an unwed woman faced in London.

That said, in the interest of crafting an engaging tale, we took a few liberties with the norms of the times. It is very unlikely that Roland and Grace would have danced the waltz in 1813, as it was considered quite scandalous and did not gain popularity until a little later in the Regency era. However, we needed to put the two in close company. We deliberately chose to host that ball at Prinny's home, as he was an early sponsor of the waltz, and most likely to have added it to the set list. We also deliberately feigned some ignorance about what a waltz really looked like in those days. As every movie and TV show set in the era has also done so, we're in good company. Incidentally, we don't recommend looking up a video of an authentic late-Regency-era waltz; some things you just can't unsee.

Fun fact: the truth about men's underwear (or lack of it) gave us such a laugh we had to share. Men's shirts had 'tails' long enough to wrap around their bottoms and tuck up between their legs for modesty and... hygiene. No, we're not kidding. Thanks to Zoe Burton for making our day with this historical fact. We're sorry if this ruins anyone's Regency-esque fantasies.

Any additional errors are ours alone!

The Ruby Dagger
A Crown Jewels Regency Mystery

Deadly intrigue meets royal expectations when murder comes for the crown.

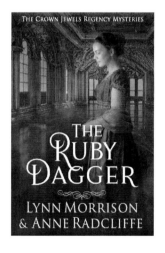

London, 1813. In the gilded corridors of St James's Palace, Lord Percy and Lady Grace face a mystery that could shake the throne itself. A murder and audacious theft of the Prince Regent's new ruby dagger thrusts them back into a web of deception and treachery.

Tarnished by his past behaviour, Lord Percy is focused on regaining favour with the Ton. When the queen demands he deliver the murderer and the stolen gift, he cannot refuse.

Lady Grace sees her chance to prove her value to the crown. She'll do anything to avoid endless weeks of ballrooms and beaus, even if that means being in close quarters with the man pledged to her best friend.

As Lord Percy and Lady Grace wade deeper into London's underbelly, love and loyalty will face the ultimate trial. Especially since this culprit is willing to spill blood.

In a society where everyone has an agenda, and half the ton is suspect, they will need to watch each other's backs. If they cannot unveil the criminal mastermind, this time it will cost them more than their reputations.

Find out in **The Ruby Dagger**. Order your copy now on Amazon.

Acknowledgments

Thanks to Melody Simmons for the amazing cover art. Thanks also to Zoe Burton for pointing out our historical inaccuracies. We ignored her advice a couple of times, and highlighted these choices in the historical notes.

Thanks to Ken Morrison, Brenda Chapman, Jody Tappan, and Bob Cousins for reading early drafts of the book and giving feedback.

Thanks to the team at Podium Audio for acquiring the audio rights to this series, sight unseen. They are such fantastic partners. We count ourselves lucky to get to work with them on bringing this story to audio listeners.

From Anne:

Since I tend to do more editing than writing, and many of you know me more in that role, I have to take this chance to give a big thank you to all the writers who have trusted me with their characters and plots over the years. Of course, that includes Lynn Morrison. Not only have I been privileged enough to watch her grow as a writer from her very first book, she was also gracious enough to invite me to write alongside her and let me slip in a couple nerdy Easter eggs and jokes. Also a big thanks to my husband who said "You're going to make me read a girl book??" and then still did it anyway. That's true love.

From Lynn:

Thanks so much to Anne for being willing to jump straight into writing this book with zero notice. There are few friends in the world who I can call when I get an absolutely crazy idea. I am so thankful to have Anne by my side in my writing journey. Thanks also, as always, to my family for not getting too mad when I missed the turn into our driveway because I was busy thinking about whatever Grace and Roland were doing.

Thanks to fellow authors Cara Devlin, Deborah Wilde, Heather G Harris, Natasha C Sass, Eryn Scott, Catherine Coles, Stella Bixby, and Reagan Davis for encouraging us to write this book, even though it was not in my writing schedule.

About Anne Radcliffe

As an American Expat living in Ontario with a husband and teen son, Anne Radcliffe spends a lot of time editing or writing in order to avoid having to become a Maple Leafs fan. Anne loves a great story no matter the genre or medium - books, graphic novels, TV, movies or video games. You can find out more about Anne on her website at AnneRadcliffe.com.

BB bookbub.com/authors/anne-radcliffe

g goodreads.com/anneradcliffe

a amazon.com/stores/author/BoD1VMVDZ1

About Lynn Morrison

Lynn Morrison lives in Oxford, England along with her husband, two daughters and two cats. Born and raised in Mississippi, her wanderlust attitude has led her to live in California, Italy, France, the UK, and the Netherlands. Despite having rubbed shoulders with presidential candidates and members of parliament, night-clubbed in Geneva and Prague, explored Japanese temples and scrambled through Roman ruins, Lynn's real life adventures can't compete with the stories in her mind.

She is as passionate about reading as she is writing, and can almost always be found with a book in hand. You can find out more about her on her website LynnMorrisonWriter.com.

You can chat with her directly in her Facebook group - Lynn Morrison's Not a Book Club - where she talks about books, life and anything else that crosses her mind.

facebook.com/nomadmomdiary

instagram.com/nomadmomdiary

bookbub.com/authors/lynn-morrison

goodreads.com/nomadmomdiary

amazon.com/Lynn-Morrison/e/BooIKC1LVW

Also by Lynn Morrison

Raven's Influence

Raven's Joy

Raven's Matriarch

Raven's Storm

<u>Wandering Witch Urban Fantasy</u>

A Queen Only Lives Twice

Made in United States
North Haven, CT
08 December 2024

61947338R00157